"You're a mi

Gemma stared at him, at his sudden stiffness, the way his brown eyes had narrowed. Alarm bells clanged in her head, but she spoke calmly. "Yes, I am."

"And you're planning to open a birthing center?"

"Yes, in your father's old offices next to the hospital." She lifted her chin, held his gaze. There had been a time when she would have backed down, apologized, tried to explain her position. Those days were gone. "Exactly as you plan to establish a family practice and reopen the hospital."

"Not exactly."

"Both facilities are for people's health."

"No, the hospital cures people and keeps them well—"

"Fortunately, giving birth isn't an illness."

Their eyes met—hers defiant, his resolute. Gemma's heart sank as she imagined the swirl of objections that were about to come at her. She'd heard them all before, fought them all before.

Somehow, it was disappointing to know she was about to hear them from Nathan.

Dear Reader,

Although I was born and raised in an Arizona copper-mining town, both of my parents were from Oklahoma, where I still have many relatives. Visits to rural southeastern Oklahoma fill me with happiness and nostalgia as I recall summers there—swimming in the creeks, exploring with my cousins or lying on the bed on the screened-in porch listening to bobwhite quail whistling in the underbrush. Although the area has never really been my home, it feels like home because of all the loved ones I have there.

Gemma Whitmire has returned to her hometown of Reston, Oklahoma, to work as a midwife and to open a birthing center. At the same time, Dr. Nathan Smith, who has no use for midwives, has come home, too, with plans to reopen the local hospital that was forced to close due to his father's embezzlement. He also hopes to make peace with his troubled family history.

I hope you enjoy Nathan and Gemma's journey to overcome their differences and find their happy-ever-after.

Happy reading,

Patricia

HEARTWARMING

At Odds with the Midwife

USA TODAY Bestselling Author

Patricia Forsythe

♦ **HARLEQUIN**® HEARTWARMING™

Recycling programs
for this product may
not exist in your area.

ISBN-13: 978-0-373-36812-9

At Odds with the Midwife

Copyright © 2016 by Patricia Knoll

Printed in U.S.A.

HARLEQUIN®
™ www.Harlequin.com

Patricia Forsythe probably would never have become a writer if a seventh-grade teacher hadn't said that Patricia's story characters were, well, crazy. Patricia didn't think that was such a bad thing. After all, she has a large extended family of decidedly interesting and unusual people who provide ideas and inspiration for her books. In Patricia's opinion, that only makes them more lovable and worthy of a place in literature.

A native Arizonan, Patricia has no concept of what a real winter is like, but she is very familiar with summer. She has held a number of jobs, including teaching school, working as a librarian and as a secretary, and operating a care home for developmentally disabled children. Her favorite occupation, though, is writing novels in which the characters get into challenging situations and then work their way out. Each situation and set of characters is different, so sometimes the finished book is as much of a surprise to her as it is to the readers. She is the author of many romance novels with many more to come.

Books by Patricia Forsythe

Harlequin Heartwarming

Her Lone Cowboy

Visit the Author Profile page
at Harlequin.com for more titles.

This book is dedicated to my beloved little sister, Betty Forsythe. Even though she never had an easy life, she brought endless joy to everyone else's.

CHAPTER ONE

FEET SLAPPING THE PAVEMENT—right, left, right, left—Nathan Smith pounded down High Street, turned west onto Main Street and took the hill that led out of town. He hadn't been this way yet on his thrice-weekly runs, but there had been a time, when he was eighteen, that he couldn't seem to take this hill fast enough. Driving the new SUV his dad had bought him for graduating as valedictorian, he'd gunned the engine, eager to leave Reston behind. Waiting for his university classes to start in the fall hadn't even been an option. He'd enrolled in some summer courses so he'd have an excuse to leave days after graduation. He'd sped down Main Street until it became Highway 6 and, since then, had kept his subsequent visits home both rare and short.

He couldn't quite believe he was back. His return to Reston had been challenging, not to mention exhausting. There were times he questioned why he'd come back, but he knew the answer. Guilt was at the top of the list, followed closely by its companion, shame.

He forced his mind to veer away from that. Even though it was the truth, if he focused on it for too long, he would never move ahead. In the project he'd started it was critical to keep going forward. There were more problems than solutions, many issues he didn't yet know how to solve. Somehow, his nighttime runs on the quiet streets helped him see his way forward. Something about the rhythm of his feet, the focus on his breathing as he ran through the cool spring evenings, helped him make sense of the daily complications of his life and the Herculean task he'd taken on.

The full moon lit his way as he ran along the pavement, then he swerved to the edge when a car came by. He waved, not because he knew the driver, but because it was expected in this rural pocket of the world. Some bred-in-the-bone habits never died.

Half a mile out of town, he crossed the bridge over the Kinnick River and slowed to a walk as he caught his breath. He'd given up his running schedule when he'd sprained his ankle a few months ago and now, when it started to ache, he knew it was time to slow down or take a break.

As he fast walked past the old Kinnick Campground, he glanced to the left and saw a light. Pausing, Nathan stood, panting lightly and using the tail of his white T-shirt to wipe away sweat as he gazed into the darkness. The camp was deserted. The Whitmires, who had owned it during his growing-up years, had left town. He'd heard they'd come in to some money. The camp, with its private, well-stocked lake, where they had once hosted hikers, birders and fishermen, had been abandoned for the past fifteen years, though he was sure the local citizenry fished the lake as if it was public property.

Nate frowned at the overgrown bar ditches on each side of the road. He wasn't sure he'd take the chance of fishing in the small lake. Weeds that had been beaten back for decades while the Whitmires were in residence had eagerly taken over the property, providing hiding places for field mice, bobwhite quail and the snakes that fed on them.

Whoever was at the campground now wasn't of the four-legged variety, though.

"Squatters," he murmured. He knew they camped out anyplace they could find, usually tucked back in these mountains, where they could grow marijuana, operate stills or cook meth. If that's what these squatters were up to, he couldn't imagine why they'd want to be this close to the highway. Of course, it was entirely possible that they were either crazy or desperate. He reached for his cell phone to call the police, but quickly realized the signal, always spotty in this area, was nonexistent tonight. He was going to have to find a better cell-phone service. It was critical for people to be able to get in touch with him.

Annoyed, he started to run again, but had taken only a few steps when he cursed under his breath and turned down the rutted lane instead. He couldn't walk away from this situation—another lifelong Reston habit. Approaching slowly, he glanced around. In the glow from the full moon, he could see that someone had been working on this place. He stopped and sniffed the air. Fresh paint. That wasn't something squatters would do, so maybe new owners had taken residence. That conclusion didn't turn him around, though, but drew him forward.

He'd always thought there was something about the smell of fresh paint that promised a new beginning, a positive change. Change was something desperately needed in this town.

The Whitmires had lived in a small century-old log cabin that Ben Whitmire—who'd renamed himself Wolfchild—had updated and renovated by hand. Nate had never been inside, but his mother had described it as "primitive." He also remembered an old tale about the place being haunted but didn't know what form that haunting took.

Someone had cleared the weeds and brush that had no doubt grown up around the door and piled it into a massive stack for burning, or maybe to be picked up by the county and turned into mulch. Abandoned tires had been repurposed into planters with some kind of spiky plants growing in them. He applauded the use of the tires. It was better than having them end up in the landfill.

"Home improvement squatters?" he questioned, even though he was quickly talking himself out of the idea that unauthorized people were on the property. He followed the path around the cabin to the back, where the light was coming from. When he turned the corner, he could hear music that sounded like some kind of wind instrument caught in an endless loop. It was as though the same few bars were playing over and over, with an occasional flat note thrown in for variety.

Wincing at the repetitive sound, he glanced around to see a floor lamp set up outside the back door with the cord snaking inside. It cast a soft glow on the surroundings—and on what looked like a woman digging a grave.

The sight rocked him to a stop, and although she hadn't seen him, Nate stepped behind a blossoming crape myrtle to see what she was doing.

A large, rectangular patch of sod had been turned over and she was busily breaking up the chunks of dirt, smashing into them with the side of the shovel blade. Too shallow for a grave. He shook his head at his own morbid thoughts.

As she worked, she sang words he couldn't understand. They were out of rhythm with the music he could now see was coming from a tablet computer set up at the base of the lamp.

The woman had curly red hair that flowed down her back and lifted when a breeze happened by. She wore cutoff jeans with black rain boots and a yellow tank top that revealed toned arms, streaked with dirt.

He needed to let her know he was there, but he was enjoying the sight of her working.

Turning around and leaving before she saw him was certainly an option, but now that he was here, he wanted to find out what was going on and, more importantly, who she was.

"Hello," he called out.

She didn't respond.

"Excuse me. Hello." He took a few steps forward, but she still didn't answer. Now he could see potted plants lined up, ready to go into the ground. She was planting something. At night.

Thinking that she might be hard of hearing, Nate stepped forward, reaching out a hand to wave at the moment she tossed the shovel aside and bent to pick up one of the potted plants lined up at her feet.

The woman turned her head, saw a hand coming at her and exploded.

Grabbing his arm, she stepped forward to throw him off balance. Then she swept out her foot to knock his feet out from under him.

Nate landed on his left side with a whoosh of breath. His hand slammed down on the sharp edge of the shovel blade, shooting pain up his arm.

The girl grabbed the shovel away from him with one hand and jerked earbuds from her ears with the other. She let them fall and they dangled from the MP3 player attached to her waistband as she moved back several feet and held the shovel out in front of her like a weapon.

"Who are you?" she demanded. "What do you want?"

"I—I saw…" Nate stopped to catch his breath.

"You saw what? A woman alone who might like some company?" She tossed her head to get her hair out of her face and moved from one foot to the other, ready to do more damage. "Well, you guessed wrong, buddy.

As you can see, even though I'm alone here, I can defend myself just fine."

"Yeah, I noticed." He rolled onto his side to sit up, but when he placed his cut hand on the ground, pain raced up his arm. Breath hissed between his teeth as he fell back.

"What's wrong?' she asked, finally seeming to realize he was hurt. "Do you need help? I can help you if you don't try anything funny."

"I can take care of it myself," he answered testily. "As long as you don't knock me down again."

Dropping the shovel, but making sure it was within reach, she came down onto her knees beside him. She slid her arm under his shoulders and helped him into a sitting position.

Nate held up his hand and tilted it toward the pale glow from the lamp.

"Oh, that's a pretty bad cut," she said. "You must have hit it on the edge of the shovel."

"Yeah, I think so."

"And you've managed to grind dirt into it."

He couldn't see her face clearly since the

light was behind her, but Nate imagined she was giving him an accusing look.

"Yeah, well, that sometimes happens when a crazy woman throws me to the ground."

"Crazy? I was defending myself!"

"I was only trying to get your attention."

"Why? So you could scare me to death?" She got to her feet and stepped back to watch him stand up, too.

"I saw the light and thought someone was up to no good."

"Yes, someone was. You!"

Nate tried to smother his temper. "I thought someone was trespassing."

"Again. You! This is private property. My property."

He paused, staring at her, then walked around her so that she would have to turn to keep an eye on him. When the light hit her face, he recognized her. The red hair— though he didn't remember it being quite this red—almond-shaped green eyes, the heart-shaped face.

"Bijou?" he asked.

"Do I know you?" She frowned at him.

"Nathan Smith," he said.

Surprise flared in her eyes, followed by a

fleeting emotion he couldn't name. Embarrassment? Dismay? She lowered her eyes so he couldn't read her expression.

When she didn't say anything else, he went on, "I thought your parents had sold this place."

"No. It's always stayed in the family." She gave a small shrug. "Obviously, no one kept it up."

He glanced around. "This is a lot of work. What are you doing back here, Bijou?"

"I could ask the same of you, Nathan, and the name's Gemma now. I changed my name the minute I turned eighteen."

"What did your parents, Wolfchild and, um, Sunshine, think of that?"

She reached up and pushed her hair away from her face, tucking it behind her ears. "They realized that I was old enough to make my own decisions and they apologized for having given me a name that wasn't cosmically suited to my personality."

Nate hid a smile as he flexed his shoulders. He'd forgotten that her parents talked like that. They had been well-meaning oddballs in this community, but they hadn't minded being out of step with everyone else in town. He hadn't thought their daughter was very much like them, seeming to be more conventional—focused on school, friends and small-town life.

"*Bijou* is French for *Jewel*," he pointed out, his gaze touching on those bright green eyes and richly colored hair.

"I know."

Lifting his uninjured hand, he rubbed his left arm. He was going to be sore and bruised in the morning. "I'm guessing you chose Gemma since Wonder Woman was taken."

One corner of her mouth tilted up as she lifted her eyebrows at him. He remembered that expression from years ago.

He held up his mangled hand. "Is there somewhere I can wash and bandage this before I head home?"

"Come inside. I'll bandage it for you."

"I'm a doctor. I can do my own bandaging."

"I know that, and I'm a registered nurse, so I'll do the bandaging. It's my house and they're my bandages." Gemma paused to pick up the tablet and shut off the music.

Nate decided not to pursue the who-will-do-the-bandaging? argument. From what he'd seen so far, he would lose, anyway.

"That was…interesting music," he ventured. "But you weren't listening to it?" He didn't have a very active imagination and didn't know why she would listen to one kind of music to block out another.

"It's Tibetan music. Frankly, I can't stand it because it reminds me of the time my dad insisted we all needed to learn to play the zither." She shook her head, a small smile on her lips. "Carly is absolutely convinced it'll help the plants grow."

He frowned. "Carly? Oh, yes, Joslin." He vaguely remembered the two of them had been best friends, along with Lisa Thomas. Glancing around at her family's property, he realized she had done what he couldn't— kept her ties to their hometown.

"Come on," she said briskly. "Let me look at that hand. It's rude to keep the nurse waiting."

Giving her a thoughtful look, he followed her inside. A nurse. In spite of her prickliness, this sounded promising.

"Don't touch the door or the facings," she said, pointing to what he could now see was a bright blue, glistening with newness. "I just painted them."

"I know. I smelled the paint."

While she scrubbed her hands at the sink, then bustled about, setting out a basin, a clean towel, disinfectant and bandages, Nate looked around the cozy cabin.

The living room held a dark blue sofa and chair with a huge, multicolored rug in the middle of the floor. A rock fireplace, probably original to the house, dominated one wall. A few sealed boxes were piled one atop the other along a wall, and a stack of paintings and photographs waited to be hung. A doorway opened onto a hallway, where he assumed the bedrooms and bathroom were.

The place was warm and inviting, not at all the den of hippie craziness his mother had claimed it to be. Also, it was rustic, but not primitive. Thinking about it now, he wondered why she had chosen that word.

"Come over to the sink," Gemma commanded and he did as he was told, standing with his hand under warm running water. He was very aware of her gently clasping his hand in her own while she turned it this way and that, keeping it under the stream from the faucet. Nate liked being close enough to catch her scent, which was faintly flowery, no doubt heightened by the work she'd been doing out back.

He was about to ask what she'd been planting when she shut off the water and grabbed a handful of paper towels, which she placed beneath his hand to catch the drips, and directed him toward the table. Its scarred top spoke of many meals eaten by many generations. The chairs were a mishmash of styles, but all seemed to be as old as the table. Nate could imagine previous Whitmires sitting here, eating, talking, laughing. The place had a settled atmosphere. In spite of the modern furnishings, glowing electric lamps and the laptop open on a living room table, he could picture a woman in a long dress coming inside, removing her bonnet and pumping water at the sink to wash up. Maybe that's what actually haunted the Whitmire farm—the ghosts of hardworking, happy people with established traditions going back generations. He shook his head at the fanciful thoughts. He never lapsed into daydreams like this.

Casting Gemma a wary glance, he ruefully decided that she wouldn't know if this was out of character for him or not. They hadn't seen each other in fifteen years.

"This cabin is nice," he said, watching her pick up a rubber bulb syringe, fill it with warm water and expertly flush his cut with a disinfectant solution. "Your family farmed this land for many years."

"More than a hundred, but my dad wasn't interested in farming so he sold most of the farmland and established the campground."

"But they stayed in this cabin, kept the family home."

"Don't sound so surprised," she said, glancing up and giving him the full attention of those remarkable green eyes. "They have roots here that they wanted to maintain. My parents may have been...unusual, but they knew how to create a happy home."

Nate didn't answer. For all of their wealth and position, his parents had never known how to do that. From his first memories, their home had been sterile, filled with icy silences. Funny, after all these years, he still never thought of the ostentatious house at the end of Pine Street as his home, only theirs. That's why it was sitting empty, falling into disrepair. Why he'd rented a small house near the hospital and filled it with furniture he'd bought himself. He had yet to include anything from his childhood home.

"And how are your parents?" he asked. "I heard they had left town, and the campground was permanently closed."

She gave him a big smile—the expression of someone talking about those she loved. "They're very well. As soon as I was launched into the world, they took the money they'd inherited from my dad's family and the sale of the farmland and took off. They've traveled the world ever since, helping out on building projects in places in need wherever they can. I see them a couple of times a year here in the States, or I go wherever they are."

"It sounds...idyllic."

Gemma laughed and her eyes lit up. "It sounds like what a couple of middle-aged hippies would do, but don't tell them I said that."

"I doubt that I'll ever see them."

"You might be surprised." She lifted his hand and examined it closely for debris, then, apparently satisfied, she carefully positioned a bandage over the cut. "This is their home, after all."

"Are you going to be here long?" Maybe she'd go out to dinner with him. There were no decent restaurants in Reston, but Dallas was only a couple of hours south and he knew there were plenty of fine dining places there. Besides, if she was as competent a nurse as she appeared to be, he might have a job for her.

"I'm back permanently."

"Really?" *More and more promising,* Nate thought. "Is your nursing license current?"

"Of course." She tilted another smile at him. "What's the matter?" she asked. "Afraid I didn't bandage your hand right? Remember, you were on my property without being asked, while I was busy working."

Deciding he'd better change tactics, he asked, "What were you doing out there, by the way? At first I thought you were burying a body."

"Planting herbs."

"In the dark?"

"It's not dark. There's a full moon, which is when these herbs must be planted."

Maybe she wasn't as different from her parents as he'd thought. "Oh? What kind?"

"Blue cohosh, for one."

He frowned. "It grows wild all around here. You only have to walk into the woods and pick it."

"I'd rather have it close by and if I grow it myself I can ensure the quality."

She was watching his face carefully. Nate felt as if he was trying to communicate in an unknown language.

"And you need these for cooking?"

"No, for pregnancy, labor and delivery. Tincture of blue cohosh stimulates labor."

Nathan went very still as those words sank in, the facts lining up before him as if they were printed on the very air.

"You're a midwife." His tone was flat.

GEMMA WHITMIRE STARED at the sudden stiffness in his face, the way his brown eyes had narrowed. Alarm bells clanged in her head, but she spoke calmly. "Yes, I am."

"And you're planning to open a birthing center?"

"Yes, in your father's old offices next to the hospital." She lifted her chin, held his gaze. There had been a time when she would have backed down, apologized, tried to explain her position. Those days were gone. "Exactly as you plan to establish a family practice and reopen the hospital."

"Not exactly."

"Both facilities are for people's health."

"No, the hospital cures people and keeps them well—"

"Fortunately, giving birth isn't an illness."

Their eyes met—hers defiant, his resolute. Gemma's heart sank as she imagined the swirl of objections that were about to come at her. She'd heard them all before, fought them all before. Somehow, it was disappointing to know she was about to hear them from Nathan.

She hadn't recognized him at first when he'd startled her and she'd thrown him to the ground. He'd been a small, skinny guy in high school, with dark hair worn long in defiance of his parents. He must have grown a good six inches since she'd seen him last, topping out at six feet, with wide shoulders and muscled arms. His hair was cut short, probably for the sake of convenience. But those eyes hadn't changed. Deep-set and steady, they looked at her as if he was trying to see into her soul.

She had admired him when they were growing up, and had a major crush on him by the time they were in high school. She'd been crazy about his good looks, his serious gray eyes and the way his thick brows came to a slight peak as if he was gently surprised by life. Whereas the other guys she'd known had been jocks or cowboys, he'd been focused and smart. Apparently, he still was.

But he was also wrong.

"Giving birth is fraught with risks. Risks that are best handled in a qualified medical facility." His voice was firm, as if he thought that stating his case strongly would have her immediately caving.

Not a chance. "Giving birth is a natural process, which women have been handling very well for quite a while now."

"That's true, but why take risks with women's lives when excellent medical facilities and qualified personnel are available?"

"It's not a risk and I *am* qualified personnel. I've been a registered nurse for ten years and a midwife for six. I've worked in every type of medical situation, every type of neighborhood you can imagine, even some pretty bad ones, which is why I know self-defense moves. Many times, a birthing center is the most affordable option for families, and you may not be aware of this, but Reston County isn't exactly overflowing with wealthy people who can afford hospital births and care. Our new birthing center is the only option for expectant mothers since we don't know when the hospital will be reopened, anyway."

"It will be soon…"

"Besides that, more than ninety percent of this country's births are in a hospital and we have such high maternal and infant mortality rates in the United States. It's appalling."

"I agree, but I can't believe that dragging home births back from the past is going to improve the situation."

"Which is exactly why they're not being dragged back from the past. Nonhospital births are proven safe on a daily basis, both at home and in birthing centers across this country."

He raised a skeptical brow. "Your birthing center has to have a transfer agreement with a hospital no more than thirty minutes away and a licensed doctor as medical director."

"I'm working on both of those things with the hospital in Toncaville until you get the Reston County Hospital reopened." She clapped her hands onto her hips. "And once our hospital *is* reopened, if you choose not to be the medical director for the birthing center, I'll respect that and continue with a doctor from Toncaville—no matter how inconvenient that might be."

He frowned, obviously not liking her tone. "You'll have to be on duty twenty-four hours a day."

"I know that."

"You think one nurse-midwife is going to be enough for the whole of Reston County?"

"Of course not. I'll be hiring other qualified personnel."

"Good luck with that." He jerked a thumb toward town. "I've got forty vacancies to fill in order to reopen the hospital."

"I have my own sources for finding qualified people for the birthing center."

"Oh? How? Did you send out flyers by Pony Express? Ask any of the locals who've ever helped bring a calf into the world to sign up?"

Gemma felt her temper heating up. Her

chin, always ready to lead her into trouble, lifted. "I've hired people and will continue to hire people who lost their jobs when Reston Community Hospital closed eight years ago. My new employees are excellent, qualified people who live in this town and wanted to continue working here but couldn't because their livelihood was snatched away. They've spent eight years driving to jobs in neighboring towns. They've missed their kids' baseball and football games, school plays, band concerts, and birthday parties because they couldn't make it home in time."

Gemma watched emotions chase each other over his face—annoyance, anger and then shame.

Nathan's eyes were fierce as he said, "And those people could have kept their jobs, continued to work here in Reston, if my father, the hospital administrator, hadn't bankrupted the place and absconded with the money."

CHAPTER TWO

ONCE AGAIN, HEAT rushed into Gemma's face, but this time, it wasn't from anger. She pressed her palms together and cleared her throat. "I wasn't… I wasn't going to say that."

"You didn't need to," Nathan said, standing up. "Everyone in town knows it."

Gemma stared at him in dismay. She hadn't meant to bring it up. It had to be humiliating for him to return here, face the critics, try to make things right. "I… I'm sorry."

The tight look on his face told her he wouldn't welcome any more references to the issue, so Gemma cleared her throat and said, "Nate, good luck with the hospital." She offered him a tentative smile, which he didn't return.

Instead, he said, "Thanks. I'll need it." He turned toward the door and paused. "And thanks for the bandage." Nathan left the way he'd come. She walked to the door and watched him jog away into the darkness, his white T-shirt leaving an impression in her vision long after he was out of sight.

Gemma stood for a moment with her shoulders drooping. She had known there would be opposition to the birthing center, but she hadn't expected to start this battle quite so soon, and certainly not with Nathan. Her heart felt heavy with dismay and disappointment.

As she cleared away the basin and first-aid supplies, Gemma wondered why Nathan was back. Why was *he* reopening the hospital? The last she'd heard, he had an excellent job at a hospital in Oklahoma City. At least now she knew where he stood regarding the birthing center.

After a few minutes, she went back outside to finish planting her herbs, making sure they were firmly in the ground, each with a small trench around it. She could fill the trenches with water, or they'd catch the abundant rain they'd had so far this spring.

It was nearly midnight by the time she finished so she cleaned her tools, put everything away and went inside for a shower. By sheer force of will, she put Nathan out of her mind and focused on thoughts of the birthing center and the positive impact it would have on the women of Reston County.

"THIS WILL ONLY take a few minutes," Lisa Thomas assured Gemma the next morning as she slid behind the wheel of her car and buckled her seat belt. "I can't wait to see the Sunshine Birthing Center. It's so great that you named it after your mom."

"She's pretty happy about it. I figured I owed her some kind of tribute for letting me bring home all those injured animals when I was little." Gemma settled into the luxurious seat, so different from the utilitarian one in her elderly Land Rover. One of these days, she would get that seat replaced and not even think about how strange it would be with the well-worn interior. She couldn't be without her rough-and-tumble Rover, though, not in this county, where roads more often resembled dried-up, rocky riverbeds.

"I'll never forget the first bird whose wing you tried to bandage. Between the splint and the bandages, that crow couldn't even stand up and constantly tipped over."

Gemma grinned. "He lived, though."

"Well, yeah, but he always flew kind of sideways after that—kept flying into your living room window."

"He did that on purpose, remember? He'd become addicted to my mom's homemade bread. He finally figured out that if he sat on the sill and tapped his beak on the glass, Mom would run out with some crumbs."

Lisa laughed, the deep, throaty sound that was so at odds with her petite frame. As usual, she was wearing a beautifully fitted and professional-looking dress. This one was the same blue as her eyes, and she wore matching four-inch heels.

"She was as big a pushover as you were. That's why he never left the area."

"Well, that and, thanks to me, he flew sideways."

Lisa grinned as she said, "Now tell me what you've accomplished toward the birthing center in the past week. Every time I go to one of those real estate conferences, I feel like I've spent time on another planet."

She pulled onto the highway and headed into town, listening while Gemma told her about the latest developments.

"We have an office with very little in it except a desk and chair, computer and phone. I've hired Rhonda Morton to be our receptionist."

"The mayor's wife? She'll certainly keep you up on all the local gossip."

"That's fine as long as she doesn't gossip about any of our patients. I've also hired Beth Garmer and Carrie Stringfellow, but they're my only nurses until we get our clientele built up enough—" She stared at the house where they had stopped. "Why are we at the Smiths' place, Lisa?"

"Nathan wants to sell it. Apparently, the house actually belonged to his mom. When she passed away, she left it to him and it's been sitting empty since his dad disappeared. I told him I'd look the place over and give him an estimate on what I think it might sell for."

Lisa swung out of the car and opened the back door to tug out a fat briefcase and a big, black binder. "Although I don't know what I'm going to use for comparative prices. This town isn't exactly a hotbed of real estate activity and there aren't too many houses like this one that come on the market. Even in this run-down state, it's worth more than all the other houses on the block combined. Did you know the foyer is white Carrara marble? Of all things to find in rural Oklahoma."

Belatedly, she seemed to realize that Gemma hadn't moved a muscle.

Lisa leaned in and gave her a puzzled look. "Come on, let's go."

Gemma responded with a big smile. "I'll wait in the car."

"Are you crazy? You'll roast!"

"It's not that hot."

"Come on. Aren't you curious to see inside the Smiths' house?"

"Not really," Gemma murmured as she joined her friend on the sidewalk.

Lisa held up her cell phone and took a picture of the front of the house before they walked through the sagging wrought iron gate and up the cracked sidewalk. Grass poked through—brave little spikes of spring in an otherwise lifeless landscape.

The general air of neglect was depressing. The front flowerbeds, which had once held Mrs. Smith's prize roses, overflowed with dead plants.

"Going to need a major cleanup before it

goes on the market," Lisa said, stepping up to knock on the door.

A few seconds later, the door swung open. "Hello, Lisa. Thanks for coming, and…oh, Gemma." Nate's dark gaze swept over her, from her neon green toenails, to her cargo shorts and sleeveless Hawaiian-print camp shirt, to the loose swirl of hair she'd pinned atop her head.

He was struggling to control his expression. "Hello," he finally said, stepping back.

She took off her sunglasses and perched them atop her head as she gave him a friendly nod.

Lisa strolled inside, seeming not to notice the tension between the other two.

"Gemma and I were on the way to the birthing center so she can show me around, but I knew you were expecting me to stop by this morning." Lisa looked over the foyer as she set her binder and briefcase by the door. "Okay if I take some pictures?"

She didn't wait for an answer, but strolled away, drawn into the once-magnificent home and toward the dining room. "Kitchens and bathrooms," she called over her shoulder.

"That's what sells houses. Kitchens and bathrooms." She disappeared around the corner.

Gemma and Nathan stood awkwardly for a moment before she pointed to his hand. "How is the cut this morning?"

"Better. It'll heal."

Since that topic of conversation had gone nowhere, she looked around at the nearly empty living room. A huge, clean rectangle of hardwood floor was bordered with scuffed dirt where a rug had obviously been rolled up and taken away.

"Looks like you're clearing things out."

"Yes. I sold all the furniture to a second-hand store over in Toncaville. Now I'm dealing with the smaller items—and the dirt." He bent slightly to dust off the knees of the faded jeans he wore with an old blue T-shirt and battered sneakers. He reached up to smooth his mussed hair and came away with a cobweb. "And the spiders," he added.

"I ran in to a bunch of those at my place, too. I didn't mind too much until they tried to join me in the shower."

"If I lived here, I'd have to pay rent to the spiders to even use the shower."

She smiled, feeling an easing of the tension, and walked over to examine a grouping of family pictures on the wall. Most of them were formal family portraits, everyone looking stiff and awkward. Gemma studied the faces of Nate's parents, both of them serious, almost grim. She could see Nate reflected in each of their faces, but staring at his father, she wondered what was on the man's mind. Was he even then siphoning money from an institution that was so vital to the community where he lived? She had no answer, so she turned her attention to the other photos. A few were snapshots of Nathan as a small boy, alone, or with an older girl. In one photo, he appeared to be about two and she held him on her hip with one arm and tickled him with her other hand. It was a happy, spontaneous contrast to the other pictures, but somehow it made her sad.

Gemma frowned, trying to pinpoint the reason for her sudden melancholy. "That was your sister, Mandy, wasn't it? I remember that she was very beautiful, and—"

"And she died when I was twelve." Nathan stepped forward and took the picture from the wall. He pulled a rag from his back pocket, wiped the picture clean and then placed it inside an open box on the floor.

"I know. I'm very sorry. I remember she used to come to our place and hang out with my mother."

Nate frowned at her. "What? When?"

Gemma paused to think. "It must have been during her senior year in high school. You and I were in second grade. I remember seeing her and my mom out in the garden, and sometimes working in the kitchen. I think Mom taught her to bake bread."

Nate didn't respond but stood looking down at the photo he'd placed in the box.

"Is something wrong, Nate?"

"No. No. It's ancient history now."

Lisa called to him from the kitchen and he left Gemma standing where she was, gazing at the family pictures and thinking that even ancient history never really disappeared.

NATE STOOD BY the picture window in the living room and watched as Gemma and Lisa headed toward Lisa's sporty little car. As they climbed in, Lisa said something that had Gemma throwing back her head and laughing as she tugged open the door and dropped into the seat. He tucked his hands into his back pockets and let his shoulders relax as he watched the curve of her neck and the way her ponytail bounced.

Gemma was everything this house wasn't— warm, inviting, happy. Somehow, having her here, if even for a short time, had made the place even more depressing.

As they drove away, he turned back to the living room, his gaze going to the wall of family pictures—although, in his mind, *family* hardly described the people who had lived in this house, especially after Mandy's death. He and his parents had been like three separate planets, each in their own orbit, never touching, rarely interacting. The Smiths had been the exact opposite of the Whitmires, whom he had often seen together in town— a tight, happy little unit of three. He remembered watching them with longing, wanting what they had, knowing he would never have it.

Mandy must have wanted the same thing. He hadn't known she was close to the Whitmires. It ate at his gut to know she'd had a whole life, areas of interest he hadn't known about, but he'd only been a kid, so how could he have known? He wondered if his parents knew. Maybe, judging by the frequent negative comments his mother had made about the "hippie crazies."

Nate shook his head, pulling himself back from the past, where he'd been too often since returning home. Whatever happened now, it was up to him to create it. He had a huge job before him and it would be helped along by selling this mausoleum. Who knew? Maybe it would be purchased by a happy family with parents who didn't mind how much noise a kid made running up the stairs, or building some crazy construction in the backyard.

Cheered by the thought, he turned toward the staircase and the last of the stored items he needed to sort through. There were a few sealed boxes in his mother's closet that he would have to look at someday. They probably contained nothing more than old business papers, but maybe there was some family history that might actually spark a sense of family in him. He snorted aloud, marveling at his need to be proud of people he'd made a point of not obsessing over.

He would finish this task, have the place cleaned and painted, then sell it and move on with his life.

"I DON'T KNOW why I let you talk me into this," Gemma groused as Carly Joslin took another bump in the road at warp speed. Her truck was headed back to Reston and the organizational meeting for the reopening of the hospital.

"I'm wondering the same thing," Lisa added, looking from one best friend to the other.

The three of them were crowded into the front seat of Carly's truck, as they'd been so many times before.

"Oh, come on," Carly answered, taking her eyes off the road to tilt her head and grin at Gemma, who was hanging on to the door handle for all she was worth. "It's like old times—taking my dad's truck, although now it's my truck, driving to Toncaville for lunch—"

"Dragging you out of antique and junk shops," Lisa broke in.

"Arriving back late, getting in trouble," Gemma added.

"Only we won't be getting in trouble this time. We're no longer crazy teenage girls…"

"We're crazy thirty-two-year-old women, and at least two of us should know better than to go anywhere with you on the day the county is doing brush and bulky-trash pickup," Lisa said.

Gemma glanced over her shoulder at the "treasures" Carly had already collected along the highway and placed in the truck bed. Twice a year, May and November, the county sent big dump trucks around to collect yard clippings to be ground into mulch, and items too large to fit into trash bins. People put out a wide assortment of throwaway items, which Carly would gleefully collect and repurpose—or "upcycle," as she called it. She hauled it all home, stored it in the barn and garage and worked her way through it until the next brush and bulky pickup. To her it was like getting two extra Christmases each year.

Lisa glanced back, too, and Carly met their skeptical looks with an unrepentant grin.

"What are you going to do with an old bicycle frame, minus tires and handlebars?" Lisa asked.

"Are you kidding? It's beautiful. I'll paint it—maybe fire-engine red—and spruce it up. Imagine how cute it's going to look in someone's front yard with live flowers in the basket…"

"Conveniently placed for the next brush and bulky pickup," Gemma said drily.

"It'll be a work of art."

"Yes," Gemma said with a sigh. "When you're finished with it, it probably will be. But some of that other stuff…the washing machine, for example."

"That wringer-type washing machine is in pretty good shape considering it probably saw its heyday when Herbert Hoover was president."

"But what on earth are you going to do with it?"

Carly gave her a smug look. "Remove the rust, oil all the parts, polish it up. Believe it or not, there's a whole society—mostly men—who collect washing machines. After I fix it up, I'll sell it to one of them."

Lisa stared at her. "Men who collect washing machines? Someday you're going to be struck by lightning for the fibs you make up."

"It's true! They've got hundreds of members—all around the world."

"That's crazy," Gemma said.

"Yup, but profitable, and besides, *I'm* a little crazy," Carly answered. "I'm surprised you still let me take the lead on these things."

"You're the one with the truck," Gemma reminded her sweetly. "And I needed a new lawn mower, which, now that I think of it, could have fit in the back of my Land Rover."

"But we wouldn't have been able to collect nearly as much useful stuff—"

"Good!" her friends said in unison.

"And I could have found you an old lawn mower, fixed it up and—"

"No."

"Well, in any case, you don't have to do your own mowing. You could hire someone to… What's that?" Carly slammed on the brakes at the same time she whipped her head around so fast, Gemma could hear her neck crack.

"It's nothing," Lisa said. "We need to keep going. We'll be late for the meeting."

"That's a chair." Carly pulled over to the

mound of discarded furniture someone had piled up at the end of the road that led into the Bordens' place. "We've got plenty of time to get to the meeting. I don't want to miss it since I hope to sell produce to the hospital kitchen."

"The chair is broken." Gemma knew it wouldn't do any good, but she had to try. She exchanged an exasperated look with Lisa. "You don't need a broken chair, Carly."

But Carly had already turned on her hazard lights to alert approaching traffic, catapulted from the truck and freed the discarded piece of furniture from a tangle of wire and sheet metal, easy for her since she was tall. She was also strong from years of working outside. Her long black ponytail swung as she held up her find.

Gemma wasn't the least bit surprised to see Carly's dark brown eyes shining in triumph as she examined it. No archaeologist unearthing a history-changing artifact could be more excited than Carly was at this moment.

"It's Duncan Phyfe style." She turned it this way and that, checking it from all angles and testing the joints. "The arms are sturdy. I can make this into something useful."

"Yes," Gemma said, joining her. "Kindling wood."

"Don't be ridiculous. Only the legs are broken. This would make an adorable swing to hang from a tree limb, or a porch beam."

Gemma tilted her head back and looked at the clear blue sky. "Repurposing, thy name is Carly."

Thrilled with her new treasure, Carly placed it in the pickup bed beside the box holding Gemma's yet-to-be assembled lawn mower. "If I attach a seat belt, it would even be suitable for little kids."

When she started to turn back to the junk pile to look for more gems, Lisa leapt from the truck. She and Gemma each grabbed an arm, marched their friend in a circle and then took her straight back to the driver's side.

"Wait!" Carly protested, straining to look over her shoulder. "There might be something—"

"Yes," Gemma answered. "Tetanus."

"Snakes," Lisa added. "Copperheads, cottonmouths, timber rattlers." She pointed to the pools of water in the bar ditch beside the road, evidence of the recent rains. "Remember they like moist places."

Carly grimaced. "Oh, yeah, right." With a slight shudder, she climbed behind the wheel. Gemma and Lisa hurried around the front of the truck and climbed in. After they fastened their seat belts, they resumed their drive to Reston.

"You wait and see," Carly said smugly. "I'll make that chair into something adorable and useful."

"I don't doubt that," Gemma answered. "But has it occurred to you that it might be a good idea to begin getting rid of some of the chairs you've refurbished over the years? You've got enough for a symphony orchestra."

"You're exaggerating."

"Not by much," Lisa added. "You've made each chair into a unique collector's item. If you wanted to, you could open a shop in Reston or Toncaville, or somewhere else nearby."

"But I don't want to. I don't want to be tied down. I wouldn't be able to work on refinishing furniture at my own pace or go out looking for new pieces. Owning a shop means having to deal with the public. The way it is now, I advertise the items I've got for sale online and people come find me, or call me up and place an order over the phone. Besides, what about my farm? My organic produce won't plant and harvest itself."

Lisa threw her hands in the air. "But with a shop your sales would go through the roof. People like to come in and browse. I know you're the ultimate do-it-yourselfer, but you could work on the farm in the mornings, then have a place in town with a back room. You could work on your projects, hire someone to work the front, arrange your merchandise. You'd be providing a job for someone. Maybe two people. A shop like that would be another way to attract tourists here. The kinds of projects you do? People from Dallas would eat that up with a spoon. They'd gladly drive up here to shop, enjoy the rustic experience, eat lunch, spend money."

Carly sent her a sidelong glance. "You planning to run for mayor, Lis?"

"I might. Someday. There's a lot that could be done in Reston if people would get their heads out of the past and think about the future." Lisa had the bit between her teeth now and was going to run with it, doing her best to convince Carly of the rightness of this idea.

"The Smiths' house, for example. It's been sitting empty all this time, but it's sound, only needs upgrading. The place has six bedrooms. It would make a perfect bed-and-breakfast."

Gemma raised an eyebrow. "I've had two encounters with Nathan Smith since I've been back. Neither one of them gave any indication he was interested in running a B and B. Besides, didn't you say he's anxious to sell?"

Lisa gave a dismissive wave of her hand. "It was only a suggestion of what could be done with that property. And furthermore, if you reopened your family's campground, you could attract tons of visitors. And the pavilion would be perfect for weddings and receptions."

"If nobody minds the giant hole in the roof," Gemma added.

Lisa didn't even pause for breath. "Your lake has hardly been fished in years. The trout are practically begging to be caught. Fishermen would be buying tackle at Wilson's Hardware, fuel and groceries at Cross-roads Gas 'n' Stuff..."

"Not gonna happen," Gemma responded with a firm shake of her head. "I've got my hands full with opening the birthing center. I can't take on anything else."

"Well, keep it in mind for the future. That's exactly what I've been talking about—planning for Reston's future. This could be a prosperous little town if people would get behind a few of these projects."

"Which you'll think up and organize," Carly said.

"Of course. Somebody has to be in charge."

"You did do a good job of convincing the mayor to find a buyer to renovate and reopen the Mustang Supermarket," Carly said.

"Having three grocery stores in town benefits everyone. Competition is a good thing."

"Having three retailers to buy my produce is also a good thing."

Smiling, Gemma settled back and only half listened to her friends. This was one of the reasons she had been so happy to move home to Reston. Besides providing a useful service to women in this rural area, she was getting to reconnect with her two best friends. Even though neither of them had anything to do with the medical field, they would be her staunchest supporters as she opened the birthing center.

Unlike Nathan Smith, Gemma thought with a sigh. His feelings about it were crystal clear and his attitude made her feel both wary and disappointed in him. She didn't know why she'd expected more from him. After all, she didn't really know Nathan anymore.

"Wow," Carly said, leaning over the steering wheel to gaze ahead as she slowed to a crawl inside Reston city limits. "An actual traffic jam."

A line of cars and trucks waited, turn signals blinking, to pull in to the high school parking lot. Junior Fedder, the deputy sheriff—short, dangerously obese and sweating profusely in the late-afternoon sun—stood at the entrance, directing traffic.

"I think that's the most movement I've seen out of Junior since that day last fall when Tyler and Bradley Saxon put a dead skunk on top of the furnace in the high school basement. Junior chased those two all the way down Main Street, but they finally lost him when he collapsed in front of Wilson's Hardware. Fortunately, he fell into a wheelbarrow so Frank Wilson was able to get him back to the sheriff's office."

As she listened to Carly's matter-of-fact recital of this story, Gemma began laughing so hard tears rolled down her face. "In the... whee-wheelbarrow?" she choked.

"Yup. Frank's wife, Tina, ran alongside, fanning Junior with a newspaper and spraying him with a plant mister." Carly grinned and waved at Junior as the truck crept past him and into a parking place. "It was a new, heavy-duty wheelbarrow that Frank had assembled and put on display. He sold out the next day when everybody saw how much poundage one of those puppies could carry."

"You lie."

"No, it's true," Lisa assured her. "Carly bought one."

Still laughing, Gemma all but tumbled from the truck. "Oh, how I've missed this town," she said, looking up at that moment to see a solemn Nathan Smith, briefcase in hand, heading toward the auditorium. He glanced her way, nodded briefly and kept walking.

The chattering crowd fell silent and stood back to let him pass. Gemma saw him pause and glance around, then mount the steps purposefully. As far as she could tell, every eye was on him, but no one had greeted him.

"Come on," Lisa said. "Or we'll never find a seat."

As it turned out, someone had saved seats for them near the front so they had a good view of the proceedings. Gemma looked around, recalling happy memories of her time at Reston High School. In spite of her unusual parents and her own obsession with finding and patching up wounded animals, she had never felt like an outsider and had enjoyed her years here. She was happy to see that, except for a fresh coat of paint and recently reupholstered seats, the big auditorium was still the same.

Two rows of chairs were on the stage and each was filled with someone important to the reopening of the hospital. County supervisors and city planners were in the back row. In the front row, white-haired, sleepy-looking Brantley Clegg, who ran the bank and would be handling the finances, sat on the far end beside Harley Morton, the mayor of Reston. Nathan, somber in a black suit and tie, was next. He sat arrow straight in the hard folding chair, his hands on his knees, his gaze on the audience, although Gemma didn't think he was actually seeing anyone.

Beside him were Tom and Frances Sanderson, wealthy landowners and cattle ranchers who had given a huge sum of money to the project. When Frances saw Gemma, she elbowed her husband and the two of them gave her happy waves. Gemma waved back. Nathan saw this interaction and shot a swift glance from the couple to Gemma.

Gemma's smile faded. Nathan would find out soon enough how it was that she and the Sandersons were so well acquainted.

"Wow," Carly said under her breath. "I wouldn't have known Nathan. He's so much taller, and in great shape. He looks like—"

"A sexy undertaker," Lisa finished for her. "I noticed that the other day when Gemma and I were at his house. Very solemn."

"I don't ever remember him being a barrel of laughs," Carly said. "And now he looks like he's made up his mind to run his head into a brick wall."

Gemma studied his face. Carly was right. He didn't appear to be looking forward to this at all. He must have felt her gaze on him because his eyes met hers. Her heart gave a little kick of anticipation but she didn't want to analyze the reason for it.

She pulled her attention from him as Mayor Morton approached the podium and went through the usual ritual of tapping the microphone attached to the antique sound system to make sure it was working, then leaning in so close to speak that it released a loud squawk. The audience groaned and several people clapped their hands over their ears.

"Oh, uh, sorry, folks." The mayor looked contrite as he jerked back. The microphone went dead and he was perplexed for a minute until a boy who couldn't have been more than fourteen jumped onto the stage and fiddled with something under the podium, then picked up the microphone and handed it to the mayor.

"Oh, thanks, Owen." The mayor nodded and finally seemed to be in his element.

He looked up and fixed his good-neighbor-and-good-politician smile into place as he surveyed the audience. "We're here as a community to reveal the plans for reopening Reston County Hospital. We've got a slide show to explain our plans and we'll take questions afterward."

"I've got a question right now," a voice called out.

Everyone turned to look at the speaker.

"Cole Burleigh," Gemma said, her lips tightening in a line of annoyance.

"Oh, for crying out loud, who kicked over a rock and let him slither out?" Carly asked as Lisa clicked her tongue in disgust.

Cole looked around the big room to make sure he had everyone's attention. He didn't look much different than he had in high school, except that he had filled out, and if he wasn't careful would soon begin running to fat. His blond hair was still thick, his brown eyes just as calculating. They narrowed as he pointed to Nathan and asked, "I want to know if Dr. Smith's briefcase is packed full of all that money his dear old daddy stole."

A murmur ran through the crowd as people turned to watch Nathan's reaction. His color deepened and he started to rise to his feet. The mayor waved him down as he turned back to Cole.

"This is neither the time nor the place for that, and—"

"Why not? It's why everyone is here, after all."

CHAPTER THREE

A WAVE OF assent rippled through the audience and Gemma's heart sank. Cole was right. People were interested in the new hospital, but they were at this meeting to try and find out if Nathan knew the whereabouts of his father and, more importantly, the missing money. She watched as people she'd known her entire life—whom Nathan had known for that long—stared at him with hardened faces.

"We'll take questions after the presentation." The mayor floundered. His gaze darted around the room as if he was looking for support, but he must not have found it if his increasingly worried look was any indication.

"But we want to know now," Cole responded. His gaze swept the room, as well. It was obvious he was loving his role, playing to his audience.

Nathan stood and placed his hand on the mayor's arm. "It's okay, Harley. I'll tell everyone what I know."

Mayor Morton appeared to swallow a huge lump as he nodded and stepped back.

Nathan took the microphone with one hand and smoothed his tie with the other. Gemma felt a spark of pride when she saw that his hands were steady.

"My briefcase contains cost projections and spreadsheets for the reopening of the hospital—"

"Do they equal the same as what ole George stole?" Cole asked, his lip curled into a sneer.

"I don't know," Nathan answered in a grim tone. "I know in general terms how much it was, as all of you do, but I never heard an exact figure of how much my father took." He glanced at Brantley Clegg, who straightened in his seat and raised his voice to state a figure that had the entire room gasping. Even Cole seemed momentarily taken aback.

Nathan nodded at the banker then turned again to the audience. "I don't know where my father is. I haven't heard from him since he disappeared—"

"A likely story," Cole began, but when he

looked around this time, he could see that he was losing his audience. People were so shocked by the full scope of George Smith's treachery that they had lost interest in Cole. Gemma saw someone reach up and tug Cole back into his seat. He sat but crossed his arms over his chest and glared straight ahead.

Nathan waited a few seconds until the crowd settled before he went on. "I'm profoundly sorry for what my father did. I promise you I knew nothing about it. However, I think it's reasonable to assume that some of that money went to pay my medical school fees. I had partial scholarships, but there are always more fees that need to be paid."

He looked down into the audience and Gemma sat up so he would look at her. She clenched her hands in her lap, wishing her strength could flow into him. In spite of the animosity that simmered between them, she wanted him to know she wasn't against him.

Nathan's gaze fixed on her for a second, then he took a breath and said, "I worked at a hospital in Oklahoma City for a few years, but I decided I had to come back here and try to make some kind of restitution. Setting up a family practice where there isn't one, reopening the hospital, getting the necessary funding, providing quality health care for the people of this county—that's how I'll pay you back. Also, I'm selling my family home. That money will go into the hospital fund, as well."

"Maybe that won't be good enough." Cole spoke again, obviously trying to regain the upper hand.

Fed up, Gemma bounced to her feet. Her red hair whipped around her shoulders as she spun on her heel. She clapped her hands onto her hips. "Cole, none of that money came out of your pocket. Why don't you just be quiet? Nathan didn't have to come back here and try to make amends, but that's what he's doing. Reopening the hospital will benefit everyone."

Cole glared at her as a murmur of agreement rustled through the room. She turned and sat down, avoiding Nathan's eyes.

Tom Sanderson stood and approached the podium. A big, strong man in his fifties, he didn't suffer fools gladly. With a nod to Nathan, he took the microphone in his tough rancher's hand and said, "Gemma is right, Cole. Frances and I have provided a large share of the funds to get the hospital going again. We'll have a much better accounting system in place, one that will be harder to defraud. If we're not worried about it, you shouldn't be, either." He replaced the microphone in its stand, then clapped Nathan on the shoulder. Nathan sent the older man a grateful look as they both took their seats.

The momentary lull gave the mayor the chance to hurry back to the podium and say, "Yes, well, all this can be discussed at length, um, later on. Right now, let's see the slides we've prepared." He nodded at the kid who'd fixed the sound system. "Owen, go ahead."

As a large screen lowered from the ceiling and the people on the stage turned their chairs to see, the young man competently checked his computer and projector. Within a couple of minutes, the presentation began and the audience settled down.

GEMMA WATCHED THE presentation and tried to make sense of the storm of emotions that buffeted her. She felt disappointed in the people, although she supposed their reaction was natural. George Smith's treachery and the subsequent closing of the hospital had affected everyone. It was the depth of their anger, the way they hadn't moved past it, that was troubling. Or maybe they had moved past it but felt they were being dragged backward once again.

And there was Nate. He was definitely being pulled back while attempting to forge ahead, trying to rebuild a vital part of the community while being resented by many of the locals. It didn't help that he was about as approachable as a daddy snake in a nest of vipers.

Her heart ached for him. In spite of his opposition to her birthing center, she felt protective toward him. She knew it made no sense, but when she looked at him, she still saw the boy he'd been, the one she knew. At the same time, she saw the man he'd become, whom she knew not at all.

NATHAN WATCHED THE SCREEN, but his mind wasn't on the presentation, which he'd seen a dozen times already. This was turning out to be even harder than he'd thought it would be. He'd hoped people wouldn't blame him for what his father had done. It appeared some of them didn't. That was a start.

While slides clicked by, interspersed with video interviews with county officials and citizen-on-the-street chats about the hospital, Nathan replayed the scene in Gemma's backyard with her digging, listening to music and singing along.

Somehow, the scene changed and became a sunny afternoon in that same backyard, but it had been different, full of pens and cages.

He and Gemma had been about ten years old. She had gushed about the baby raccoon she'd found abandoned and taken home. He wanted to see it. His mother never allowed any pets, not even a goldfish.

At the Whitmires', he'd been astounded by the variety of animals in her personal menagerie. Her father, Wolfchild—Nathan recalled snickering whenever he heard that name—had built all the pens and cages. He had glowed with pride as Gemma had shown the animals. There had been several puppies and dogs, abandoned on the road outside the campground, and cats and kittens left behind. The citizens of Reston County had quickly figured out that the Whitmire family were pushovers when it came to unwanted animals. It was public knowledge that Gemma would find good homes for all of them.

There had also been a fawn wounded by an arrow, several birds with broken wings or legs, along with the baby raccoon, who had been darned cute. They'd all needed rescuing and Gemma had...

Nathan sat up so suddenly, many people in the audience stared at him.

Did Gemma think he needed rescuing like some wounded animal? His gaze went straight to her and she met his eyes with a questioning look.

Sitting back, he crossed his arms over his chest. She was wrong, and he would make that clear the first chance he got. But right now, he had to deal with the rest of the town.

He understood why the people of Reston were mad at his father. He was, too. He had tried to find George, tried to figure out where he'd disappeared to along with the money. What he'd told the audience at this meeting was true. He'd never known the exact amount because he didn't want to know how great a larceny his father had committed.

He'd never known that George had a gambling problem that had gotten completely out of hand when Mandy, and then Nate's mother, died. Nate admitted, to his shame, that he hadn't known what his father was capable of because he hadn't really known his father. All he'd known was that George spent long hours at work and never took a vacation—rarely a day off. Now Nate knew why. It was called cooking the books and his dad was a master chef.

The county sheriff and some state investigative agencies had searched for George and had tracked him to Las Vegas, but the leads had petered out. They speculated that he'd changed his name and obtained false identification. They would wait until he resurfaced—but that hadn't happened in all of these years.

Wherever George was, he had almost certainly gambled all that money away. If he'd been a lucky gambler, he probably wouldn't have needed to steal in the first place.

Harley returned to the podium and asked, "Does anyone have any questions?"

Of course they did and the next hour was spent in heated discussions about money, personnel, building and equipment upgrades, contract bids for the work, and a dozen other issues. The county supervisors, city manager and banker all answered questions. Finally, someone brought up the other issue Nate had been dreading.

"What about the birthing center?"

HARLEY'S GAZE WENT directly to Nate. Gemma watched consternation flit across his face. It was obvious that he didn't want to answer that question.

"Dr. Smith, how will the birthing center be involved with the hospital?" Harley asked.

"The same as with any other hospital. When complications occur, the mother will be transferred to the hospital—"

"Although such occurrences are rare," Gemma broke in, springing to her feet. She hurried up the stairs and across the stage to the podium. Swinging in beside Nate, she eased Harley aside, confiscated the microphone and gave a bright smile as she said, "With every mother and baby, our goal is to make sure they receive the best care possible. We ensure this by frequent checkups and careful monitoring throughout the pregnancy, along with a comprehensive birth plan and education." She cast a quick glance at Nate. "As you probably know, in Oklahoma, birthing centers can only deal with low-risk pregnancies. We will make every effort to guarantee that a low-risk pregnancy stays that way. We will answer any and all questions the parents may have, and we'll make it as safe and as memorable as possible. After all, birth is a once-in-a-lifetime event," she concluded to chuckles from the audience.

Nate retook the microphone and kept his gaze on Gemma as he said, "The birthing center will be monitored by the medical staff at Reston County Hospital."

"Well, doesn't Reston County Hospital have to actually open first?" Gemma asked sweetly, leaning in and raising her voice. "The Sunshine Birthing Center will be open within a few weeks. Until Reston Hospital reopens, we'll transport patients to the hospital in Toncaville if necessary, and our medical director will be one of their physicians. We'll hold an open house so everyone can visit our facility and if we have any expectant mothers—and if I remember correctly, there are *always* expectant mothers around here—please feel free to call and make an appointment. Even if you ultimately choose not to use our services, we're happy to talk to anyone." She gave the center's phone number and as she did, Nathan clenched his jaw.

Belatedly seeming to sense the tension, the mayor stepped in between Gemma and Nathan. "Um, that's all the time we have right now, folks. I'm sure you'll have more questions. Call my office and we'll try to help you as best we can."

Gemma was disappointed in Nate's reaction, although she didn't know why it surprised her. She was ready to leave, to rejoin Carly and Lisa, but she found herself gathered into a hug. She looked up into Frances Sanderson's smiling face.

Laughing, Gemma returned the hug.

"Gemma, we're so happy to see you back in Reston, at last," Frances said. Curvaceous and beautiful with shoulder-length silver hair, she was dressed in a crisp white shirt, black jeans and chunky turquoise jewelry.

"It's only because of you that I'm here."

"It's only because of you that we have a healthy grandson," Frances countered. She glanced up when Nathan paused beside them and treated him to one of her sparkling smiles. "Dr. Smith, you're very fortunate to be able to work with Gemma."

Nathan looked at her, then at Gemma, who hid a smile. He probably didn't know Frances very well and wasn't aware that she rarely acknowledged negative situations, choosing instead to see the world through rose-colored glasses.

"Um, yes," he agreed, but his dark eyes said something completely different.

"Tom and I are having our annual Memorial Day picnic at our place and we've invited all the hospital and birthing-center donors and potential donors. Of course, we want you to come. We intend to wring every last cent out of them and having you there will make us look legitimate." She told them the time, wiggled her fingers at the two of them and went to rejoin her husband.

Maybe Frances was more shrewd than she appeared.

"The Sandersons are contributing to the birthing center?" Nathan asked, his gaze following Frances as she charmed her way, one by one, through the people on the stage. Tom followed in her wake, shaking hands and exchanging a few words with everyone. Gemma knew that was one of the reasons the two of them were so successful—they worked as a team.

"So far they're the major contributors."

"Because you saved their grandson?"

Gemma crossed her arms at her waist and tilted her head to the side as she considered him. "Careful, Nathan, your skepticism is showing. I am a trained and experienced midwife." She couldn't control the testiness in her voice.

"So you keep telling me." He glanced away, then back again. "Thanks for shutting down Cole." The words came out as if they were dragged from him. He turned away, grabbed his briefcase and hurried from the stage.

Gemma pressed her lips together and looked down as she slowly followed him off the stage. It was as if he couldn't stand to be around her, but it wasn't strictly because of their professional differences. This was deeper, more personal.

YVETTE BURLEIGH WATCHED the crowd exiting the auditorium. She'd made the mistake of leaving Cole alone while she went to the ladies room. He had wandered off with some of his like-minded cronies. Now she couldn't find him and she'd left her truck keys at home so she couldn't even crawl inside, prop up her feet and wait for him. Her ankles were swollen, her back hurt, the baby was doing gymnastics on her bladder and if he didn't stop it, she was going to need the bathroom again before they got anywhere close to home. She patted her belly. Sometimes that calmed her unborn son. She moved into the shade and took a deep breath. Settling her back against the wall, she tried to relax.

On a daily basis, she found herself swinging between elation about the baby and profound depression fueled by fear that she would be a terrible mother. Her own hadn't been much of a role model, bouncing in and out of Yvette's life as she'd grown up and been passed from one relative to another and then to foster homes. Yvette was terrified she would do that to her son, except that her baby would know who his father was—a man with a stable family. Cole's mom and dad were bossy and overbearing and most of the time she was scared of them, but they were thrilled about the baby. They were planning to purchase nearly every top-of-the-line item their grandson would ever need and Yvette had been completely left out of all the discussions, shopping and decisions. Apparently, her only part in this was to produce the actual baby.

Having grown up in unstable and sometimes dangerous households, she hated conflict and didn't want to get into any arguments with her in-laws. She wished she had a friend or two, girlfriends she could go shopping with to choose things for herself or for her son, but there was no one.

And then there was Cole.

He had a good job helping run the family sale barn, where livestock was auctioned off to the local ranchers. Her son would never want for anything except maybe tenderness and gentle understanding from his father. She didn't know exactly how a father was supposed to act, but thought it wasn't like her loud, arrogant father-in-law, or her convinced-he-was-right husband.

Knowing all of that, she was happy and scared and worried all at once.

Hormones, Yvette thought. All this confusion was nothing but hormones, but that didn't make it easier to handle.

"Hello, Yvette. How are you?"

Her eyes sprang open and she stood up straight. Carly Joslin strolled up with Lisa Thomas and the woman Yvette now knew was Gemma Whitmire—the one, along with Nathan Smith, who Cole hated and wouldn't say why.

Embarrassment flushed Yvette's face. She knew her husband had made a fool of himself. He didn't seem to be bothered by it, but she was. It wasn't the first time he'd done it, and she knew it wouldn't be the last. It was mystifying to her. Even though he seemed to think his opinion was the most important one, he usually wasn't like this at home, but whenever they were out in public he turned into a different man, one who had to be the authority on everything, the loudest voice, the know-it-all. They'd met online, had been married less than a year and she feared she'd made a dreadful mistake. She was ten years younger than he was. There was no one she could talk to about her marriage. She wasn't from Reston, had few friends here, and her family—what was left of it—was hundreds of miles away.

She knew Carly and Lisa wouldn't say anything about Cole's antics, but she didn't know Gemma so she braced herself for whatever she might say. The other woman seemed pretty outspoken and sure of herself if the way she'd grabbed the microphone from Dr. Smith was any indication.

Yvette liked that. She admired strong women, mostly because she knew she wasn't one.

Carly introduced the two of them and Gemma gave her a warm smile. "Congratulations on your upcoming birth," she said as she ran a practiced eye over Yvette's belly. "You're about seven months along?"

"Yes." She rested her palms on her stomach and her son gave such a strong kick, her hands bounced. Everyone laughed. "He's pretty lively today."

Gemma pulled a card from her handbag. "Since you're so far along, you've probably got a doctor and a birthing plan all ready to go, but if I can do anything to help, please call."

"Oh, thank you." Yvette took the card and tucked it into her pocket, then glanced up in time to see Cole bearing down on them, his face hard. "I've got to go. It was nice meeting you, Gemma," she said hurriedly, turning away and moving rapidly toward the truck.

Cole detoured away from the women and was at the vehicle before her, unlocking the door. He braced a hand under her elbow, helping her in even as he growled, "Why were you talking to them?"

"I was being polite. Carly and Lisa are always nice to me…"

"Stay away from Gemma," he ordered, slamming the door, then stalking around to the driver's side and jerking the door open.

"That might be hard to do, Cole. This isn't exactly a big city."

He started the engine and put the truck in gear. "You can if you make a point of it, Yvette."

Her lips tight, she looked out the window as tears filled her eyes. She'd made a terrible mistake and she had no idea how to fix it.

She knew she could leave, but where would she go? How could she support herself and the baby? If Cole and his parents even let her take the baby. She had only a high school diploma and no job skills outside of the do-you-want-fries-with-that? variety.

She wished she could talk to Gemma. She had so many questions about the baby and about childbirth that her doctor tried to answer, but he was too busy to spend much time with her. Dr. Smith seemed nice enough in spite of what Cole said, and he seemed honest. Cole wouldn't allow her to talk to either of them. She didn't know what she was going to do.

GEMMA PUT A hand to her throat as she stared after Cole's truck in dismay. "Oh, my goodness. Is that girl even a day over nineteen?"

"Not by much," Carly answered, and told Gemma what she knew of Cole and Yvette's courtship and marriage.

"She looks exhausted, overwhelmed and…"

"Terrified," Lisa supplied. She also studied the retreating truck with a worried look. "You don't think Cole is…"

"Abusive toward her?" Carly mused, then shook her head. "I don't know. I hope not."

"I hope she calls me," Gemma said. "I know I can help her."

Her friends exchanged a look. "Still rescuing kittens," Carly teased gently.

"Yup. I'll never change." For some reason, Nathan's solemn face came to mind. She wished things were different, were better between them, but maybe that was something that also wouldn't change.

"Come on," Carly said. "I did promise to assemble your lawn mower since I'm the gardening expert in the group, but do you two mind if we take a quick drive down Sky Mountain Road? There are a bunch of houses along there that might have put out—"

"No!" Gemma and Lisa answered in unison.

Laughing, the three of them climbed into the truck and headed toward Gemma's.

NATHAN WATCHED GEMMA drive away with her friends and envied how easily she had slipped back into daily life in Reston. He wondered how long it would be before that happened for him. Or if it ever would.

Even though he was trying to do the right thing by the people of his hometown, they resented him because of what his father had done. He knew it was going to be a long, hard road to win back their trust. He wanted to do it on his own, though.

Fortunately, he'd had a minute to catch his breath and collect his thoughts when Gemma had jumped to his defense. He was grateful to her for telling Cole to shut up, but it rankled that she'd had to. He didn't want her to rescue him.

A hand clapped onto his shoulder and he glanced up with a start to see Tom Sanderson grinning at him.

"Dr. Smith, I want you to meet my son, Trent." The man beside him was a carbon copy of his father, but thirty years younger. Nate and Trent shook hands as Tom continued. "He couldn't make it to the meeting. My wife is heading home so I'm going to fill Trent in on what happened. You want to join us? You look like a man who could use a beer."

Nate looked from father to son. The family had moved to the area about five years ago, so they didn't have any firsthand knowledge of George Smith's crimes. Old friends might have abandoned him, but it was probably time he made some new ones.

"Yes, sir," he said. "I sure could."

CHAPTER FOUR

"What do you think, Gemma?" Lisa asked, setting the small carved figure on an end table and positioning it just so. Gemma's mom had sent it from Botswana, where she and Wolfchild were helping build a school.

The figure was a precise circle in ebony, with the mother's head bent down toward her child, arms cradling the baby, whose face was nestled into her neck.

"It looks good there, but I think it would make the perfect logo for the Sunshine. I could have it on the reception desk, and also painted on the sign. I'll have to find someone to do the artwork, though."

She glanced hopefully at Carly, who was relaxing on the sofa with a glass of iced tea. She shook her head. "Sorry, Gemma. I can put colors together and paint a basic design, but something that detailed is outside my skill set." She tilted her head as she considered it. "Although I guess I could learn."

"Marlene Fedder," Lisa suggested. "Junior's mom. She took up painting about five years go, and she's really good."

Lisa set down the piece. Carly picked it up and ran her fingers over it, letting them rest on the back of the baby's tiny head. Sorrow touched her face before she handed the carving back to Lisa and resumed sipping her tea.

Lisa and Gemma exchanged a look, but didn't comment. Lisa rewrapped the piece and fitted it back into its box, then she ran her hand over the tabletop.

Gemma saw the gesture and smiled. "It's clean, Lisa. You polished it five minutes ago, remember?"

Lisa answered by wrinkling her nose. "Can I help it if I like clean surfaces, uncluttered spaces?"

"You've earned that quirk," Gemma assured her. Lisa had been raised in the home of her loving hoarder grandparents and was determined to never go down the path of too many possessions taking over her life.

"We should celebrate the last of your unpacking," Lisa said, curling up on the sofa opposite Carly and pulling her feet beneath her.

Gemma sat sideways in the armchair, her legs dangling over one arm and her head resting on the other.

"Let's order a pizza from Crossroads," Carly suggested. "That's one of the good things about living in a small town. You can get gas, groceries, new socks and a pizza all at the same four-hundred-square-foot store." Before Lisa could object to the number of calories in a typical Crossroads pizza, she held up her hand. "Try to think of it as a crust-based salad. They do buy my onions and peppers, you know."

Lisa rolled her eyes, and Gemma laughed. While her two friends haggled over the pizza toppings, she relaxed and thought over the events of the past few days. When their dinner had finally been ordered, she said, "At the meeting yesterday, did either of you know there would be that much hostility toward Nathan?"

Carly shook her head. "No. I thought people would be too excited about the reopening to care about anything else." She shrugged. "But I'm probably not the one to ask. Most of my conversations center around vegetables or reclaimed furniture."

"I thought people might be hostile," Lisa admitted. "A few have made comments. Everyone was curious. I think most of them expected him to come in driving a Rolls-Royce, move into the family mansion and lord it over the rest of us."

"Probably what Cole Burleigh thought," Gemma said.

"Looks like the good people of Reston suspected he'd profited a lot more than he did, maybe even colluded with his old man," Carly said.

"Well, then, they just didn't know him." Gemma spoke more sharply than she intended to and her friends gave her assessing looks.

"That's the second time you've come to his defense," Lisa pointed out. "Wasn't he the one who had nothing good to say about your chosen profession?"

Gemma squirmed uncomfortably and focused on the ceiling. "I'm used to that. Almost every midwife is." She paused. "He didn't have to come back here. No one expected him to...make up for his dad's crimes."

"And?" Lisa prompted.

"I don't know why he's doing it."

"Because it's the right thing?"

"Maybe to prove he's not like George," Carly added.

"I guess so," Gemma admitted. "But he had a good job in Oklahoma City. No one there knew or cared about his father, or Reston. Whatever his reason, I think it's tearing him up."

"How can you know that after seeing him exactly three times?" Carly asked.

"It's a…feeling I have."

Out of the corner of her eye, she saw her friends exchange a look, one she knew well, that said, "Gemma is on another rescue mission."

She pretended not to notice.

"YVETTE, THIS IS the changing table I picked out for you," Margery Burleigh announced in tones that seemed to invite applause. "Bob assembled it."

Yvette thought that much was obvious since he had bandages on three fingers. He had brought the table in on a hand truck and now waited, red faced and panting, for his wife to give him further instructions.

Forcing a smile, Yvette looked at the oversize, curlicue carved piece of furniture and wondered how they would fit it into the nursery. It was too big, and…overwhelming.

In fact, it reminded her of Margery—outsize and overdressed.

Her mother-in-law seemed to think her place in the community was much more important than it really was. She considered herself to be an expert on everything, including childbirth and child raising, though she'd only ever had one son, and that when she'd been past forty. Now in her seventies, she was set in her ways and unlikely to change. She drove a Cadillac and dressed up every day in spite of living on a place with livestock, and raising her own chickens. Yvette had never seen her in a pair of jeans, and suddenly had a momentary vision of the big, ugly changing table dressed in denim.

"Um, thank you," Yvette finally said. "It certainly looks…useful."

If Margery was annoyed by the faint praise, she simply breezed right past it. "The crib you said you liked in that online store won't do. You're going to get the one that matches this changing table and can convert into a toddler bed, then into a full-size bed later on. When the other children come along, we'll get them ones to match."

"Other children?" Yvette asked faintly. How many was she expected to have? Besides, she had already ordered the crib she wanted.

"It's not easy being an only child. Ask Cole. I couldn't have any more babies or we would have filled the house up." Margery seemed to recall something and fixed her piercing, critical gaze on Yvette. "You do already know that. You're an only child, right?"

"Yes, I am."

"That settles it, then," Margery exclaimed as if they'd been having a heated argument. "You'll want a big family."

Yvette wondered how Margery could possibly know that. She never asked what Yvette wanted or thought, or hoped for. She simply made ironclad statements and stared down anyone who tried to argue with her. Bob went along with whatever she said and backed her up. Cole was intimidated by them, although he could be exactly like Margery.

Margery turned her attention to her husband. "Go ahead, Bob. What are you waiting for?"

"For you to quit flapping your gums," he answered.

Dismayed, Yvette watched him wheel the latest monstrosity down the hall and into the nursery with his wife sailing along behind, handing out orders.

Cole had disappeared somewhere, probably because he knew his parents were coming over. No doubt, he was steeling himself for their upcoming trip to a rodeo in Tulsa—just him and his parents. Yvette was expected to stay home and represent the family—and Burleigh Livestock Sales—at the Sandersons' barbecue.

She wasn't quite sure why Bob and Margery weren't on the hospital committee, or part of the fund-raising campaign, except that if Margery couldn't be in charge, she wouldn't want to be involved. From what Yvette had seen, Frances Sanderson was far more likely to charm people into giving than Margery, who'd try to bully people's wallets out of their pockets.

Yvette had liked what she'd seen of Frances and Tom, and was eager for the weekend. She was also looking forward to peace and quiet in the house and not having another baby item foisted on her.

She wished she was brave enough to tell them no, she didn't want all the items Margery was buying, but shc wasn't.

THE MUSTANG SUPERMARKET had recently reopened under new management. The outside looked great, if orange and brown were a person's favorite colors, Nate thought. At least it was clean with shining windows and a freshly resurfaced parking lot—which had a puddle in the middle big enough to swallow a compact car.

The puddle had always been there, filling up with every rainfall for as long as he could remember. He didn't know why they hadn't graded the lot before refinishing it. Maybe someone had objected. The puddle was as much a part of Reston as the First Baptist Church, the Elks Club and the high school gym.

Nate stepped out of his car, slammed the door and stared at the puddle, recalling a time when he'd spied the water, made a break for it and jumped in, feet first. He'd been about five. His mother had been horrified. Since she didn't want to get drenched in dirty, sloppy water, she'd sent Mandy in to get him. Mandy had been giggling uncontrollably, which he now saw had been equally humiliating for his mother. She didn't like the attention a muddy little boy and a laughing teenager would bring. She had hustled them back into the car and hurried home without getting the groceries they'd come to buy.

Glancing up, he saw that all movement in the parking lot seemed to have slowed. People who had been walking in to the store, or out to their cars, had paused, their faces turned toward him, watching as he pocketed his keys and started toward the entrance. He nodded to people as he went along and that seemed to break the spell as everyone went back to their own business.

He wondered what his mom would think of this kind of attention.

At the sound of hurrying footsteps, he looked back to see Gemma bearing down on him.

"Good morning, Nate," she sang out, giving him a big smile.

With her red hair flying around her face, and her lemon-yellow summer dress, she looked like a burst of sunshine—a good match for the name of her birthing center. All eyes were on her as she walked quickly toward him—as were his. It wasn't simply that she was attractive. She was absolutely full of life.

"How are things going?" she asked when she caught up to him.

"Um, fine." He realized he needed to quit staring at her, so he pulled a shopping cart out of the lineup and went inside, taking a moment to appreciate the scents of new paint and the pine cleaner used to wash the floors.

Gemma grabbed a carry basket and looped it over her arm as she fell into step with him. "I only came in for a couple of things," she informed him as if he'd asked. "You should try the deli. They make excellent sandwiches. Carlin Houck runs it. You remember her, right?"

He gave her a dry look. "Well, I've known her since kindergarten, so I think so. I may have been gone a long time, but I don't suffer from amnesia."

When her cheeks reddened, he softened his tone. "I'll try the deli."

People were giving them sidelong looks or outright stares, obviously eavesdropping as she continued to chatter on about the wonders of the Mustang Supermarket. A number of people smiled at her enthusiasm.

When Mrs. Arnstein, their high school math teacher, saw them, she hurried up and gave them each a hug, then stood back to look at Nate.

"It's wonderful to see you. I'm glad you're back." She beamed approval at him.

"I'm glad to see you, too, Mrs. Arnstein," he said, and meant it, touched by how happy she was to see him, unlike nearly everyone else in town. If it hadn't been for her patient tutoring, he never would have passed his junior year. They chatted for a few minutes and when she left, he felt a warmth he'd barely known since he'd returned to Reston. He looked at Gemma, who was watching him as if he'd done something brilliant.

They continued on, with Gemma waving to people or stopping to speak with them as she accompanied him up and down the aisles. It was almost as if she was acting as his... What? Bodyguard?

"And did you know that Lisa was instrumental in getting it reopened? Even provided the mayor with names of potential buyers."

Nate stopped with a package of pasta in his hand and treated her to a suspicious look. "Are you trying to sell me on the community, or the community on me?"

Gemma blinked. "What do you mean?"

"I don't need you to escort me through the grocery store so people won't be mean to me."

Heat rushed into her face again. "I—I wasn't..."

"Yes, you were and I don't think you can help it. You're a born rescuer, but I don't need your help."

"As—as a medical professional, I naturally see the need to...help people." She floundered.

"I'm not in need of medical help and I don't need you to inject yourself into my life, shield me, or stand between me and trouble."

Gemma looked away, then back at him. "In that case, goodbye and have a nice day." Turning, she marched away, back straight, head up.

THE SUDDEN JERK of the steering wheel and the ominous *thunk-thunk-thunk* noise coming from the front right tire told Gemma she had a flat. She pulled off the road and climbed out to take a look. It wasn't simply flat. It was pancaked.

Rolling her eyes, she bent close to inspect a ragged split on the sidewall, then looked down at the turquoise full-skirted sundress she had put on for the Sandersons' barbecue. The chances of keeping it clean while she changed the tire were nonexistent. She could wait for some Good Samaritan to happen by, but she'd been driving on this road for ten minutes and hadn't seen another car.

Hands on hips, she stared at the tire and considered her options. She could call Lisa or Carly, but they both had things to do before going to the party—Carly was delivering some freshly harvested produce, and Lisa was holding an open house on the other side of the county. There wasn't a garage in Reston and getting someone out from Toncaville would take too long. Besides, she knew how to change a tire. She simply wasn't dressed for it.

"When am I going to learn to always

carry a change of clothes?" she muttered as she opened the back of the well-worn Land Rover and began rummaging around for the jack. After setting it on the ground, she began working on removing the spare. Even after using an old scrap of T-shirt to wipe the bumper, her chore was made more difficult because she had to arch her body away from the vehicle in an effort to keep her dress clean.

When she heard a car pulling up behind her, she turned with a relieved smile to see Nathan Smith behind the wheel. Her smile froze in place, then collapsed altogether as he leaned over the steering wheel and grinned at her.

NATE HAD KNOWN whose vehicle it was as soon as he'd spotted it. He'd seen it around town with Gemma behind the wheel, hurrying from one place to another.

But she wasn't rushing around now. In fact, *she* needed *his* help. The way her smile faded when she spotted him brought out a puckish sense of humor he hadn't exercised in a long time. He shut off the engine and stepped out of the car.

"Need some help?' he asked as his gaze took in the flat tire, the jack and the open back of the Rover.

She gave a careless wave. "Oh, no, thanks. I can handle it. I've changed many tires."

"In a dress?"

"I'm sure it'll be fine. I can keep my dress clean, and—"

"How? By taking it off?" he asked, nodding toward a herd of cattle grazing in an enclosed pasture by the road. "You'd give those cows quite a show."

That startled a laugh out of her, but he knew she wouldn't give in. He could almost hear her thinking… *Of all the people in the world to happen by, it had to be Nate.*

"I don't want to hold you up. You're probably on your way to the Sandersons', too, and—"

"I've got plenty of time." Before Gemma could say anything else, he gently placed his hands on her shoulders and moved her aside.

"Wait. Aren't *you* afraid of getting dirty?"

Nate gave her a considering look. "You're right," he said, then began unbuttoning his dark blue shirt.

GEMMA'S HEART FLUTTERED and her mouth went dry when he flipped the shirt around and settled it on her shoulders as if she was a human clothes hanger. The faint spicy scent of his cologne lifted to her nose—and weakened her knees. Determined to be strong, she grasped the door frame and breathed in a gulp of air.

Three cars passed in quick succession, their occupants whipping their heads around to see what was going on.

Now someone shows up, she thought. The news about the two of them beside the road—him with no shirt—would be all over the county within minutes.

Her voice croaked a little as she said, "Aren't—aren't you afraid *you'll* shock the cows?"

"Gemma, you seem to think fears rule my life. I'm sure they're not bothered by half-naked men." He smiled—the happiest expression she'd seen from him. "You're a nurse. I'm sure you've seen men more than half-naked."

Heat washed up her face and he chuckled as he turned to examine the flat and then continue the struggle with the spare tire.

Dumbfounded, Gemma stared at him. She hadn't seen him since they'd met at the Mustang a few days ago and he'd accused her of injecting herself into his life. What had happened since then? She wasn't quite prepared to question his change in attitude. She was simply going to enjoy it.

Nate removed the spare and bounced it on the ground. Only it didn't bounce. It went as flat as the right front one. He glanced up. "Gemma, when did you last check this tire?"

She tucked her hair behind her ears and slanted her gaze away from his. "Oh, not that long ago. Maybe a year or two."

That brought a snort of laughter as he slung the tire back into the Rover, replaced the jack, found a rag to wipe his hands and slammed the hatch. "Gemma, it's time for you to pay attention to your tires. You'll have to call a tow truck, but since it's a holiday weekend, it might be a while before anyone can get here."

Nate plucked his shirt from around her shoulders and said, "You'll have to ride with me. You can try to call a tow truck on the way—if you can get a cell-phone signal."

Gemma opened and closed her mouth a

couple of times as she watched him button his shirt and tuck it in. Riding with him made perfect sense. She knew that, but the crazy reaction she was having made her wary of spending any more time with him. Still, what choice did she have? She cleared her throat. "Okay."

She grabbed her purse and the turquoise jacket that went with her dress, then locked her Rover and walked to where Nate stood holding the car door open for her. As she sat down, she said, "Thanks for your help, Nate."

"Always glad to rescue a lady in distress," he answered in a jaunty tone that had her giving him an odd look. He was making a joke at her expense, she thought, recalling the way he had called her a born rescuer. She wasn't going to deny it.

"I'm a big believer in payback," he said. He slid behind the wheel, pulled onto the road and continued to the Sandersons'.

She eyed him skeptically. "Payback?"

"You know, someone does something good for me, like protecting me from the evil shoppers at the Mustang Supermarket, I want to help that person."

Gemma made a point of looking out the window as if she was vitally interested in the trees they were passing. "Oh, will you please let that go?"

"Not yet," he assured her.

She rolled her eyes and instead, she managed to get a cell-phone signal, find the number for the garage in Toncaville and make arrangements to have her car towed. To Gemma's relief, the tension between them seemed to have disappeared and their conversation was easy and natural as they finished the drive to the barbecue.

The big two-story ranch house that Tom and Frances had built a couple of years ago stood at the curved end of a U-shaped driveway. Another house was under construction across the road. Gemma guessed it was intended for the Sandersons' son and his family. Cars and trucks lined the edge of the drive and filled the area in the middle. Nate parked the car and once again held the door for Gemma.

As they walked toward the house, she said, "You realize that everyone will think we came together, don't you?"

"We *did* come together."

"I mean like on a date."

"Would that be so bad?" He grinned again and took her elbow as they headed toward the back of the house and the huge covered patio, where everyone had gathered.

Gemma bit her lip, trying to keep up with his disconcerting changes in attitude. She hated feeling off balance, and the way he shifted from solemn to standoffish, from disapproving to teasing, kept her from knowing where she stood with him.

She held up a hand. "Okay, so we're on the same page here—you don't want to feel as though I'm rescuing you, trying to get people to like you, but it's okay if everyone here thinks we're on a date?"

He nodded. "Pretty much."

Her eyes narrowed. "You're teasing me, aren't you?"

His lips formed into an ironic twist. "And I must be really bad at it if it's taken you this long to figure it out."

CHAPTER FIVE

GEMMA WAS TRYING to think of a response when Frances hurried up to greet them. She was wearing a brightly patterned dress and her hair was done up in the type of smooth chignon that Gemma thought was the essence of classiness, and which she could never achieve with her own curly, flyaway hair.

Their hostess gave them each a quick hug and said, "Come get something to eat. My goal is to not have *any* leftovers to deal with." She pointed them toward buffet tables set up near the back door of the house and whirled away in a splash of color to greet the newest arrivals.

"She better be expecting lots more people if she hopes to get rid of all this food," Gemma said, surveying the tables full of barbecued ribs, roasted corn on the cob and countless side dishes.

Nathan picked up a plate. "I'll do my share."

The two of them filled their plates and turned to look for seats.

"Nate, Gemma, over here," a male voice called out.

Gemma turned and was delighted to see Trent and Mia Sanderson waving them over. They both stood to give Gemma hugs, then Trent shook hands with Nate and introduced his wife. There were two other couples at the table, people she didn't know, who Trent also introduced.

Mia Sanderson was tall and willowy with olive skin and long, straight hair, which she tossed over her shoulder as she sat down. She wore a yellow dress that bared her shoulders and complemented her skin tone.

Gemma smiled at her. "You look a lot better than you did the first time I saw you."

"That's because I'm not in excruciating pain," Mia answered, indicating the baby monitor that sat beside her plate. "Max will be awake in a few minutes, so excuse me while I wolf down my food. I haven't finished a meal at a normal pace in six months."

Her husband scooted her chair closer and put his arm around her shoulders. "I'd feed him if I could, honey, but I don't have the right equipment."

Mia batted her eyelashes at him and said, "There's always some excuse."

"Mia," Gemma said, "I know you're from Los Angeles and Trent lived in Texas and then here. How did you two meet?"

Mia and Trent looked at each other and smiled.

Mia said, "In Las Vegas—"

"I was there for a bachelor party," Trent added.

"I was a model working at an auto show." Mia lifted her hand in a smooth, sweeping gesture as if showing off the elegant lines of a vehicle. "My job was to stand by a new car in a tight evening dress and try to convince people that their lives wouldn't be complete unless they owned one of those fabulously expensive status symbols. We had to memorize a script. I know more ways to describe horsepower, torque and fancy sports cars than you can imagine."

"We were staying at the same hotel," Trent added. "We met in the elevator—"

"Where Trent showed me what a true gentleman his mom and dad had raised. He gave me his suit jacket because I'd lost my dress and I was in my underwear."

Everyone at the table stopped eating and stared.

Gemma held up her hand. "Back up a minute. How did you lose your dress?"

Mia smiled. "I didn't really lose it—the auto-show people took the dresses for cleaning and there'd been a mix-up with our luggage—mine and my roommate's bags. That left me to go down, wearing a sheet, to claim our things."

"Yeah," Trent said, wiggling his eyebrows. "But you wore that sheet like a boss. We got married four days later." Trent tightened his arm, rocking her close to him.

"And had Max eleven months later."

"On the side of the highway," Gemma added.

"During a lightning storm."

A baby's wail sounded from the monitor and Mia excused herself to go get her son. Everyone continued eating and the conversation drifted to other topics for the next half hour, until she returned carrying a chubby little boy who had his mother's dark hair and eyes and his father's smile.

"Okay, now that you're back, you can't stop there," one of the other ladies at the table said as Mia handed the baby to her husband and contemplated her plate of cold food. "Why wasn't Max born in a hospital?"

"There wasn't one nearby," Trent answered without looking at Nate. He held up his finger in front of his son's face and Max grabbed it with both of his tiny fists. Before he could maneuver it into his mouth, Trent lifted him up a few inches, then dropped him down onto his well-padded bottom, causing the baby to give out a deep, rolling chuckle. "Max came two weeks early. Mia's labor moved a lot faster than we expected. We were both new at this. Mom and Dad were out of town so we were trying to make it there on our own, but the storm hit at the same time Max decided he was tired of waiting around. I pulled over to try and help, but it was way beyond my calf-delivering skills."

"Then Gemma showed up and saved the day," Mia added.

"I was on my way into Reston to visit my two best friends when I saw a truck stopped and two people inside. One of those people was about to pass out," she added with a grin.

"Hey, I was new at this dad business, remember?" Trent protested.

"I'd never seen anyone with a face that pale who still had a heartbeat," Gemma teased. "But, as it turned out, Max arrived without any further complications, an ambulance found us and got Mia and the baby to the hospital."

"None of that would have happened if we'd had a hospital closer," Mia said. "I was so scared. I'm so grateful that medical facilities are opening up here. Having a midwife, of all people, show up just in time was a true miracle."

The others at the table nodded as they exchanged glances. Being without a hospital had affected everyone in the community.

"Midwives can be helpful in an emergency birth like that," Nate said.

Gemma shot a glance at him as Trent said, "She was more than helpful. She saved Mia's life. Max was fine, but Mia's blood pressure was dropping fast."

Before he could say anything else, Frances swept up to their table and encouraged everyone to have dessert and then mingle. "The music's starting up in a few minutes and then I fully intend to charm your wallets right out of your pockets," she said with a smile as she took her grandson from Trent. "I'll take Max with me. Nobody can resist an adorable baby. Also, I expect all of you to be dancing and having fun."

Everyone at the table stood and moved to the dessert buffet, except Gemma, who stepped back and watched Nathan. She wondered what he thought about the story of Max's birth. His statement that midwives were helpful in emergency situations was troubling, though not surprising. She doubted that he would ever change his mind.

As if her thoughts had conjured him, Nate appeared at her elbow. "Care to dance?" he asked.

"Um, yes." What else could she say? Besides, she wanted to enjoy this different side of him while it lasted.

The band was playing a slow tune, which appealed to most of the older guests and to Gemma since it would give her a chance to talk to Nate. It would be a different story once they started up with the Texas two-step. She knew her people and when that song started, everyone, young and old, would flood the dance floor.

As it turned out, Tom Sanderson and Brantley Clegg pulled Nate aside for some kind of discussion regarding the hospital, leaving Gemma feeling disappointed enough to begin eyeing the dessert table.

"Oh, there you are." Carly's voice drew her out of her unhappy thoughts and Gemma turned to greet her friend. Her gaze went up and down Carly's lithe frame.

"You actually wore a dress," Gemma said, approving of her red knee-length skirt with its matching sleeveless top. Carly's long black hair wasn't in its usual ponytail but was down in a shiny wave across her shoulders.

"Well, it *is* a party. Even I know how to dress for a party," Carly answered with pretend huffiness.

"With cowboy boots."

"Hey, I actually polished these," she said, turning her feet this way and that so Gemma could admire the effect. "They're my best ones, and you know I don't wear heels. Why bother when I'm already five foot ten?"

"How long does it take to polish a pair of boots like that?"

"The length of time it takes to watch an episode of *Real Housewives of…*somewhere."

Gemma gaped at her. "You never watch reality TV. What did you think of it?"

"I think those women need to go out and start digging in a garden if they want things to get real very fast."

Gemma grinned. "You're probably right. Well, all the polishing paid off. You look gorgeous."

"Thanks. It's so nice to have a compliment. I hear so few from my vegetables." Carly glanced around. "I saw your Land Rover on the side of the road. Glad you got a ride here and that flat didn't happen on the way to a baby emergency."

"No baby emergencies yet. No expectant moms yet." With a shrug, she added, "I'm hoping to get some when we open the birthing center and begin prenatal classes. Moms won't want me to deliver their babies until they know they can trust me." She went on to tell Carly about her two flat tires and Nate's help.

When Gemma got to the part about Nate removing his shirt, Carly laughed and said, "Anyone who saw you two will have spread the news all over the county. Gossip will have you married off by midnight."

"I know." Gemma sighed. "I hadn't actually forgotten about small-town and small-county life, but I guess in my case, I was hoping it didn't apply."

"Good luck with that."

Glancing up, Gemma spotted a man across the room and went very still. She took a second look before she said, "Carly, did you know Luke is here?"

Carly didn't turn around. "Yes. As a matter of fact, he came by my house earlier to drop off something his grandmother left me. Brought it all the way from Dallas since he was coming to his aunt and uncle's party, anyway."

"Oh, really? What did his grandmother leave you?"

"An antique trunk."

"That was nice of her, considering you and Luke are no longer married."

Carly shook her head. "What Luke and I had was so short and so long ago, it can hardly be called a marriage. More of a… ripple in the streams of our lives. His grandmother was always sweet to me, though, and I'm honored that she remembered me."

Gemma nodded even as she studied her friend's carefully neutral face. It was a long time ago, but she knew the hurt from Carly's broken marriage had never really gone away. That's why she worked so hard, at so many different projects. At first, she'd done it to forget, but now it was a habit.

Looking for a change of subject, Gemma surveyed the crowd and asked, "Where is Lisa?"

"Over by the swimming pool, having one of her usual arguments with Ben McAdams over the direction the city of Reston needs to take."

"I hope she keeps her cool and doesn't push him in."

Carly laughed. "When has she ever kept her cool where he's concerned? She's always ready to throttle him or defend him to the death. Remember when we were in seventh grade and she made us help her break him out of jail?"

"I'll never forget. I know the sheriff only wanted to scare Ben into being more responsible with his BB gun, but I was convinced the law was coming for us."

"I think it worked. After that, he never shot at anything except tin cans."

Gemma laughed as Carly turned to see who else they knew, then froze in place. "Oh, no," she said under her breath.

"What? What is it?"

"The band is playing the Texas two-step and Bunky is headed our way."

"No-o-o," Gemma moaned, her toes curling into her open sandals. "Oh, please, you dance with him. I almost needed to see a podiatrist after the Christmas party at the chamber of commerce, remember? And at least you're wearing boots."

"I'm too tall for him. He likes dancing with someone his own size, but his wife refuses to, so it's up to you." Carly looked around for an escape route and slipped behind a row of flowering bushes.

"But he's got two left feet," Gemma called

after her, pitching her voice low. "And no sense of rhythm."

Carly's laughter drifted back to tease her.

Dalton Bunker screeched to a halt in front of Gemma and grabbed her hand. "Glad you're here, Gemma girl. You're my favorite dancing partner."

She didn't have a chance to disagree, plead a headache, or make up a sudden emergency or impending natural disaster before he'd dragged her onto the dance floor and whirled her into his arms so fast she was sure she experienced whiplash.

The band was playing a rock and roll tune from the 1960s that seemed to fire up Bunky's blood even more than usual. "That's what I call real music," he declared ecstatically as he swooped her into a combination of a two-step and a hip-swing jive step that he'd made up himself. It involved many spins and dips. Gemma simply went with it and tried to keep her toes out of the line of fire, although she wasn't always successful.

The other dancers quickly became adept at staying out of reach of Bunky's enthusiastic moves. Faces whirled past in a blur, but she saw Nate standing at the edge of the dance floor, staring at her, openmouthed.

It took her a minute or so, but she finally figured out the crazy nonrhythm that Bunky danced to and even managed a few moves of her own, which delighted her partner.

When the music finally stopped, Bunky gave her a big kiss on the cheek and basked in the applause from the audience. As he took a bow, Gemma slipped away to find a place to hide. When she spied a patio table and chairs near the corner of the house, she gratefully slid into a chair and pulled off her sandals, even as she noticed she wasn't alone.

Yvette Burleigh sat in one chair, her feet propped on another. The light in that corner wasn't great, but Gemma could see the younger woman's feet were quite swollen, as were her face, arms and hands.

Trained to keep alarm out of her face and voice, Gemma smiled and said, "Hello, Yvette. It's so nice to see you again. How are you feeling?"

"I've been better." Yvette adjusted her position in the chair. "It's getting harder to move around. And I've still got two months to go."

Gemma leaned over to examine Yvette's ankles. "You seem to be retaining a great deal of fluid. Have you been to see your doctor?"

"I've got an appointment on Tuesday." Yvette twisted again, trying to get comfortable. "I called his office, though, and he said some fluid retention is normal."

"Some is, but not this much."

Yvette rested her head on her palm. "And my head hurts so bad. Maybe because I don't sleep much, either."

"It's probably not a good idea for you to wait until Tuesday to get checked—"

"I don't want to go to the hospital." Fear quavered in Yvette's voice as her eyes filled with tears.

"I can check you out right here, if that's okay with you." Gemma kept her voice upbeat. "I promise that I'm qualified."

"I—I know you are." Yvette glanced around. "I've…asked people about you. Yes, please see if my baby's okay, and me, too, of course."

"I'll go get my bag," Gemma said as she pulled her sandals back onto her feet. They seemed to have recovered from Bunky's missteps as soon as she had someone else to claim her focus. "I'll be right back."

She had taken several steps around the corner before she recalled that she didn't have her car and, therefore, no medical bag.

Redirecting her steps, she went looking for Nate. When she spotted him talking to Tom, Brantley and a group of other men, she wasted no time in hurrying up and pulling him aside.

"Is your medical bag in your car?"

"Of course. What's wrong?" His gaze swept the area, looking for someone in distress. "Has there been an accident?"

He didn't wait for an answer, but excused himself from the group and started for his car at a rapid pace as Gemma scurried along beside him, explaining about Yvette.

"I'm sure it's the beginnings of preeclampsia, but I need to check her blood pressure to be sure. Also, she's got a severe headache, doesn't sleep and I don't think she's eating right. There's a full plate of food in front of her that hasn't been touched."

Nate shot her a swift glance. "We need to call Emergency Services, get her to a hospital and on the proper medication."

"She doesn't want to go to the hospital, seems terrified of the idea."

"She may not have a choice." Nate stopped at his car and pulled his bag from the trunk. "Where is Cole?"

"I don't know, but let's try to keep this quiet. She's terrified and I seriously doubt that Cole gives her much support or help with her fears."

Gemma led the way back to the quiet corner where Yvette waited. Although she sent Gemma an alarmed look when she saw Nate, she sat quietly while he checked her blood pressure and Gemma slipped an oximeter onto her finger to check her oxygen-saturation level.

While they waited, Gemma asked Yvette if she'd eaten anything.

"No. I wasn't hungry. I know it's a barbecue and everything, and the Sandersons are so nice, but…" Her voice faded away. "I'm a vegan. I know it's crazy with Cole's family owning the cattle sale barn, but have you seen baby calves with those big brown eyes? And baby chicks? They're so cute and fluffy."

They had the results in a couple of minutes. Gemma took her hand. "Yvette, your blood pressure is sky-high and your blood oxygen is too low." She lifted her head as she heard Carly's voice coming from around the corner. "Excuse me a second."

She hurried away, gave Carly some instructions and returned in time to hear Nate say, "We need to get you to the hospital." He put his things away and snapped his bag shut decisively. "And get you on the proper medication."

"No. No hospital, please." She looked from Gemma to Nathan, begging for understanding. Gemma's heart went out to her. She'd seen this before, but she couldn't let pity for the patient overwhelm her professional judgment.

"Where is your husband?" Gemma asked. "Is Cole here?"

"No. He and his mom and dad went to a rodeo in Tulsa. A cousin of Cole's is riding his first bronc in a big competition. They won't be back until tomorrow night. I'm here with my neighbors, Roland and Becky Hall, to represent Burleigh Livestock Sales. They can take me home."

"They need to take you to the hospital,"

Nate responded. He stood with his hands on his hips, head thrust forward as he observed her. "Or we can call an ambulance."

She shook her head again. "I don't trust hospitals. Every member of my family has died in a hospital. And, yeah, I know it's not the facility's fault, or the staff's, but... I don't trust them. None of my family members came out alive..." Her voice faded away as she gave in to her terror and tears overflowed her eyes. "Please," she whispered.

Gemma plucked a paper napkin from the holder on the table and handed it to Yvette as she said, "This won't get better on its own. You're very close to having a serious case of toxemia, which is a threat to your life and your baby's."

Yvette dabbed at her tears and said, "I don't want me and my baby to be pumped full of drugs."

"These would be *life-saving* drugs." Nate sounded frustrated as he looked from Yvette to Gemma.

"Tell me what to do and I'll go home and do it."

Nate shook his head. "It's not that simple—"

"Yes, it is," Gemma interrupted. "Yvette, have you got any eggs at home?"

"Of course. My mother-in-law raises chickens. And they're right down the road from us. But I'm a vegan. Cole eats them."

"Yvette, it's time to stop thinking about baby calves and their big brown eyes. Imagine a vicious old bull chasing you around a field, and then imagine him as a juicy hamburger."

"What do you mean?"

"You're not getting enough protein. For the sake of your baby—and yourself—you need to go on the 'crazy egg diet.' Twelve eggs in twelve hours."

Nate stared at her. "Eggs? You've got to be kidding."

"It works. I've seen it many times. The albumen in the eggs stabilizes the blood pressure and relieves the headache."

Nate gestured around the corner. "Can I talk to you over here, please?"

He stalked away and Gemma followed him, her annoyance growing as they moved out of Yvette's earshot.

"Eggs instead of competent medical care?" He shook his head again as if he couldn't believe what he was hearing. "Who's going to monitor this 'crazy egg diet,' which, by the way, is sounding increasingly crazy?"

"I will, of course. This diet was created in the 1950s by Dr. Tom Brewer and has helped thousands of women, tens of thousands. By this time tomorrow morning, Yvette will be much better."

Nate frowned at her. "The Brewer pregnancy diet. Yes, I've heard of it, but it's no substitute for medical care. I can't, in good conscience, let you take a chance with her life."

"This will *save* her life, and you can't force her to go to the hospital." Gemma flung her hands wide. "She's almost hysterical at the prospect."

"It's still the right thing to do."

Gemma regarded him for a few seconds. He was as angry and convinced of the rightness of what he was saying as she was convinced of what she was saying. "Listen, Nate. I'll take her home and get her started on this right away. Lisa and Carly will come, too. If there's even the slightest hint she's in more distress, we'll take her to the hospital ourselves or call an ambulance. I'll take a blood sample and send it to the lab in Toncaville to be checked, and then another one in the morning to show the improvement and confirm that the crazy egg diet is the right choice."

Nate's eyes were narrowed, his lips fixed in a straight line.

At that moment, Carly returned with a plate of deviled eggs and a glass of water. Gemma nodded toward where Yvette waited.

"So you're starting it already?" Nate asked, following Carly.

Gemma marched along right behind him. "She has to eat something and it might as well be eggs."

"I want to do this egg thing, Dr. Smith," Yvette said as she picked up half a deviled egg and took a bite. "If Gemma says it will help."

Nate looked from Yvette to Gemma, then he picked up his medical bag. "I guess I know when to quit," he said. He fixed his angry gaze on Gemma. "But you call me if she gets worse in any way and I'll make arrangements for her to be admitted to the hospital in Toncaville."

Yvette emitted a faint squeak of distress, but Nate turned on his heel and walked away. Gemma stared after him.

CHAPTER SIX

THE NEXT MORNING, Yvette waved goodbye to Gemma and Carly, shut her front door, then went down the hallway to the full-length mirror to look at her ankles. They were almost back to normal and her face no longer looked like a balloon. Her headache was gone and her blood pressure was in the acceptable range. Gemma had told her to get a blood-pressure cuff at the drugstore and check her pressure every day.

She had become pretty sick of eating eggs, but it had paid off just as Gemma had promised. Gemma had awakened her every couple of hours to feed her more eggs—boiled, scrambled, fried…she'd had them every way possible. The blood sample Lisa had taken to the lab this morning had proven the egg strategy had worked.

Returning to the kitchen, she picked up the diet that Gemma had printed out for her.

Good-quality protein, fresh fruits and vegetables in abundance, milk, lots of water and salt in reasonable amounts. She was supposed to eat twenty-six hundred calories a day and gain more weight. The women in her family had always been skinny—mostly because they were more interested in drinking than in eating. She was no exception even though she never touched alcohol. Skinny was the way Cole liked her, too, but she had to ignore any complaints he might have. Her heart gave a nervous flutter at the idea of defying him so her thoughts skittered away from that and focused on the paper in her hands. Beef, pork, chicken, turkey, oily fish, white fish.

"Yvette, the vegan ship has sailed," she murmured. A trip to the grocery store was called for.

She put down that list and picked up the one Gemma had written of the classes she was offering. Prenatal and antenatal care, preparing for childbirth, controlling pain during childbirth and breast-feeding.

Yvette wanted to take them all. Some were offered during the day. She could go to those because Cole would be at work. After she took a few classes and felt more confident, she would tell him, though. She would.

As grateful as she was for the care Gemma and Carly had given her, as well as Dr. Brewer's pregnancy diet, she was even more grateful that she now had a couple of friends. Three, actually. After Tom Sanderson's nephew, Luke, had carried her to Lisa Thomas's car. Lisa had driven her and Gemma home, where it had taken both of them to get Yvette out of the car. The memory made her smile because all of them had ended up in hysterical laughter. In the meantime, Carly had delivered the blood sample to the lab thirty miles away. Yvette was touched that someone she barely knew was willing to drive so far and then come back to spend the night. Lisa didn't stay overnight but promised to rush back if needed.

Yvette envied how the three of them had fun together. From what she could tell, it had been going on their entire lives. They told stories of their childhoods that made her laugh even as she longed for such happy memories. When she had asked about memories of Cole, they had gone silent for a minute, exchanged a look, then Carly had told her about the springtime tortoises he had collected until his mother had found some in the bathtub and ordered them all back down to the creek. That sounded exactly like something her mother-in-law would do. Pets outside were fine, but forbidden in the house.

This was the house in which Cole had grown up and it was still decorated exactly as his mother had done it. Her in-laws had built a bigger, fancier place a couple of miles away and let Cole have this one. He wanted nothing changed. All the walls were icy white and scuffed in many places. The carpeting was beige, every stick of furniture was some shade of brown. The sofa was beginning to show its age and was dotted with spills and stains, compliments of Cole's drinking buddies. She had tried to scrub out all the marks, but they resisted her efforts, mocking her with their stubbornness.

Because she'd grown up in a family usually teetering on the edge of poverty, in badly maintained rentals or in foster homes where nothing belonged to her except the clothes on her back, Yvette had yearned for a home of her own. She'd never thought about a career, only a job that earned enough for her to have a place of her own, no matter how humble, that she could make beautiful. She knew how to sew. It was the only way she'd been able to afford decent clothing during her teenage years. When she'd first seen Cole's house, she had immediately begun making plans, envisioning ways to make it inviting, even cozy, with fresh paint, curtains, throw pillows and slipcovers.

She might as well have saved those dreams for another lifetime, she thought.

Cole had forbidden her to paint the nursery, even though she had already purchased the paint, a cheerful shade of blue, and all the supplies. He said white had been good enough for him growing up, and it would be good enough for his son. And now the room was filling up with the ugly, outsize furniture Margery had bought.

Yvette wanted color in her life, so she had turned to gardening. She rested her hands on her belly and stared dreamily out the window at the yard. The roses were blooming, as were the gladioli, warm splashes of color against the green. She had cut armloads of them and displayed them all over the house. She didn't know much about gardening, but she wanted to learn, and to plant a vegetable garden.

Carly had told her about the organic vegetables she grew, harvested and sold, and about the shop her two best friends had convinced her to open. She planned to sell the furniture and accessories that she collected and refurbished, as soon as she found someone whom she could hire to help her out. It sounded fun. Yvette wished she could be that employee.

Now that she was here in Reston County, living in a sturdy, though unglamorous, house, married and expecting a baby, she should be happy. Sometimes she was, but lately, she'd begun to realize that safety and security weren't what made happiness. There were many other aspects to being happy that she hadn't found when she'd married Cole. Because she hadn't seen respect and unquestioning support displayed in a marriage, she hadn't known to expect them, but she knew there had to be something more than what she and Cole had.

The rattling of the back doorknob had her stuffing the papers from Gemma into the waistband of her slacks, smoothing down her top and turning to see Cole coming in with an enormous teddy bear wearing a cowboy hat.

Cole looked so proud of himself that Yvette couldn't help smiling as she said, "Is he going to require his own room? Because we're running short of space in the nursery."

"Nah, he can have a corner. Someday, when our kid is being a brat and has to sit in time-out, they can keep each other company."

Cole removed his own cowboy hat and hung it on a peg by the back door, then sat the bear in the middle of the kitchen table, where it loomed, smiling, as he took Yvette into his arms and kissed her. He was careful to turn her slightly sideways first so he didn't squash the baby.

Yvette leaned into him, realizing how much she had missed him. "I'm glad you're home. How was the rodeo?"

"Let's just say the country's bronc riders don't have to worry about my cousin Jarrett. He got bucked off in three seconds flat."

"Is he okay?" She didn't know much about bronc riding—or "busting broncs" as Cole usually called it—but she knew it was dangerous, and that the rider was supposed to keep his seat for eight seconds.

"Yeah. Only thing hurt was his pride." He paused and studied her face. "It's a good thing you stayed home, though. A rodeo arena isn't the place for a pregnant woman, what with the hard seats and dust. Were you okay here? How was the Sandersons' party?"

"Fine," she said with a smile, resting her head on his shoulder. This was the man she had come to love, the one who showed concern for her. She knew this was the moment when she needed to tell him everything that had happened last night before he heard it from someone else. This was when she needed to tell him how Gemma had saved her and his son. He had a right to know about it, and about the classes she planned to take—while he was in a good mood and was glad to see her.

"I met some nice people. It was fun." She stepped from his arms. "Let's see if we can find a place for Cowboy Bear."

"Good name for him. Maybe I should get him a Dallas Cowboys T-shirt so little Cole Jr. will know which team is the best." Hooking one arm around the bear and the other one around her, he urged her down the hallway to the nursery, talking all the while about the rodeo, the traffic in Tulsa, what he'd had for dinner the night before and the hard bed at the hotel where he and his parents had stayed.

Yvette decided it would be rude to interrupt him.

COLE GLANCED OVER his shoulder at the blanket that was neatly folded and placed at the end of the sofa, and the pillow that rested atop it.

Someone had been here.

Yvette never sat on that sofa because of the stains she'd tried and failed to get out. For a girl who'd grown up in poverty she could be really prissy about some things, and that couch was one of them. It looked like someone less squeamish had slept there. But who?

Jealousy kicked at him, but he fought it down. She wouldn't cheat on him. She was seven months pregnant with his baby. Besides, she knew she had a good thing going here—the nicest place she'd ever lived, on a hill that looked down on Reston Lake, and money like she'd never had before.

But who had been here?

"You're already starting your classes at the birthing center?" Carly asked, giving Gemma a sideways glance as they drove back toward Reston.

"I made the decision last night while I was up cooking eggs. There are other expectant mothers like Yvette who don't know what's going to happen, and reading all the books in the world isn't as good as talking to other mothers and getting the benefit of their expertise."

"Not to mention getting information from an experienced midwife. Do you think she'll call you when she's ready to deliver?"

"Not if Cole has anything to do with it. And she's got a good doctor." Gemma turned in the seat and propped up her knee as she leaned against the door. "In fact, he might not even let her come to the classes."

She yawned and looked over at her friend, who appeared fresh and bright as a dew-covered rosebud. Carly, who could fall asleep anywhere, had made herself comfortable on the living room sofa, after covering it with a sheet, but Gemma had slept little in the recliner. She had been monitoring Yvette's condition, preparing eggs for her and watching her eat them, while attempting to report in to Nate every few hours. She had managed to check in a couple of times, but another storm had kicked up during the night, so cell-phone service was even worse than usual.

Gemma tugged at the skirt of the sundress she'd been wearing since yesterday afternoon. She covered another yawn as she said, "Yvette is petrified of going to the hospital, though, and I don't know what she's going to do when it comes time to deliver. The classes might help."

Carly nodded and continued driving.

They talked about other things and Gemma nodded off, waking only when Carly's truck bumped over the unpaved driveway to the Whitmire property.

"IT WILL BE a while before this place sells, Nate, even with the cleaning and painting you're planning." Lisa ran her hand along the banister, once kept highly polished by Nate's mother, but now dull with grime.

Nate nodded. "I know, but there's nothing I can do about that. It's the price of living in a town where the median income is low."

"You're right." Lisa shrugged. "I'm sorry, too, about how long the roof repairs took."

"That couldn't be helped. We've had so much rain, it delayed everything."

"As long as you're not worried, I won't be, either." She held up some of the more flattering photos she'd taken of the place. "I'll leave these on the table by the door, in case you want them. When the place is ready for showing, I'll take more photos and make up flyers, and I'll contact you when someone wants to see the property."

She departed with a friendly wave and Nate was left standing on the staircase, where he'd been tacking down a loose section of the carpeting. He didn't want anyone catching a heel in the loose carpet and taking a tumble. But he was stalling and he knew it. Soon, he would have to hire someone to do all of the cleaning, repairing and painting. Nate turned and sat down on the stairs as he thought about it. He knew there were local people who could use the work, but he didn't want them in the house yet.

In spite of the Sandersons' efforts to befriend him and make him feel welcome at their barbecue, and Gemma's apparent desire to shield him from the town's ire, he felt out of place. At the town meeting, he had learned that the people of Reston still resented his father's crime. In turn, that made him reluctant to let them in the house. He knew that didn't make sense because they would be trooping through by the busloads once he put the place on the market, if not to seriously consider buying, then to simply look at what had once been Virginia Smith's pride and joy.

Nate looked down at the worn, dirty carpet that she'd had steam cleaned twice a year, then over at the carved banister whose intricate design had been a stranger to dust during his formative years. She'd rarely hired help except for big jobs. He could recall the immense satisfaction on her face when she'd achieved the exact amount of shine she wanted on the brass andirons in the formal living room. He could never recall her looking at him with that kind of satisfaction.

"Oh, get over it, Smith," he muttered. "Time to let go."

Once the house was spruced up, he would never have to come here again. All the paperwork would be handled at a title company. And after it was sold, all his energy could go into the hospital and building up his medical practice.

He had emptied the house of everything except the few items he wanted to keep and three boxes from his mom's closet that he hadn't yet sorted through. They were waiting by the front door. Standing up, he went down the stairs, crossed the foyer and picked up a couple of packed cartons. Now was as good a time as any to put them in his car.

With some maneuvering and rearranging, he wedged all of the keepsakes he was saving into the backseat and the trunk. He was done, but he needed to make one more walk-through to make sure everything was out.

He climbed the stairs and walked through his old bedroom, where rectangles of unfaded wallpaper showed the places his sports and heavy-metal-band posters had been. He couldn't remember now why he'd loved heavy metal so much except that his dad had hated it. At the time, that had seemed like a good enough reason.

The guest rooms and his parents' room were empty. He closed those doors and moved on to Mandy's room, where he hesitated with his hand on the knob. Except for the thorough cleaning his mother did a couple of times a year, she had left it untouched, a memorial to her only daughter. Nate had felt as if he was betraying both of them when he'd cleared it out.

Turning the knob, he stepped inside and took a slow walk around the room, coming to a stop by the window, which overlooked the weed-filled backyard. Then he turned back to view the world his sister had created for herself.

This room looked as if it was from an entirely different universe, not simply from another family. At some point during her last year in high school, Mandy had torn off the wallpaper and repainted every wall, the trim and the door. The colors she had chosen were bright yellow and neon orange. Maybe it had been an attempt to warm up this house, or at least her corner of it. She had also filled her room with posters of the rain forest. She had sewn burlap curtains and brought in pots full of plants, which horrified their mother, who feared water damage to the furniture.

He had helped Mandy paint, and his inexpert wielding of the brushes and rollers hadn't seemed to bother her at all. He'd loved the color, so warm and brilliant, and the eye-popping shade of the orange trim had made them both laugh.

A thought surfaced through his bout of reminiscence and a shiver ran up his spine. He rubbed his hands over his face as if to wake himself up. That's why he'd always liked the smell of fresh paint. It brought back happy memories of Mandy, but he'd buried them for so many years because the bad memories of the last few years of her life were so overwhelming.

Nate could remember Mandy talking about what he realized now were ecological and global economic issues. He'd only been eight years old and hadn't understood her arguments or the reason she was so different. He walked to the closet and opened the door. Pink and purple stripes had been her choice in her younger years, but by the summer before her senior year, she had made the big change. As a little boy, he hadn't known what caused it, but now he thought he did— she had been determined to be involved in the world, so different from their secretive father and withdrawn mother.

The sound of footsteps in the hallway pulled him around.

"Lisa?" he called out. "Did you forget…"

"It's not Lisa. It's me." Gemma appeared in the doorway and greeted him with a tentative smile. She was dressed in shorts and a peach-colored top—a glow of color in this gloomy house. Like Mandy's room.

"I came over to tell you how Yvette is doing. The front door was open so I came on in."

He shrugged. "You could have called. Cell-phone service seems to be working today."

"I didn't think of it since it rarely does." She strolled into the room, glanced at the walls and smiled.

"I'm changing my service provider. People need to reach me." He paused. "Did you get your car fixed?"

"Yes." She smiled. "Four new tires and a new spare."

"That ought to keep you on the road for a couple of years."

Gemma nodded then turned slowly and took a careful look at the empty space.

"This was your sister's, wasn't it?" She turned to him with eyes full of sympathy.

"Yes. I was making sure everything was out."

Gemma walked to the window and looked at the yard. "East-facing window. When the sun rose, it must have made this room seem as if it was on fire." She smiled at him over her shoulder.

"It did."

"Sad to think that someone who created this room, was so vibrant herself, is gone."

"Yes." The sorrow in her voice echoed what he'd been feeling all day.

Seeing Gemma here somehow made his memories of Mandy even sharper, though the two of them had looked nothing alike. It took him a moment to put a name to the quality they shared. They were vibrant, he thought. He didn't think he'd ever used that word before, but it perfectly described this room, the way his sister had burst out of her family-imposed cocoon and blossomed in her last year at home. Mandy had cultivated that liveliness. Gemma had been born with it. Having her here made him yearn for what he'd missed with Mandy and what he couldn't have now.

He wasn't willing to drag anyone else into his little pity party, so he gestured toward the open door. "Shall we go?"

"Oh, of course."

He shut the door carefully, closing in the only bit of warmth this house had ever known, then followed her down the hallway and the stairs. At the bottom, she turned to him and said, "About Yvette. She's much better." Gemma told him everything that had happened and gave a rundown of the woman's vital signs along with the results of her blood tests.

Nate nodded as she talked. This was easier, he thought. Easier to slip into his professional persona and leave his homegrown ghosts behind for a minute.

When Gemma was finished, he said, "I looked up Dr. Brewer's pregnancy diet. It's more than lots of eggs. Do you think she'll follow it? Yvette said she's vegan."

"I explained pretty carefully what the consequences of toxemia are. It scared her."

"Last night should have scared her."

"Believe me, it did. I think she'll follow the Brewer diet. She's also going to take some classes I'm offering."

Nate raised an eyebrow. "Does Cole know?"

"I don't think so."

"Expect trouble from him."

"After the last time I saw him, I will, and you should, too."

"I will."

Silence stretched between them. With her flaming hair, colorful shirt and neon toenails, she would be the center of attention in any room. And she was exactly where he wanted his attention to be. It wasn't only her clothing or her hair, but she glowed with life. He'd seen it at the Mustang and at the party. People were attracted to her, drawn by her humor and compassion, the way she put other people ahead of herself—as evidenced by the crazy dance she'd done with Bunky. It was part of her personality that came out as genuine warmth toward others—and as her need to rescue them. Him.

Gemma gave him a polite smile and reached for the doorknob. "I'd better go. The Sunshine Birthing Center opens in a couple of days and there's still lots to do."

"Sunshine…" Nate said the name hesitantly as the questions that had been bothering him came up yet again.

"What about it?"

"Not it. Her. The first time you came over here with Lisa you said Mandy had visited your mother out at your place."

"That's right. Many times. I was only eight but I remember that my mom and dad showed her our garden and taught her about plants. She and my mom baked bread. My mom is famous for her bread. Why?"

"I didn't know about it, that's all. I didn't know what she was doing." Except that she was hanging out at the "den of hippie craziness" as his mother had termed it.

Gemma frowned as if she was trying to twist her thoughts with his. "You were also eight years old. Did you pay a lot of attention to what your big sister was doing?"

He took a minute to answer. He had talked

more about Mandy in the past ten minutes than he had since she died. He felt as if he was forcing open a rusted door.

"We were…close." To Mandy, Nate had never been the pesky little brother. She took him everywhere she could in town, which made him wonder why she'd left him behind when she'd gone to the Whitmires'. Nate shoved his hands into his back pockets and looked down, studying the marble floor. "And then suddenly, she was gone from home more than she was here."

"She must have found something that appealed to her. She and my mom weren't that different in age. Mom had me when she was only nineteen, and, well—my mom was fun. She still is."

"I guess that was the attraction for Mandy."

"And she didn't tell you she and my parents had become friends? Why does that matter?"

"Something changed her. She had a different focus. One that created conflict between her and my parents. I didn't know before what caused it, but now I do."

Her eyes widened and she clapped a hand to her chest. "And you hold *my* parents responsible? Don't you think that's kind of a stretch? Mandy must have been pretty smart. Wasn't she valedictorian of her class?"

Nate watched defensive anger flare in her eyes and shook his head. "I don't know. It was a long time ago, but—"

"It still haunts you," Gemma stated.

"It's…being in this house." Stepping forward, he held the door for her and when she walked out, he followed her, then closed and locked it.

Gemma stopped to look back at the entryway, and the room beyond. "I don't think it's this house, Nate. It's only a building, after all. Maybe you shouldn't even come here." She put her hands on her hips, the stance of an annoyed woman. "This can't be healthy. Wouldn't it be better to stop digging up the past? The best thing you could do is move into the future. Make new friends." She gestured to encompass the property. "Leave this behind."

"That's my plan."

"But you don't have to do it alone. There are people who could help you. *I* could—"

"No." He shook his head. "No."

Gemma's expression changed from anger

to hurt. Her lips trembled when she said, "All right, then."

With a wave of her hand, she hurried down the sidewalk and climbed into her Land Rover.

Nate watched her drive away as regret kicked at him. He'd been wrong to take his frustration out on Gemma. No matter what his own problems were, the two of them had to live and work in this town. They were in the same profession, so he needed to come to terms with what was going on in his own head. He had too many questions about his family, his past, his sister and her death. Issues he'd successfully buried for years had been resurrected the minute he'd returned to Reston because they were the kinds of things that never stayed dead.

"Like zombies," he muttered, an ironic twist to his lips.

He took another look at the house then headed to his car with firm steps. Gemma was right about one thing. He needed to leave this place behind, but he didn't need… emotional help to do it. Only physical labor.

He would pay Lisa to hire workers to clean and paint this place. It was time to let it go.

All the memories he had of this house were bad ones, so what did it matter if people came in and fixed it up? He had a medical practice to establish and a hospital to reopen. Who knew? Maybe having a crowd inside might exorcise some of the ghosts.

GEMMA DROVE AWAY with tears stinging her eyes. She didn't understand what was going on in Nate's mind and she wondered if he even knew. What she had said wasn't strictly true, anyway. A house was more than a building. That's why she'd moved back into the cabin where she'd grown up. She wanted to bask in the happy memories and create new ones for herself. It was obvious that Nate didn't have those kinds of recollections.

But how could he blame her parents, especially her mother, for the way his sister had changed? Did he think they weren't good enough to have associated with Mandy? How could he think that? His father had been a thief, for goodness' sake. And why did it matter now?

Gemma was confused, upset and unable to find a way through the tangle of emotions. She needed to get to the Sunshine Center, but that could wait awhile. Right now, there was only one thing to do. Turning her car around, she headed straight for Lisa's office.

Twenty minutes later, she was sitting on the love seat in the Reston Realty office, a glass of sweet tea in her hand and a plate of cookies on her lap. Lisa's receptionist, Sandy Borden, made the best sugar cookies anywhere, and always kept some in the office for clients or their children.

Sighing, Gemma took a bite and savored the buttery sweetness. "This is just what I needed. They could only be more perfect if they were dipped in chocolate."

"Wait until Christmas," Lisa answered, looking up from her computer screen. "I didn't know there were so many ways to decorate sugar cookies. What's this all about, anyway? I haven't seen you eat this much sugar since...well, I never have."

"Dr. Nathan Smith."

"What a coincidence. I'm filling out the forms to list his house for sale. What happened?" Lisa saved her work, closed her laptop and came over to the love seat. She chose a cookie from Gemma's plate and sat down beside her.

Gemma described her encounter with Nate.

"I get that he doesn't respect midwifery, but I have no idea why. And I don't understand where all the rest of this is coming from, like the questions about how well my parents knew his sister. Why does that matter now and…why do I care?" She took another bite of cookie.

"Because, one way or another, you have to work with him."

"I've worked with objectionable people before. Remember Dr. Gilbert Grab-hands?"

Lisa snickered. "The fastest booty pincher in the West. Whatever happened to him?"

"A group of nurses threatened a lawsuit and he retired in a hurry."

"But is Nate really objectionable or are you ultrasensitive because of the Cole Incident?"

"I don't know. Maybe." Gemma sipped her tea and thought about it. Cole Burleigh was a bully, always had been, which was another reason she was concerned about Yvette. His parents had held him back, starting him in kindergarten a year late so he would be bigger, more developed by the time he reached high school and would be able to play varsity football. Many parents in football-crazy towns did that. But Cole wasn't the star player they had envisioned. He'd been injured in practice, had broken a leg that healed but was always vulnerable to new trauma since he was still growing. In spite of his dad's most intimidating efforts, no doctor would release him so he could play again. The Burleighs knew that without high school experience on the field, he would never make a college or professional team. They looked for someone to blame but couldn't find anyone, or anything, except circumstances. Bigger than everyone else in his grade, and now bitter, he'd used his size and strength to intimidate his classmates—at least the ones who were smaller than him.

And one day, in the fall of their senior year, he'd set his sights on Gemma. Cole must have been watching her for weeks, looking to see where she went, what she did and where he could get her alone…

GEMMA ROLLED THE truck to a stop beside the pavilion's overflowing trash cans. She

grimaced at the mess. This was her least favorite chore, but since her dad let her use
the truck for it, she didn't mind. Her driving
skills were improving. She had just parked
without the bunny hop that often accompanied her stops.

Since this was the last stop on her route
around the small lake, she jumped out,
grabbed gloves and trash bags, and began
picking up the scattered refuse. When the
bins were empty, she scanned the area, even
walking down the boat ramp a ways to pick
up some smashed paper cups.

With her head down, she walked back to
the top of the ramp, searching for pieces of
plastic, which were always a challenge to
keep out of the water and away from the
fish. Satisfied that she had everything, she
headed for the truck, tossed the last bag into
the back and reached for the door handle.

"Hey, Bijou."

Cole Burleigh's voice rocked her to a stop
as her eyes widened in surprise. He ambled
down the pavilion steps toward her. She realized he must have been hiding behind one
of the big pillars that held up the roof.

"Cole, you scared me to death. What are you doing here?"

He grinned his cocky, I-always-get-what-I-want grin. "I came to see you."

Her nose wrinkled as she frowned at him. "Why? You see me every day at school."

"Maybe I want to see you in private."

The way he tilted his head and lifted his eyebrows made her step back several feet and regard him warily. "Why would you want to see me in private?"

He held out his beefy hands, palms up, as if he was presenting her with a gift, then he jerked his chin at her in a come-hither manner he must have been practicing before a mirror. "You're gonna be my new girlfriend."

Dumbfounded, she stared at him. "What?"

"Bijou, you're gonna be my new girlfriend. I've decided you're the one."

He took another step toward her and she took another step back. Cole frowned as if he hadn't anticipated that reaction.

"Cole, I'm not interested in having you, or anyone, for a boyfriend."

His lips curled. "That's a lie. I've seen you looking at me in Mrs. Arnstein's class."

"She makes you sit right in front of her so

she can keep an eye on you. Of course I have to look at you. Everyone does. And you always sit turned halfway around in your chair to make *sure* everyone does."

That stopped him for a moment as he assessed her reaction. "Come on, Bijou. You know you want me."

"No, Cole. I *don't*."

Her emphasis on the last word had his fury springing to life. His brows drew together and his mouth twisted. He lifted his hands again, but this time, they were extended as if he was going to grab her and shake her. His voice was a growl as he said, "Nobody says that to me, Bijou."

She jumped backward but came up against the truck bumper, which threw her off balance. At the same time, Cole made a grab for her but missed as she slid sideways and cringed away from him.

From nowhere, another figure flew at them, forcing himself between Gemma and Cole.

"Leave her alone, Cole!" Nate Smith threw up his hands as Cole swung a fist at both of them. Nate—smaller, lighter and quicker than Cole—grabbed Gemma's arm and jerked her away, at the same time putting up his forearm to protect her.

Cole, already off balance, spun around from the force of his intended blow. His big feet tangled and he stumbled toward the edge of the boat ramp, where it was slick with moss. He tried to regain his balance, but his forward momentum carried him to the bottom, arms pinwheeling, shoes skidding until he splashed into the water, facedown.

Gemma and Nate gave startled laughs. Cole didn't stay down for long, but came up soaking wet and shaking his head like a bull.

That made them laugh even harder until he turned with murderous rage in his eyes and started toward them.

"Nate," Gemma yelled. "Get in the truck."

She ran toward the driver's side and got in while Nathan jumped in beside her.

With shaking hands, she started the engine and got them going, remembering to ease off the clutch smoothly as she switched gears and stepped on the gas. The tires fought for purchase and loose gravel shot out from beneath them. When she heard an angry roar, she realized the flying pebbles had hit Cole, but she didn't stop. Within seconds, they were away from the pavilion area and on the lane leading to the Whitmires' house.

She glanced in the rearview mirror to see Cole stomping after them but growing smaller in the distance.

"Bijou, are you okay?" Nate asked.

"Yes, I think so." Emotions surged through her, but the dominant one was elation that she had escaped Cole.

She stopped in front of the cabin and shut off the engine before turning to thank Nate. He didn't give her the chance. He jumped out of the vehicle and hurried away without a backward glance. Openmouthed, she stared after him. He hadn't even waited for her to thank him. Maybe he was afraid Cole was coming after them. She looked back the way they'd come. Cole probably *was* coming after them.

Heart pounding, she jumped from the truck and rushed inside to tell her parents what had happened…

RECALLING THE COLE INCIDENT NOW, Gemma smiled at Lisa. "I'll never forget the sight of my dad, Wolfchild the Peace Activist, rushing from the house with blood in his eyes, looking for Cole."

"I wish I'd seen that," Lisa said, biting into a cookie. "As well as Cole falling on his face in the lake."

"That *was* pretty funny, and I think that's why he still hates us. Nate and I laughed at him. He was also mad that the sheriff took a report on the incident, even though Cole was the only one hurt, and then it was only his pride. His parents were horrified to have their son's name on a police report, which then got printed in the paper because Cole was legally an adult."

Gemma paused, thinking it over. "I was glad Nate talked to the sheriff, but I never understood why he wouldn't let me thank him."

"Because, even then, Nate was an enigma, and you had that major crush on him."

"Yes, but I got over that pretty quickly."

Lisa tilted her head and searched Gemma's face. "Did you, Gemma? I've always thought you never got over it. He was the one who got away. Now you're both back here, and—"

"He wants nothing to do with me."

"I don't think that's the problem. I think

there's a lot more going on, and you're only part of it."

Lisa stood and returned to her desk while Gemma sipped her tea and thought about what she'd said. Gemma wanted things to be different, better, between her and Nathan, but they were getting worse because whatever Nate was dealing with was eating him alive.

CHAPTER SEVEN

"I'm sorry, Dr. Smith, but the hospital kitchen isn't even close to being up to code and it will take a while to get it there. Adding that to the other upgrades means it will be six to eight weeks before we can open this facility." Clifford Vogel handed Nate a list of the necessary repairs. Now that Cliff and his construction crew had opened up the walls and spent hours examining the place, Nate had a better idea of the extent of the work that needed to be done—as well as the additional time and money required.

Nate read the list and sighed, then gave it to Tom Sanderson, who looked it over and passed it to Brantley Clegg.

Tom whistled between his teeth. "I didn't know there was that much to be done."

"And that much more money would be needed," Brantley added.

"It's been sitting for eight years, right?"

Cliff asked. "That's eight years of neglected regular maintenance on top of the necessary upgrades. However, we can start right away. This afternoon, in fact."

Nate nodded. "Okay, that would be—"

"Better wait until tomorrow morning." Tom inclined his head toward the building next door. "Gemma's open house is tonight and since she shares the parking lot, we better not have it tied up."

"Whatever you say. We'll get started first thing in the morning." Cliff gave them a wave and climbed into his truck.

As he drove away, Tom turned to Nate and said, "You're going to Gemma's open house, right?"

"Of course." Nate answered with a smile he didn't feel. "I'll see you and Frances there."

When he was gone, Brantley Clegg said, "In spite of the amount of money they've put in to this, and all the fund-raising they've done, Tom and Frances are doing a good job of not trying to control this project."

"I know." Nate wondered where the older man was going with this.

"But once it gets rolling, other benefactors

might not be so willing to keep their opinions to themselves."

"So I should look out for people wanting to tell me what to do?"

"That's right. It's all part of being accountable."

Nate knew it was all part of being the son of the embezzler who had hurt this town so badly. He'd thought he was developing a thick skin, but sometimes comments still stung, even though Brantley was trying to be kind.

"When we started this project, we knew we would have to practice transparency in every area. Right?" Brantley asked.

"Yes, of course."

"This is when it starts. As soon as large amounts of money are being spent, questions will start."

"Which means we have to have the answers. And the receipts."

"Now you're catching on." With a wave, Brantley headed up the street toward the bank.

Nate stared after him for a second, then, aware of the growing heat of the day and the spike in humidity, he went into his office, where his new receptionist, Stacie, handed him his messages. He gave her a brief smile and glanced around at the empty reception area.

"Don't worry, Doctor, you'll be getting tons of patients soon. After all, you're the only doctor in town. It will take people a while to make the switch, but pretty soon they'll decide they'd rather drive five miles to see the doctor instead of thirty."

"I'm sure you're right," he agreed, but he really wasn't so sure. She was new to Reston, not terribly experienced and already knew the people of this town better than he ever had.

His office had been open for a week, and he'd had a few patients. He knew his practice would increase after the hospital opened, after people got to know him, after he could start living down what his father had done. Attending the open house for the Sunshine Birthing Center would be a good start. He hoped he could get Gemma alone for a minute and tell her he was sorry for making her the target of his confusion and regret.

"In fact, you have a new patient in exam room one right now," Stacie informed him.

"Oh, who?"

"Wayne Fedder, Jr.," she answered. Nate thought it was interesting that her cheeks reddened when she said it. "Here's his chart."

Curious, Nate looked over the chart, including the vital signs his nurse had recorded, and noted Junior's high blood pressure and fast pulse. He wondered how Junior would feel about blood tests for diabetes and thyroid issues.

Junior looked up when Nate walked into the room and shut the door behind him.

"It's time, Doc," Junior said.

"For?" Nate pulled his stethoscope from his pocket and listened to Junior's overworked heart and laboring lungs.

"For me to get healthy."

"That's good to hear," Nate said, pulling up a stool. "But what brought this on?"

"I can't pass my department physicals anymore, so the sheriff gave me six months to get in shape. And, there's Stacie."

Nate nodded toward his outer office. "Stacie Richards? My receptionist?"

"Yup. Says she won't marry me until I get healthy, 'cause she doesn't want to be a young widow if I can't outrun the bad guys.

I need you to give me some kind of diet to follow, but it has to be simple. I'm a lousy cook so I gotta be able to find healthy stuff that gives me energy and doesn't make me wanna puke."

Nate chuckled. "That's a tall order, but let me see what I can find in my files. I'll be right back—and you'll be getting a complete physical today so we know what our goals are. I hope you've got plenty of time."

Junior scooted back on the examining table and made himself a little more comfortable. "Yeah, I do. Reston isn't exactly a hotbed of crime."

After rifling through his files, Nate came up with a plan he thought Junior could live with, especially if the incentive was getting Stacie to marry him. When he returned to the exam room and handed the papers to Junior, he said, "You'll have to start exercising, too."

Junior gave him an alarmed look. "I've seen you out running at night or in the morning. I won't be ready for that for a while, even with bad guys chasing me."

"Walking is good. Maybe Stacie will go for a walk with you."

Junior's face lit up. "That'll work."

The next hour was spent on the kind of physical Nate enjoyed doing because it gave him time to focus on his patient, getting to know him and his complete medical history.

Finally, with an order for lab tests in hand, Junior stood to leave. "And, Doc?"

"Yes?"

"Most people in town know you had nothing to do with what happened to the hospital funds—with your dad's felony. It hurt the town, the whole county, but folks are glad you're reopening the hospital, and that we've got a doctor again. Try to remember that once something like that has happened, people don't find it so easy to trust."

Humbled, Nate nodded as he realized how much he'd needed to hear someone say that. "Thanks, Junior."

The deputy set his hat at a jaunty angle and grinned as he shook Nate's hand and opened the door. "And so you know, Doc, I intend to kiss your receptionist on the way out."

Nate laughed. "You have my blessing."

GEMMA WAS THRILLED with the turnout. The reception area was so packed that guests spilled onto the sidewalk out front and into the parking lot. Lisa and Carly had cleared a path and moved the cookies and punch outside, which had attracted even more visitors, including some who had only been driving past.

Gemma was busy handing out brochures, which gave phone numbers, a list of the upcoming classes and answers to frequently asked questions. Smiling, she reveled in the crush, answered many questions that were in the brochure and directed guests to where Rhonda was showing off the birthing rooms, which were set up as comfortable bedrooms.

Around eight o'clock, Gemma pulled Lisa aside and said, "The turnout has been phenomenal, but the crowd seems to be thinning out now."

"That's because we're almost out of cookies and punch. Do you want me to run to my office and unearth the sugar cookies from Sandy's secret stash? I know where she hides it."

Laughing, Gemma said, "No. Otherwise, these people will never leave."

Lisa turned away to speak to someone and Gemma proudly surveyed the inviting decor of the clinic. She had researched the best colors for relaxation and calmness, so every room had been painted some shade of blue or green. The reception area, where she planned to hold classes for the time being, was a shade called wellwater, a cheery but restful turquoise. The chairs were a mix of those from Carly's collection. Each had been refinished, painted or upholstered to Carly's perfectionist standards.

The African carving of mother and child sat on a shelf behind the reception desk and was reflected in the logo on the stationery and the sign over the entrance. It was also painted on the door. Marlene Fedder had never painted on a glass door, but she'd been willing to try it. In fact, she'd done a wonderful job.

Happy with the way things were going, she rechecked the list of people who had signed up for classes. Yvette Burleigh's name wasn't on it since she hadn't been at the open house, but there was still hope that she would attend. Gemma had talked to Yvette twice since she and Carly had spent the night at the Burleighs' and Yvette had assured her that she was following the Brewer plan carefully.

Yvette hoped she could attend at least one of the classes. Gemma had translated that to mean "If Cole doesn't stop me."

The room suddenly went silent and Gemma looked up to see what had happened. Nate Smith came through the door and nodded to the crowd, then stopped to look around the reception area. Concerned, she took several steps toward him, but after a momentary lull, everyone went back to their conversations.

Nate made his way to her. She took a quick glance around the crowd, checking to see if anyone looked ready to confront him, but all her guests were otherwise occupied, so she relaxed and gave Nate a polite smile. "Thanks for coming, Nate."

"If I end up being the medical director, I need to know what we have here." He glanced around. "Nice crowd." He paused, focusing on the wall behind a row of chairs. "Interesting artwork."

Gemma smiled. "That's my favorite thing in the entire place." The wall was dotted with small, brightly colored handprints and footprints. "Those are thanks to Devon and Dylan Morton, Rhonda and Harley's twin grandsons. They're three."

"Colorful" was all he said before turning away. "I'd better go…mingle."

He'd said that word in the same tone he might have used to say "pull weeds" or "scrub toilets."

"At this rate, he's never going to get the town to trust him," she murmured. Even though she was still annoyed with him, she knew she couldn't let this awkwardness continue. It wouldn't benefit anyone. Scooting up beside him, she took his arm and turned him toward a group of people who were new to the area.

Nate gave her a look that seemed to question if she was still trying to rescue him, but she only answered with a smile.

Within a few minutes, she was pulled away by an expectant mother holding a two-year-old on her hip. She wanted to ask about a class on dealing with sibling jealousy.

"I don't know much about that," Gemma answered. "It's not part of childbirth."

When the woman's face fell, she added, "But I'm sure I can find someone to teach that. I can see where it would be very helpful." She handed over the clipboard. "Give me your name and number and one of us will get back to you."

The woman put down her son and quickly wrote her information on the clipboard before the little boy found something more interesting to do than stand beside his mommy. She thanked Gemma, scooped his hand into hers and walked outside.

Gemma stared after her, thinking this was where she'd been going wrong, and so had Nate. People liked sharing their expertise. She could get Mona Zahn to teach a class on helping toddlers accept a newborn. The woman had eight well-behaved kids. There were other ways they could help. She and Nate, if she could convince him, needed to get the entire community involved with the rebuilding of the health-care facilities. She was sure it would also improve his standing in the community.

Excited by the idea, she turned to look for him but was pulled away by Mrs. Page, her fifth grade teacher, who wanted to congratulate her on what she had accomplished.

When the crowd finally began to thin out, Gemma once again looked for Nate and found him heading for his car. She hurried after him.

"Wait up, Nate. I want to talk to you about something."

He paused, keys in hand, and waited for her, squaring his shoulders and facing her as if expecting a confrontation.

"I'm going to get the community involved in the birthing center."

"Unlicensed people delivering babies?"

Impatiently, she waved away that comment. "Of course not. Don't jump to conclusions. In teaching classes, or whatever else I can think of, and I think you should do the same thing with the hospital."

"In what way?"

"You want people to accept you, right? You want to build up your practice and prove you're a good doctor, right?"

"Yes."

"Then, instead of the contractor and the hospital board and you taking care of all the details, the local people can help."

He frowned, leaned against the side of his car and crossed his arms over his chest. "With what?"

Gemma pointed back toward the Sunshine

Center. "Painting. Murals on the walls, sewing curtains or throw pillows for the lounge, things like that. This hospital never had a gift shop. Well, now we can, by resurrecting the hospital auxiliary. Those were people who answered the phones and handed out books and magazines to patients, but they could stock a gift shop, sew or knit gifts or build birdhouses—volunteers to direct people to where they need to go. It was a small operation before, but it could be expanded."

"It's one floor and has only thirty rooms for patients," he pointed out, then tilted his head. "This isn't another of your ideas to make me popular, is it?"

"Popular?" she scoffed. "This isn't middle school, Nate."

"But is that what you're doing? Rescuing me? Again?"

Her face heated up and she glanced away. "Why can't you accept my suggestion, Nate? Take it for what it is?"

He didn't answer, but asked another question of his own. "You can't help yourself, can you?"

"Not when I see the right thing to do—the way to help someone. Not when I see what someone needs to do to…help themselves." It was so clear to her. Why didn't he understand?

"Most people would call that being bossy."

"Maybe. It's still a good idea. It couldn't hurt." She cleared her throat. "As I was saying, we could get volunteers to show people around."

"It's not that hard to find your way around."

"You know what I mean," she said, rolling her eyes. "If the community buys in, if they feel like it belongs to them, it will help them forget about the past. And I know who could head up the painting, too. Marlene Fedder."

"Doesn't she still work for the post office?"

"She's retired and looking for something productive to do. She painted the logo for the Sunshine." Gemma gestured over her shoulder. "If you give her a call, I'll bet she would help. And she's an artist. Paints landscapes. She would be the perfect person to be in charge of the murals, although you'll have to make sure she involves as many people as possible."

"Oh, I will, huh?" His lips twitched.

"Yes, and you'll have to make sure the

board…" Gemma paused, finally taking a good look at him. "Are you laughing at me?"

He grinned. "Absolutely not."

She put her hands on her hips. "While I have to admit this beats your usual sour expression, I don't appreciate being laughed at."

"I'm not laughing. I'm…admiring your enthusiasm."

Gemma gave him a dubious look. "But will you do it? Will you talk to the board and the contractor about this?"

"I don't know, Gemma. I'm not sure it's a good idea."

GEMMA'S MOUTH DROPPED OPEN. "You've got to be kidding me. Don't you realize that the more help you've got, the sooner you can get this place open again?" She jerked her thumb toward the darkened hospital entrance.

"Don't you realize that there aren't many people in this town who would want to help me?"

Her face fell. "Which brings us right back to what we were talking about a minute ago. It's why you have to change their minds—

point out that it will benefit them, benefit everybody."

Nate bit his bottom lip to keep from smiling because, just like that, she was off again. She really *couldn't* help it. The rescuer in her needed to keep pulling people out of trouble, protecting them, and that was the last thing he needed. He hadn't come home to Reston so people would feel sorry for him. He'd come because he'd hoped to do some good to make up for George's perfidy. And he didn't need anyone, least of all Gemma, standing between him and his detractors. Still, she might have a good idea here.

And she was so beautiful, impassioned and captivating. Right now, all of her passion was focused on him. Something in his gut squirmed at that knowledge. Since he'd grown up in an undemonstrative family, he didn't know what to do with the kinds of emotions she stirred in him, but he knew he couldn't simply go with them, let them take over. Besides, it wouldn't be fair to her or to him.

Nate kept his arms crossed over his chest as she tried to convince him of the rightness of her plan. In the yellow-hued glow from the old-fashioned streetlight, her eyes glittered and her expression changed from serious, to pleading, to annoyed, while her tone of voice matched each shifting emotion. Her hands shot out to encompass the town, then formed fists at her sides before clamping onto her waist once again. It was quite a show of what an impassioned woman looked like.

He couldn't remember a time when he'd relaxed and enjoyed anything this much. He already knew he would do what she asked. What she said made sense and aligned perfectly with what Brantley Clegg had said about being accountable to the citizens. He simply enjoyed having her try to convince him.

"So, what do you think?" she asked when she finally wound down. "Don't you think it's a good idea? Won't you at least consider it?"

"I'll consider it," he said. "If you'll consider having dinner with me."

She stared at him. "What? When?"

"Now. Tonight."

Gemma scooped her phone from her pocket and glanced at the screen. "It's almost nine o'clock."

"Are you hungry?"

"Um, well, yes. All I've had since noon were some cookies and punch." She glanced toward the birthing center.

"Carly and Lisa put everything away while we've been talking," he said. "All you have to do is turn off the lights and lock up."

"All right, but the only thing left open in Reston is Mary Alice's Café."

"You're right, but if we have one of her meat pies this late, we'll be popping antacids all night. I...know a place nearby. The cook's pretty good."

"Oh, where?"

"My place."

Again, she gave him that look where a corner of her mouth lifted and her eyebrows rose. "First, you being shirtless on the road to the Sandersons' barbecue, and now dinner at your place. The gossips are going to have a field day with this."

"It's bound to happen. We both work in health care. It's only natural that we'd see each other."

"That's true."

He waited while she thought it over. He couldn't blame her for hesitating. He'd let his demons from the past cloud his judgment and he needed to apologize.

Finally, she nodded. "Oh, okay then. I'll follow you in my Rover. Where is your house?"

"At the end of Sycamore. The old Volney place. Their son rented it to me."

She nodded and hurried back to lock up. Nate watched to make sure she was all right. As soon as she climbed into her Land Rover, he got into his car and drove home.

He waited for her by the door and was stunned to realize that he was nervous, his stomach fluttering in a way it never had before. When he opened the door and reached around to flip on the light, he gave the living room a quick glance to see if it was as cozy and inviting as hers. Not a chance, he decided, but he held the door for her, anyway.

GEMMA GAVE HIM a smile and stepped inside, eager to see his place and not quite believing she was here. As she might have expected, the furnishings were top-of-the-line, but all done in neutrals. There was a brown leather sofa with a matching chair and some nice brass lamps on substantial square tables. The biggest surprise of all was the row of orchids blooming on the wide windowsill. They were the hardy type, not some delicate beauties that would fade and fail with the slightest of adverse conditions. They were blooming in shades of dark red, purple and yellow.

"These are beautiful," she said. "But, orchids?"

"A patient gave me one a couple of years ago and I discovered I could manage to not kill it, so I tried another and another."

Gemma nodded sympathetically. "Gateway orchid. You get one, and then you have to have another and another. I'm the same way with my herbs…and with purses. I love buying purses, and if I can find one on sale, or in a thrift store, even better. I love a bargain even better than I love a new purse. I used to have dozens." She sighed. "But I've managed to cut down to about twenty."

"Where do you store them?"

"In the guest room closet. I lined them all up on the shelf. Unfortunately, when I want one, I have to get the ladder and climb up to get it."

"You appreciate something more if you

have to work for it," he pointed out drily as he walked into the kitchen.

This time, she was certain he was laughing at her, but she really didn't mind. Nate brought her a glass of wine, which she sipped as she wandered around the living room, reading the titles of the books that filled the bookcases on three walls. Fleetingly, the hundreds of books reminded her of Lisa's grandmother. Mrs. Thomas had owned so many books, along with dozens of unusual keepsakes, that it was impossible to walk through their house. In contrast, Lisa had gone the other way, keeping a book only until she had finished reading it, then giving it away unless she thought she'd read it again. She was the same way with everything. Anything in her house had to be loved and used often.

Nate had his books arranged in basic subject areas so it was easy to locate the medical books, or the ones on astronomy or paleontology. His interests were varied, but confined to one field: science. The only novels he had were medical thrillers.

After she finished looking over his books, Gemma went into the kitchen, where she found Nate wearing a chef's apron and expertly chopping vegetables.

He glanced up. "Grilled salmon and sautéed vegetables," he announced. "Be ready in about twenty minutes. No dessert, though. I can cook, but I can't bake."

"No problem. I've eaten enough cookies lately." Gemma sat down at the table. "Anything I can do to help?"

"No. I've got it."

"A man who cooks," she said, marveling.

"I like to eat and I don't want to go out to restaurants every night."

That made sense for an introvert like him, Gemma thought. He had to be around people but needed time alone to recharge. Of course, that didn't explain whatever else was going on in his mind—his opposition to midwifery and his questions about the friendship between Mandy and her parents.

"So you think that if we ask the community to help, they would actually do it?" he asked.

"Why not? It would benefit everyone."

"Yes, it would." Nate paused as he placed their food on plates. "Thanks for the suggestion, Gemma. I know I haven't always listened to you, but this time, I am."

She gave him a sweet smile. "Which shows that even the most stubborn people can change."

He nodded, and they talked about the project all through dinner. It was nearly eleven o'clock by the time they finished.

Nate had turned his chair sideways and leaned back, his legs stretched out before him, crossed at the ankles. He was slowly twisting his wine goblet. Light caught the faceted glass, sending small rays over his fingers. It was the most relaxed Gemma had ever seen him—and the most vulnerable. His hair was mussed from where he'd run his fingers through it when they'd talked about the need to upgrade the hospital's two operating rooms. His eyes drooped with tiredness, but he seemed free of the strain that had been his companion lately. It made him approachable, and oh, so attractive.

She knew it was time for her to leave, but she wasn't quite ready yet. "How is your practice, Nate? Do you have new patients coming in?"

"Yes, but it's slow," he answered, and they

talked about the challenges of a small-town medical practice.

Considering what had gone on between them since they'd both moved back to Reston, Gemma was surprised at her reaction to him, and her reluctance to leave, but she had a class to teach tomorrow, so she stood and said, "Thanks for dinner, Nate. It was delicious. You're an accomplished chef. I've got to go get some sleep or I won't be worth anything tomorrow."

"Like I said, I like to eat." He followed her to the door and reached for the knob just as she did. His hand covered hers.

Their hands sprang apart and Gemma looked up with a nervous twitch of her lips. Any humorous quip she might have been able to construct died when she looked into his eyes. Want and need welled up in her, chased by doubt.

He was a mystery that only grew.

Memories of the youthful crush she'd had on him resurfaced, adding a poignant sweetness to those needs, but more recent memories followed, ones that weren't nearly as sweet.

His lips tightened in the way she was coming to recognize as a prelude to something unpleasant. "Gemma, I'm not staying."

"What? What do you mean?"

"I'm not staying here permanently. I agreed to come reestablish the hospital and a family practice, but someone else can take over in the next year or so. I'll go to Houston. A friend has invited me to join his practice. But I couldn't do it until I'd finished here."

Gemma shook her head. "I don't understand why you would go to all this work if—"

"To make up for what my dad did, and then forget everything about this town and move on."

"So you can put Reston and everyone in it behind you?"

"Yes, and you don't have to worry about rescuing me from those who dislike me. I won't be here that long."

"I… I see." She looked down, trying to assimilate this news and deal with the pang of sorrow and regret that pierced through her.

"I'd appreciate it if you'd keep that to yourself. Brantley knows, and so does the hospital board, but I don't want it to come out until people in town know they can trust me to do what I've promised before I leave."

Even though dismay filled her throat, Gemma nodded.

"Thanks, Gemma, and thanks for coming. I'll…walk you out." His dark eyes were troubled, cautious, as they'd been almost every time she'd seen him. The approachable man of a few minutes ago had gone, stepped behind a secure door where he must keep his softer emotions hidden away, along with the depth of his troubles.

"Oh, um, thank you." She stepped away and fumbled for the knob. This time he didn't help her with it, but swung the door inward as she stepped outside, then followed her to the Land Rover.

"Good night, then," he said in an unreadable tone as she climbed inside.

Gemma thanked him again for dinner and drove away, her emotions leading her thoughts into a tangle. Before she turned the corner, she glanced in the rearview mirror and saw him still standing there, arms crossed over his chest, staring at the ground.

The loneliness of his stance almost had her turning her car around and going back, but common sense prevailed. This wasn't the right time.

CHAPTER EIGHT

Y<small>VETTE WALKED OUT</small> of her first prebirth class with one of the other attendees, a tall, vivacious girl about her own age.

"So I said yes. We went out three times before I realized his name was Kelvin Summers, not Sutter, like I'd thought, but by then, I was in love. I married him and became Misty Summers. I sound like I should be a weather reporter."

Yvette laughed. Unlike her, Misty was talkative and funny. She had a warm personality that had drawn the other girls to her. There had been four in the class, all first-time mothers with lots of questions that Gemma had patiently answered, sometimes more than once. Yvette had exchanged phone numbers with them and they had plans to get together again, both before and after their babies were born. Somehow, it made it all a little less scary to know they were in the same boat.

"I only hope my husband doesn't want to name our daughter Stormy or Windy, or something like that."

"You don't have a name picked out?" Yvette asked.

"We can't seem to agree on one. I like Natalie Elizabeth and he likes Sadie Rebecca, but then kids would probably tease her and call her Shady R. Summers. We'd better make a decision soon." She sighed. "Little miss will be here in a couple of weeks."

"Tough choice," Yvette said. "They're both beautiful. As soon as we knew ours is a boy, Cole decided we needed to name him Cole Junior."

"It's a good name," Misty said in a breezy tone. "But..."

"What?"

Misty shrugged. "I talk too much, but I've always thought kids should have their own names, be their own person, not an extension of Mom or Dad."

Yvette nodded thoughtfully. "I've never thought about it like that before."

Misty grimaced. "I probably should have

kept my mouth shut, but that's so hard for me. Anyway," she said, returning to their previous topic, "I'll probably let Kelvin have his way. If he's the one to name her, it will make him feel more connected to her while I'm sleeping and he's walking the floor with her at night." With a laugh, she waved good-bye and headed for her car. "I've got to get back to work at Phil's Dollar Store. This is my last week before I stay home and start nesting."

Smiling, Yvette watched her drive away. All the other girls in the class had jobs, but they'd been able to get off to attend this class. She liked that. She'd never had a boss who would have allowed that to happen. She glanced up the street to where Carly would soon be opening her boutique for repurposed furniture and what she called "upcycled art-work." In fact, that's what she was calling her shop—Upcycle. The frame of an old child-size bicycle, painted bright red, would hold the sign out front.

It seemed like it would be a fun place to work, but she knew she wouldn't be the one working there. Cole had made it quite clear that he didn't want her to have a job. Besides, she had a much more important occupation coming in a few weeks.

She turned toward her own vehicle and was brought up short when she caught sight of her husband. Cole was bearing down on her, dodging the trucks and piles of construction equipment that now crowded the center of the parking lot. His fixed expression told her he was angry. She had been on the receiving end of such anger before, though never from him. Since she had no idea how this was going to go, she braced herself.

"Yvette, what are you doing here? Didn't I tell you not to have anything to do with Gemma Whitmire?" he demanded, coming to a stop in front of her. Before she could answer, he went on, "How do you think that made me feel? Driving past and seeing you coming out of there, doing exactly what I'd told you not to do?"

Fear shivered through her, causing her son to shift in her womb. She rested her hands on her belly to calm him.

"Answer me." His brow was furrowed, his eyes narrowed and his mouth twisted into a knot. He was a good-looking man, but anger made him ugly.

Yvette could barely find her voice. "I… know what you told me, and I… I know seeing me here makes you mad."

"What are you doing here?"

"Ta-taking a class, learning ju-just how my body is changing and what to expect during labor."

He threw his hand out dismissively. "You could learn that from reading a book. You know I told you to stay away from Gemma, and yet here you are. How do you explain that? And I want to know who was at the house with you the night I was in Tulsa."

Looking at him, Yvette saw the face of every man who had ever stood over her and tried to intimidate her—her father, her uncle, her stepfather—usually before a fist came her way. Then she looked down at her swollen belly, where her son was growing, waiting to come into this world where he would have to be nurtured and protected. By her.

It was her responsibility to make sure he knew how to respect women and that had to start with respecting his mother. He couldn't do that if she was weak.

Even though her heart was pounding,

Yvette stiffened her spine. "I don't have to, Cole. I'm sorry…"

"You should be," he shot back, a smug look of triumph beginning to bloom in his eyes.

"…that I didn't tell you I was taking this class, but that's all I'm sorry for."

He gaped at her. "You don't think you owe me an explanation?"

"No. It's my body and, right now, this baby is entirely mine. I have to decide what's best, and that's what I'm doing. And what's more, I'll be taking more of Gemma's classes. I've already signed up. So you know, I have one on Tuesday and another on Friday, unless Gemma has a patient in labor, then the schedule will be changed."

His mouth opened and closed a couple of times. "But—but my mom could tell you anything you need to know."

"Your mom knows a lot, which I'm sure she'll tell me." Yvette was tempted to say, "whether I want her to or not," but knew she had to fight one battle at a time, so instead, she finished up with "She isn't a medical professional."

"Well…there are other places that you could—"

"Not here in Reston. And why should I travel thirty miles, in this condition, to another class, another midwife, when I can drive five and learn what I need to know? And as far as someone being at the house the night you were in Tulsa? It was Gemma, along with Carly Joslin. Lisa Thomas was there for a while, too. I got sick at the Sandersons' barbecue and they took me home and cared for me. I didn't tell you because I know how you feel about Gemma. But she's a nurse and a midwife. Isn't it better for me and this baby to be cared for by a professional rather than my trying to figure this out on my own?"

He blinked and shook his head. A feeling of power like she'd never known before surged through Yvette. She was winning this argument.

"You should have called me, told me you were sick that night."

"And I would have if not for your insistence I stay away from Gemma."

Cole seemed to have no answer for that, but he tried to get back on track by gesturing across the street to his truck. "Get in. I'll take you home."

"No. I've got my car, and I have to go to the grocery store. I need milk—" she pointed to her belly "—to grow this baby, which, by the way, I might have Gemma deliver."

Standing on tiptoe, she kissed his cheek and headed for her car. She imagined that she could hear her son applauding.

COLE STARED AFTER HER, his thoughts scrambling. He couldn't believe what had happened, was stunned at what Yvette had said. He had never expected this, hadn't planned for it.

Yvette had been exactly what he wanted in a wife—sweet, soft-spoken, obedient. After they'd chatted online for a while, he'd gone to Wichita to meet her. She'd had two part-time jobs—working in a fast-food place and a grocery store—and lived with three other girls in a crummy apartment. Her car had been a joke, held together with duct tape. The front bumper had been wired on with what looked like a couple of rusted coat hangers.

She'd been impressed by his truck, his money and his good job. As soon as she'd said yes to his proposal, he'd bought her a newer car, along with the biggest diamond he could afford. She'd been so sweetly grateful that he knew he'd made the right decision in spite of what his mom and dad had said about the horrors of marrying someone he met online. He didn't care because he'd waited a long time to find a girl like her and he wasn't going to let her get away. When he finally made his parents understand that, he and Yvette had been married in a small ceremony his mother had arranged and he'd brought his bride back to his family home, where they'd both been happy, especially after they'd discovered she had become pregnant soon after the wedding.

Now she was defying him. He wanted her to have the best medical care, but she already had a good doctor and seven different books on childbirth and babies. He didn't understand why she needed Gemma's help.

At first, he'd wanted to keep Yvette to himself, but then he wanted her to have friends because that would make her want to stay. He didn't want those friends to include Gemma Whitmire, though. Everything had been fine until Gemma had returned to Reston.

Fear hit him in the pit of his stomach. What he hadn't counted on was that someone who had been so easy to win might be just as easy to lose. If he lost her, it would be all Gemma's fault. He considered going into Gemma's precious birthing center and confronting her, but that might drive Yvette further away. He wasn't about to let that happen.

GEMMA STOOD BY the window of her clinic and watched Cole and Yvette. She didn't know what they were talking about, but she saw Cole point toward her center, a furious look on his face.

When Yvette kissed her husband on the cheek and headed for her car, Gemma felt a spark of pride. Cole hesitated, as if he couldn't decide exactly what to do. Gemma reached out and secured the dead bolt and watched as he stomped back to his truck.

Gemma hoped Yvette was taking charge of her life and her pregnancy and that Cole wouldn't stand in the way of her self-worth and independence. The night she and Carly had spent at Yvette's house had taught her a great deal about the younger woman. She'd had an unstable life before she'd met Cole and was so grateful to him for all he'd done for her. Gemma feared that wasn't the best start to a relationship because it made Yvette too dependent on her husband.

Rhonda had gone home for the day and Gemma was ready to follow, when her phone rang. She picked it up and was delighted to hear her mother's voice.

"Hi, honey," Sunshine sang out. "I finally got a chance to call you."

Gemma sat down at the reception desk. "I'm so glad you did. How are things going? How's Dad?"

After assurances that Wolfchild was fine, Sunshine said, "We've been so busy, but the project is going well. Roof goes on tomorrow. What about you, honey? What's happening?"

The first thing that popped into Gemma's mind was "I'm constantly thinking about Nathan Smith," but she kept from saying that aloud.

"Gemma? Are you there? Did we get cut off?"

"Yes, I'm here." She talked about everything that had happened in the past couple of weeks. "I've seen a lot of Nathan Smith and…it hasn't always been pleasant. He's struggling with family secrets, I think."

"What do you mean?"

Gemma explained about Nate's question regarding Mandy.

Sunshine made a sound of distress. "That was a tragedy and since Nathan was only twelve when Mandy died, it must have had a terrible effect on him."

"He didn't know you were friends with her."

"There was no reason he would have known. Mrs. Smith didn't approve of us and our lifestyle—although, thinking about it now, I realize it wasn't personal. She didn't like anyone who was different, or who was comfortable in their own skin…or that she couldn't control."

"Sounds like a miserable way to live."

"I think it was, and by the time Mandy was seventeen, she knew it and wanted something different."

"So she made friends with you."

"And Evelyn and Randy Frost, who raised pigs, remember them? They also made their own sausage. I think that experience turned Mandy into a vegetarian."

"I imagine so."

"She visited Mrs. Poole and learned how to quilt. Her senior year in high school was a year of learning and exploring and it panicked her parents. They could see they were losing her."

"What did they think was going to happen when she went off to college?"

"Honestly? I think her mother planned to go with her and would have if Nate hadn't been so young, and, well, she didn't leave her house much."

"Wow. I had no idea."

"No one knew what happened with Mandy, even a few years later when she came back home, nine months pregnant, and died in childbirth. I saw her during that time, but she didn't talk to me." Sunshine paused. "I still don't know exactly why, but she seemed to be...drifting."

"What do you mean?"

"It was as if she was floating along and everything would work out fine if she ignored it."

"That's so sad."

"Yes, it was. It was hard to stand by and watch. I felt helpless and I'm sure it was even harder for her parents."

"And Nate," Gemma added.

They chatted for a few more minutes, then Gemma talked with her dad, and when they hung up, she was left with even more questions than she'd had before. She was beginning to understand Nathan's home life as a boy, and the effect Mandy's death had on him.

She stood and walked to the window, gazing across the parking lot to Nate's office.

It shook her to realize the depth of her feelings for him. In spite of their professional differences, she was drawn to him as she never had been to any man. She saw now that she always had been. It wasn't his looks alone, although she couldn't deny that was a factor. She was drawn to the yearning in him to be better than his father had been, to right old wrongs. He was battling ghosts from his past, though, and she had already seen that he wouldn't welcome her help.

ON SATURDAY MORNING, Cole went to work and Yvette began getting ready to help at the hospital renovation. She and Misty Summers would sit at a table in the shaded entrance and hand out painting assignments. She could hardly wait to spend the day with her funny and outgoing new friend.

Yvette hadn't told Cole of her plans—he might try to stop her. Since the day he'd caught her at the Sunshine, he'd seemed wary of laying down the law, but the old version of her husband would be back soon. It was like waiting for the other shoe to drop.

When she heard a truck pulling in to the driveway, she hurried to see if Cole had returned.

But it wasn't Cole. She stared in dismay as her father-in-law's truck backed up with a tarp-covered load in the bed.

Margery's car pulled in as well, because she refused to travel in her husband's truck, claiming the ride was too rough. She emerged from her Cadillac like a queen arriving to personally direct an army of minions. Except she had only one minion, and he didn't take direction well.

Bob unhooked the cords holding the load in place and pulled back the tarp to expose a crib. No doubt, it was the one that would convert into a toddler bed, Yvette thought, then into a full-size bed and, if Yvette's son was lucky, an escape pod to get away from his grandparents. She heartily wished she had an escape pod.

This thing was as ugly as the changing table—dark-stained wood, carved with curlicues and what looked like some crazy-eyed animals. Also, it was massive.

"It looks like a tricked-out jail cell," she murmured.

Yvette's heart sank at the sight of it, and her son set up a ruckus, moving and kicking in a way he never had before. Quickly, she leaned against the back of a chair for support and rubbed her hands over her belly, trying to soothe him.

He was obviously reacting to her distress, and it reminded her of her vow to protect him. Unborn or born, she had to do her best for her son, had to show him what a strong woman was. Even though her heart quaked at the thought of confronting the Burleighs, she knew it was time.

Hands firmly over her baby, she walked out to the driveway. "Good morning," she called out.

"Good morning, Yvette. We've brought the crib. Bob will unload it and put it in—"

"No." To her annoyance, Yvette's voice broke. She cleared her throat and tried again. "No."

Margery didn't give her the slightest attention. "We'll take away that crib you bought. It's completely inadequate, and—"

"No." This time, Yvette raised her voice.

Finally, her mother-in-law turned to look at her. "What do you mean 'no'?"

"I'm—I'm happy with the crib I bought. It's exactly the right size for that room, and… easy for me to move if I need to…and it's the one Cole and I picked out."

That wasn't strictly true. Cole couldn't have cared less about the crib. There had been a ball game on when she'd been shopping online for it, but his parents didn't need to know that.

Margery clapped her hands onto her hips and stepped forward. Yvette's heart thumped, but she stood her ground.

Bob waited by his truck, a fascinated audience.

"What are you talking about, Yvette? I told you I had the baby's crib all picked out."

"But I don't want it." Power surged through her. "I've already got the one I want for my baby. I assembled it myself," she added proudly. She looked at her father-in-law. "And, Bob, you can take back the changing table and the rocking chair. They're much too big for that room. I'm—I'm going to order the ones I want. They're the color I want, smaller and lighter, and they match the crib."

For the first time since she'd known him, Bob Burleigh smiled at her. Respect sparked in his eyes. "Sure, Yvette. I'll move them out to the carport right now and be back to get them after I take this load home." He started inside.

Margery squawked as if she'd choked on a chicken bone, her wide eyes rolling from Yvette to Bob and back. "But—but… I picked out what he needed, and…"

"No, you picked out what you want my son to have, but he's my son and Cole's, so thank you, but we'll get what he needs."

She almost felt sorry for Margery, who seemed to be having trouble making sense of Yvette's words. "You don't want us to buy things for our grandson?"

"You're welcome to buy anything you want as long as we approve."

Margery's mouth opened and closed a couple of times but no words came out.

Yvette smiled, experiencing a surge of warmth she never thought she'd feel for this hardheaded woman. Thoughts, ideas and certainties flooded her mind. Now that she wasn't bound by fear, she knew exactly what to say.

"You see, Margery, I... Cole and I want our son to love you for who you are, his grandmother, not for what you can give him."

"What?"

"I want you to bake him those wonderful cakes you know how to make. I want you and Bob to hold him on your laps and read hundreds of books to him so he'll always remember the sound of your voices, and associate reading with love. I want Bob to take him down to the creek, teach him about frogs and turtles, take him to the lake, and teach him how to fish. I...*we* want you to teach him about raising chickens, talk to him about his family history, his ancestors, show him what to be proud of. Margery, there's barely a handful of people in my family I can be proud of, so it's up to you."

Yvette watched to see what effect her words were having. She hadn't even known she felt like this, had these desires, until this moment. Maybe it was only hormones talking, but saying these things aloud had flooded her with the knowledge that this was what she wanted for her son. Even though she and Cole had never talked about this, she knew he would support her.

Confusion warred with tenderness in Margery's expression. Tears filled her eyes and she dabbed them away with the heel of her hand. "Yvette, that's... I don't know what to say."

"That's a start," Bob said as he carried the rocking chair out and set it down. "Margie, girl, we're about to start a whole new chapter in our lives. Let's don't screw it up." He walked over and gave Yvette the first hug she'd ever had from him. "Yvette, you've shown more maturity in five minutes than my son has in his whole life. I'm proud of you."

Yvette returned his hug. No man in her life had ever said he was proud of her.

Yvette smiled at him, and then at Margery, whose expression was sliding into joyful acceptance. "All—all right then, Yvette. Okay if I arrange a baby shower for you? Only close friends and family, so you can get to know everyone better? We can take pictures and start a photo album to show the baby when he gets bigger."

"That would be perfect," Yvette said as her son settled down in her womb.

GEMMA ARRIVED AT the hospital for the beginning of the Extreme Paint Over, as Marlene Fedder and her committee were calling it. She'd been thrilled when Nate had taken her suggestion and convinced the hospital board to go along with it.

"I can't believe Marlene pulled this off in just over a week," Lisa said, looking at the cans of paint and variety of brushes, rollers and tarps arrayed along the walls of the hospital interior.

"She was all over this as soon as the hospital board asked her to do it," Gemma said. "She's been working night and day. Of course, it helped that the contractor got the walls cleaned, repaired and primed in that time."

"It also helped that she recruited every artist, art teacher and crafter in the county," Carly added.

"Including you," Lisa said.

Carly gave her friends a pitiful look. "I know. I'm exhausted and we haven't started painting yet."

They laughed, then stopped to admire the way the entire project was organized.

The murals on each section of wall had been faintly outlined, and the necessary paint colors were lined up along the baseboard, each one sporting a number that corresponded to a number on the design.

"Oh, I get it," Gemma said. "It's like a giant map, or paint-by-the-numbers picture."

"That's right. Marlene thought up the whole concept. Apparently, she'd been dreaming up these murals for years, or ones like them, but didn't have any place to paint them. I can't believe the good people of Reston don't have something else to do on a Saturday, but they've signed up in droves, some for only an hour or two, some all day. After they finish, the actual artists will go through and do the shading and final touches. Many of the committee members thought the whole idea was crazy, but Marlene strong-armed everyone into seeing things her way." Carly shook her head in wonder. "Forget Reston. We need that woman in Washington."

"I agree." Gemma looked down at the card she'd been handed at the door by Misty Summers and Yvette Burleigh. She had been delighted to see that Yvette looked wonderful today—glowing, in fact—and so happy. "I'm assigned to the emergency room."

Carly held up her card. "I'm in charge of the crew over at Pediatrics. We'll see how good I am at painting aquatic life and bubbles."

"I've got the main lobby and reception area," Lisa said. "No idea what the design is supposed to be. See you later."

Gemma and Carly watched her walk away. "Designer top, leather shorts and wedge sandals." Gemma sighed. "Those are her painting clothes?"

She glanced down at her own T-shirt and jeans, already stained with the blue paint she'd used on the doors and trim of her house.

"For her, that's dressing down," Carly answered. "And I read that wedge sandals give your feet better support than flats do."

"You have the most interesting store of random facts in your head."

"I've got to have something up there to balance all the gardening information." With a wave, Carly headed to the pediatrics area.

Gemma walked toward the emergency room. She was familiar with the route because she had visited it whenever one of the creatures she was trying to rescue had been frightened and hurt enough to turn on her. She'd been pecked by birds, scratched by cats and bitten by dogs—and one baby raccoon. Those bites had instigated some moments of terror until it was determined the animals were free of rabies. She had also fallen out of a tree and broken her arm when she'd been trying to save a nest of baby birds whose mother had been attacked by one of the cats she'd rescued.

The place was beginning to fill up and the person in charge was getting people organized. Gemma hurried to join them.

CHAPTER NINE

NATE ARRIVED LATE in the morning and was making his way through every room in the hospital to observe the work being done. Gemma had been right. People were enthused about this project, ready to help and wanted to see it through.

He saw Carly in the nursery, painting happy animals on the walls. Nate continued on his way, making the emergency room his final stop because that's where Yvette had told him Gemma would be. In the days since he'd last seen her, he hadn't stopped thinking about her. When he'd been seeing patients, meeting with his staff, the hospital contractor or the hospital board, she had been on his mind.

Besides the hospital board, she was the only one he'd told about his long-term plans. Maybe he should have said something sooner, been upfront about doing what needed to be done in Reston and then moving on. But she was pulling at him somehow, and he wanted a complete break with the past. He was determined to go.

Gemma was sitting cross-legged on the floor in front of the nurses station, adding shades of green and brown to a pastoral scene of trees and what he thought must be the Kinnick River. Her hair was pulled up in the ponytail that seemed to be her go-to style. She was leaning forward, her concentration complete as she worked.

Examining the scene she was painting, he realized it wasn't the Kinnick River alone, but also her family's campground, lake and cabin. She was painting a river of happy animals on the walls. Bubbles with children's faces rose from the water. He smiled, wondering if she planned to paint in the cages and pens for all the animals she'd rescued. It was a good idea. It tied the mural into the surrounding area, besides being designed to bring calmness to the emergency room. He hoped it succeeded. He'd never worked in such a small emergency room, or such a small hospital, for that matter, and he had visions of the staff stumbling over each other during a crisis.

Nate paused and glanced back the way he'd come, thinking of all the people he'd seen in the past half hour, and all that they'd accomplished. He hadn't worked at a hospital that was such an integral part of the community. His community.

Gemma was painting her own memories into the mural in here. The children's faces that Carly was adding to the bubbles floating up from the river where frogs, fish and hippos frolicked—were they children she knew?

Probably, and everyone else might be doing the same thing. They might not like him and they might even continue to blame him for what his father had done, but this hospital was important to them in a way he hadn't understood until Gemma had given her impassioned speech about getting the community to help.

That was something his father hadn't understood, either, which might be why he'd embezzled the funds that supported the hospital. Robbing the schools and the churches would have had the same result. He'd effectively cut the heart out of the town, but now everyone was working hard to bring it back. He was grateful to be part of it.

"Doesn't that hurt your back?" he asked.

Gemma glanced up. She had green paint on her cheek. His smile widened.

"Oh, hi, Nate. Yes, it does, but we don't have any stools, benches or even chairs. Almost all the hospital fittings were sold to satisfy the creditors."

He suppressed a wince then said, "You were right."

She took another critical look at the work she'd been doing, then turned, ready to stand up. She gave him a saucy look. "Of course I was, but right about what?"

Nate reached out a hand to help her up, then watched as she stretched her legs, placed her hands at her waist and carefully worked out the knots in her back muscles.

"Getting the town involved in the renovations," he said.

She tilted her head and grinned at him. "I love to hear you admit it."

At that moment, Frances Sanderson swept into the room. "Oh, here you two are. The hospital board has decided that we need to honor Marlene and her crew for getting all of this organized and carrying it through. Unbelievable how much is being done in one day. Anyway, we're having an ice-cream social tonight at the high school gym. Everyone who's helped is being invited. My daughter-in-law is printing flyers so everyone will know. It'll be a great opportunity for—"

"Fund-raising," Gemma supplied with a grin.

Frances gave her an indulgent smile. "You know me so well. See you tonight at eight." She strolled out with a wave.

"She's like a force of nature," Nate said as he stared after her. "She never stops."

"She can't stop, not now that we know everything is going to cost so much more than we thought it would."

BEFORE GEMMA COULD CONTINUE, Misty Summers walked out of an emergency room cubicle. She looked around at the cheerful work being applied to the walls, then reached behind her and used both hands to support the small of her back.

"This looks beautiful," she said.

"Hi, Misty," Gemma said. "Where did you come from?"

"I've been lying down in there for a couple of hours," she answered, pointing to the cubicle with one of the only beds left in the place. "I had to find a rag to wipe off the dust.

Don't worry, I opened the window to let in fresh air and closed the door to keep out the paint fumes." She yawned. "Yvette said she could handle the assignment table."

Gemma frowned and immediately put down the square of cardboard she was using as an easel, along with her brush.

"Are you feeling all right, Misty?" Gemma put her arm around the other woman's shoulders for a hug, then checked her pulse.

"I've got a backache and some cramps from sitting on that metal folding chair, handing out painting assignments. That's why I got up and started walking around. That made me feel worse, so I came in here to lie down. I guess I fell asleep in spite of the ache. I should have insisted right away that Kelvin find me a more comfortable chair. He's gone home to get one now." She sighed. "I've enjoyed being pregnant, but I'm ready for it to be over."

"Growing a baby is hard work, and takes a ton of energy—"

A sudden gush of water pooled at Misty's feet.

"Oh, no," Misty said. "Gemma, does that mean my water just broke?"

"Yes. Your daughter is tired of waiting, too. She's ready to meet her sweet mama so she's going to arrive today."

"Today?" Misty squeaked out the word.

Gemma made her voice soothing. "That's right and everything's going to be fine. You're seeing Dr. Hedley over in Claybourne, aren't you?"

"Yes."

"We should give him a call and tell him you're coming to the hospital."

"I don't remember his number. It's in my phone in Kelvin's truck. He took it to get me another chair. I don't know why he's not back yet." Misty barely had the words out before a pain hit her. Eyes wide, she reached for a nearby table to support her. Gemma kept a firm but gentle grip on her arm and Nate hurried to help hold her up.

"How long have you had the backache and cramps?" Nate asked.

"Since about eight o'clock—as soon as I sat down in that metal chair."

"Although you weren't aware of it, your daughter has been doing a lot of work in the past four hours to get ready for her grand entrance." Gemma gave her a warm smile.

"It was very considerate of her to let you get some rest because you have hard work ahead of you."

"It felt exactly like the backaches I've had every day. I thought labor would be worse, like the pain I just had." She looked from Gemma to Nate. "You mean my baby might come faster than I thought?"

"We don't know yet."

Her eyes full of tears and terror, Misty said, "But I'm not ready yet. I still have two weeks to go."

"A due date is simply a medical estimate. Remember, we talked about that in the class a few days ago? Your baby has other ideas," Gemma said, maintaining her calm manner. "She's chosen her own birthdate."

"What's Kelvin's phone number?" Nate asked. "I'll call him. I'll also find a wheelchair. There's got to be one here somewhere." He turned away as soon as Misty gave him her husband's phone number and came back a few minutes later with the wheelchair. "He's on his way," he assured them. "He's also going to call Dr. Hedley."

Misty sank into the chair as another pain hit her. Gemma and Nate exchanged glances as her back arched and her body bucked against the chair. In the middle of her groan of pain, Misty made a strong, grunting noise from the back of her throat.

"I don't think we have time to wait for Kelvin to get here," Gemma said, switching to a brisk, no-nonsense tone while maintaining her warm manner. She glanced up at Nate to include him in what she was telling Misty. "That grunting noise you made during your contraction tells me your labor might be progressing faster than expected. Let's go over to the birthing center, where we can check you out. Then the decision can be made on what needs to be done."

"Oh, okay," Misty said.

They quickly learned why the wheelchair was still in the emergency room—any weight on the smaller front wheels made them grind to a halt. Nate had to tilt it onto its larger back ones to get it to move. Bent over in this awkward position, he pushed the wheelchair out of the emergency room and across the parking lot to the Sunshine Birthing Center. Gemma hurried ahead to unlock the door. Once inside, she led the way to the nearest birthing room. Between them, she and Nate got Misty onto the bed.

"I'll examine her while you go wait for Kelvin and get him over here."

Nate looked as if he wanted to argue but then seemed to remember that this was her house, and her area of expertise, little though he might think of it. Besides, arguing would simply waste time. He nodded, asked Misty for a description of her husband and his truck and went outside.

Within a couple of minutes, Gemma had confirmed her earlier prognosis. "Misty, you're dilated to ten and the baby is crowning."

"That—that means she's coming right now, doesn't it? Oh, where is Kelvin?"

While her patient fretted, Gemma tried to make her comfortable. "He'll be here soon, but right now, you have to concentrate on what's best for you and your baby. You're strong, Misty. This is hard, but you can do it."

Gemma attached a heart monitor to the baby's scalp. As soon as she saw a reading on the monitor, she said, "Misty, your baby's heart rate is strong and fast, like it's supposed to be."

"Oh, good. So she's okay?"

Another pain had Misty crying out and clutching at the bedcovers. When Gemma checked again, she saw that the baby's head had moved back up in the birth canal. The next pain brought it back into sight, then it disappeared again. Three repetitions of this disappearing act told her that the baby's shoulder was stuck beneath her mother's pelvic bone.

Gemma ran through the reasons this might have happened. If Misty had been lying on her back while resting in the cubicle, the baby could have slipped into the wrong position. Excusing herself, she hurried out of the room and called for Emergency Services. Even though Gemma knew she could deliver the baby safely, Misty and her daughter would need in-hospital care as soon as possible.

Coming back into the room, she said, "Misty, your daughter's shoulder is stuck under your pelvic bone."

"Oh, no, did I do something to hurt my baby 'cause I didn't know my labor was starting?" Tears ran down Misty's face. "Is she going to die?"

"Certainly not. Nobody is going to die. We simply have to change your position and get you up on your knees."

"What's happening?" Nathan asked from behind her.

Gemma answered as Kelvin Summers pushed past Nate and ran to his wife's side. Misty reached up and grabbed her husband's hand, wringing it as another pain hit.

"Shoulder dystocia."

"May I have a look?" Nate asked, squirting hand sanitizer onto his hands and quickly donning gloves.

Gemma stood close and spoke quietly to him. "The skin on the baby's head has darkened. Blood flow has slowed."

"I can see that." After a brief but thorough examination, he said, "The baby is in distress. We need to perform a cesarean section."

"Yes, yes, let's do that," Kelvin said as Misty let out a scream of pain.

"Yes, do it," Misty groaned, her eyes rolling in panic. "I'm going to die. My baby's going to die."

"No. The baby's not in distress. Her heart-beat is still strong and isn't even dipping into a dangerous range. A C-section isn't neces-sary," Gemma insisted. "If we change your position right now, we can solve this without surgery. I've done it many times."

When Nate started to object, she gave him a severe warning look and said, "Will you step into the other room with me, please?"

Nate followed her into the tiny space she was using as an office.

Gemma turned to him once they were alone. "I can handle this."

"Surgery is the best and fastest option," Nate said. "I shouldn't have to tell you how serious this is. There's a possibility of hem-orrhage or other serious injuries."

"And the possibilities are increasing the longer we argue," Gemma answered testily. "For a C-section, you'll need an anesthesiol-ogist and an operating room." She threw her hands wide. "Do you see that here? The near-est ones are half an hour away. I've already called 911. An ambulance is on the way. If everyone, including you, will calm down, I can solve this by getting her up, and—"

"Getting her *up*? That will put her at even more risk."

The horrified father-to-be appeared in the doorway. "Hurry, Doc. She's dying!"

"Nobody is going to die," Gemma said again with even more emphasis. "Are you going to help me or not? We're running out of time. I've called Emergency Services, but this baby is going to arrive before they get here."

Nate leaned in close and spoke in a low tone of controlled rage. "I'll help, but I'm also going to call your medical director and get him over here. If I find this patient has been harmed in any way, I'll make sure this place gets shut down." Raising his voice, he turned to Kelvin and said, "Call her doctor and tell him to meet you at the hospital in Claybourne."

Fury and disappointment fought to surface, but Gemma forced them down. Even though this was her birthing center, she felt helpless and disrespected. Reminding herself that she was a professional and had promised to do what was best for her patient, she pushed her hurt feelings aside.

"Come on," she said.

While Kelvin called Dr. Hedley, Gemma spoke soothingly to Misty and helped her turn onto her knees with Nathan's assistance. She then checked to make sure the cord wasn't around the baby's neck, and also that the baby's hand or arm wasn't up by her head. She relayed this good news to Misty, then moved with caution to slightly rotate the baby into birth position and waited for nature, and gravity, to bring the little one into the world. All the while, she kept up an encouraging conversation with Misty, assuring her that she was strong, she was doing a wonderful job, that she could deliver this baby.

Baby Summers emerged after a few more contractions and Nathan was the one to catch her. Gemma helped Misty lie down again, and he handed over the crying, wiggling newborn. Gemma avoided his eyes and placed the tiny girl on her mother's chest, then checked Misty for signs of hemorrhage.

Kelvin's knees collapsed under him and he landed in the wheelchair as Misty cradled her daughter and cried, "My baby, my little girl. Oh, you're so beautiful."

By the time the ambulance arrived, Misty

had delivered the placenta, the baby had been washed and swaddled in a clean blanket and beanie, and Kelvin had remembered how to breathe—though he still looked shell-shocked.

When they'd headed to the hospital, Gemma turned to Nathan and said, "You can call our medical director now. I'm sure he'll want to hear all about how I did exactly what I was supposed to do in spite of your obstructionism. I'll get you his phone number." She started toward her office and then turned back. "After that, I'm inviting you to leave. I understand that you want to shut me down, but this is my birthing center, I know exactly what I'm doing and you're not welcome here."

Nate looked as if he wanted to argue, wanted to come back with an angry response, but after a moment of studying her furious expression, he turned and headed back to the hospital.

WIELDING HER HOE with a viciousness she didn't know she possessed, Gemma worked her way down one row of herbs and up the next as she uprooted weeds that had sprung up while she'd been getting the birthing center open. The few pepper, carrot and lettuce plants she and Carly had put into the ground were thriving in spite of her neglect.

An hour later, she was almost finished. Her wrath had begun to dissipate when she heard an approaching car. Carrying her hoe, she walked around to the front of the house, where she saw Nate's car pull up. She turned around and went back to work.

When she heard his footsteps following her, she didn't even bother to glance up as she said, "Physically, I'm not capable of throwing you off my property, so I hope you'll leave on your own."

He was silent for such a long time, she finally had to look up. His hands were in his back pockets. He rocked onto his heels, the picture of an uncomfortable male about to do something he didn't want to. "I was hoping I could talk to you."

"Why bother?" she asked furiously. "You won't listen to me. Talk to my medical director. Or did you already?"

He glanced away, examining the rows of blue cohosh and other herbs. "I didn't call him. I…came to apologize. I overreacted."

"Ya think? Why is that, Nate? Believe me, I've been in this situation before with doctors who think midwives are incompetent."

"I don't think you're incompetent." He held up his hand as he said it. "If anything, I admire your professionalism—"

"But not my knowledge and expertise. Not what I do, and do very well."

Heartsick, she turned away and continued attacking weeds. It could wait, but she needed something to keep her occupied while her mind replayed the events with Misty over and over and she tried to make sense of them.

"Yes, I realize your education and training have been different than mine," she went on, hoeing ruthlessly. "That you're an MD with an emphasis in family practice, and that you've probably delivered hundreds of babies, but the Sunshine Birthing Center isn't some fly-by-night, pop-up operation run by ignorant…harpies."

"I don't think that, Gemma."

"Then what is it, Nate? Why don't you have any respect for me and what I do?"

"It's not you. It's not personal. It's…" His

words dropped away as his face worked, full of pain and despair.

"What?" She threw her hand into the air. "I won't know if you don't tell me."

"A midwife killed my sister."

"What? What do you mean?" She lowered her hoe to the ground as her arms went weak with surprise.

NATE SCRUBBED HIS hands over his face and through his hair, then dropped them to his sides. He knew he looked haggard and disheveled, but he didn't care. Even though he felt justified in his opinion of midwifery, he hadn't handled the situation with Misty, or with Gemma, well. He'd let his history and his emotions cloud his judgment—something he'd been strictly trained not to do.

After a minute, he went on. "Mandy went to college at OSU but dropped out after her first year. She and our parents had a huge fight over it. I didn't understand everything that was going on. I was only nine when it happened. I only knew one night there was lots of yelling and door slamming—something my mother never allowed—and Mandy saying she wanted to explore the world, or at least the US. She had inherited some money from our mom's father when she turned nineteen, a couple of months before. It was about two hundred thousand dollars and she must have thought it was all the money in the world. Now I understand it meant freedom to her, the first time she'd ever had money without strings tied to it. It meant…" His face spasmed. "Having a life where she didn't have to care what anyone else thought, didn't have to ask for money. My dad kept a tight hold on the purse strings."

Gemma frowned and Nate shook his head. "Ironic, isn't it? George was tight with his own money but was willing to steal other people's. Turned out, he wasn't tight at all. He'd simply gambled it all away. He had no money, but none of us knew that at the time. Mandy's funds from our grandfather had come straight to her so Dad couldn't touch them." He grimaced. "Sadly, I wasn't as lucky. My inheritance disappeared down the gambling sinkhole. There was absolutely nothing left by the time I was old enough to take control of it."

"That's what addiction is," Gemma said sadly. Even though she was still furious with him, she couldn't help sympathizing. "Any kind of addiction is a bottomless pit where money disappears."

They were both silent for a few moments, then she asked, "What happened after... Mandy and your parents fought?"

"The next morning, before the sun was even up, Mandy slipped into my room to tell me goodbye. I cried and begged her not to go, but she said she had to. She said she couldn't stay in that house, and she couldn't do what they wanted her to anymore. It was killing her. I didn't know what she meant, but by the time I was eighteen, I did. She had packed a duffel bag of her things and that's all she took. She said she'd write to me, but I never heard from her."

"Oh, Nate. I'm sorry. I didn't know..."

He waved away her apology. "No one did. My mom and dad were horrified, said she'd been influenced by other people in town."

"Like my parents," Gemma added.

"I guess, but I didn't know that then. The worst influence was a boyfriend she'd met while she was at university. He wasn't a student, but he was worthless, jobless, even homeless. In fact, that's what my dad called him—Les. I didn't know what his real name was until much later. Brett Vaugrun." Nate shook his head and gave a snort of disgust.

"Once we found that out, Dad started calling him Les Vagrant. Turns out he was the son of one of the wealthiest families in the state. They were big in oil and gas wells, but their son wanted to find himself and took my sister along to help him do it. The truth is, his family was fed up with him and had cut him off. Looking back, I think he saw this inexperienced young girl who had a little bit of money for the first time in her life and he grabbed on to her, told her whatever she wanted to hear. He was ten years older than she was, wasn't good-looking, but there must have been something about him, something he said or did, that attracted her. He'd been arrested numerous times. My dad got a copy of his arrest record and we all saw his mug shot.

"I don't know what she was looking for, what she hoped to gain. Since there was such a big difference in our ages, I never really understood what she wanted." Nate paused. "But that guy... If Mandy was looking for some kind of knight in shining armor, he wasn't it."

"Maybe she was looking for something or someone different than what was available in this rural town."

"I guess," Nate said, then added emphatically, "But she was *smart*, didn't need someone like that. Old Les Vagrant must have been a helluva con artist."

He gazed into the distance, looking back to that dismal time. He was barely aware when Gemma took his arm and urged him into the house, to a chair at the table. She turned on an overhead fan and poured glasses of cold orange juice for both of them. She then took out some sliced ham, cheese and crackers, arranged everything on a plate and placed it before him, along with carrot and celery sticks.

"What is this?"

She raised an eyebrow. "Obviously, it's a snack. I suspect you haven't eaten, your blood sugar is low and you need protein."

"Yeah, I guess you're right." Absently, he sipped from his glass and ate a little of the food, suddenly realizing he was famished. He hadn't eaten or drunk anything in many hours. His mind worked, trying to organize his thoughts and not let the memories swamp him before he finished what he had to say. He had been over this so many times, but even with the maturity and clarity of adulthood, he'd never been able to find his way through the tangle of emotions and events that had happened.

Gemma took a drink of her juice and said, "Go ahead with what you were saying, Nate."

"After my sister left, my mom closed Mandy's bedroom door and locked it. We never talked about her—not that my family was big on communication, anyway. My parents put out the story that she was studying abroad and wouldn't be home for a while. I don't know how many people actually believed that."

"But Mandy came home, right?"

"Yes, when I was in seventh grade. She opened the front door and walked right in as if she'd only been gone for a few hours. She was almost nine months pregnant. We learned later that Les, er, Brett Vaugrun, had spent all the money she'd inherited and taken off. Maybe it was a good thing that it had taken him three years to spend it all because it must have taken her that long to realize what he was, and to make the decision to come home. She no longer had her car. The boyfriend must have sold it or kept it. Mandy hitchhiked home. Almost nine months pregnant and she'd hitchhiked from Fort Smith, Arkansas."

Gemma made a sound of distress and he saw the concern in her eyes. That almost stopped him because it was too much like pity, but he kept going.

"But Mandy wasn't alone. There was a woman with her, a midwife. Her name was Brendyce—she only went by one name—and she was going to deliver the baby when the time came. Strangely, my parents welcomed Mandy home with open arms and they were…tolerant of Brendyce."

He fell silent for so long, lost in the memories, that Gemma finally prompted him. "What happened?"

Nate glanced up. He'd almost forgotten she was there. He gazed at Gemma's honest, open face—from which she'd scrubbed the streak of green paint—and her bright, intelligent eyes. She was nothing like the slovenly, pushy Brendyce, but he couldn't help connecting the two of them in his mind.

"I was thrilled that she was home. Yeah, I

know it's not cool for a twelve-year-old boy to love his big sister, but I loved her and I hadn't seen or heard from her in three years, so that made it even more special when she came home. She was…different, though."

"In what way?"

"She seemed disconnected, as if she knew she was going to have a baby, but she acted like it was happening to someone else. At first, she didn't talk about what had happened with her boyfriend, but he wasn't around so my parents guessed he'd taken off and she later confirmed that." Nate glanced up. "Not that my parents ever talked to me about it. I quickly learned to eavesdrop."

He paused again as if he was trying to organize his thoughts. "As I recall, she didn't have so much as a box of diapers or a baby blanket, but she wouldn't let anyone buy anything for the baby. She said she had plenty of money. She'd buy whatever the baby needed, but that wasn't true. She had nothing. She spent the next few days wandering around in the woods as if she was looking for something. Sometimes Brendyce went with her, but usually Mandy was by herself. I know because I followed her."

"What did she do?"

Nate was battered again by the anger and confusion he'd known then. "She went out to your family's campground, sat by the lake... didn't talk to anyone, although I saw your mom try to get her into conversation a couple of times."

"I know my mother tried to talk to her." Gemma told him what her mom had said about the way Mandy seemed to be drifting. "Strange that I never knew any of this until now."

"Well, it seems that where my sister was concerned, there was an entire part of your parents' lives that you didn't know about."

She drew back, hurt, but he was so deep in his own remembered pain that he couldn't veer from the recollections that were pulling at him.

"She went into labor the week after she came home. Even though our hospital was open then, there was a doctor on duty and she could have been there in less than ten minutes, she was adamant about wanting a home birth for her baby." Nate frowned. "Which was another thing I didn't understand. She'd never been any happier in our home than I had. Why have the baby there? It didn't make any sense. None of it made any sense.

"Anyway, I don't know if she'd had any prenatal care or not, but I can see now that neither she nor this Brendyce person were ready for what was about to happen. It was the middle of the night. Mandy screamed in a way I've never heard anyone scream before or since." He paused. "Things went downhill from there—fast. We learned later that Mandy's baby was turned sideways in the womb and couldn't be born. A C-section would have saved both of them but Mandy, and her supposed midwife, waited too long." The memory was tearing at him.

"As forceful as my mother was, she wouldn't go against Mandy at first. Finally, I was the one who called the ambulance, but it was too late. Mandy and the baby were both gone by the time they reached the hospital." His hand clenched into a fist. "That was twenty years ago, but we had a good little hospital then. Doctor Young would have known exactly what to do. There was no reason for her and the baby to die."

Nate looked down at his hands. "That was

the main reason I decided to become a doctor, although I always knew family practice would be my field."

"What did Dr. Young say? What went wrong? I'm asking because it sounds like gestational diabetes along with other issues."

"That was exactly it," Nate said. "Diabetes."

"Were there mental problems, too? Is it possible that she lost her grip on reality when her boyfriend dumped her?"

"Almost certainly."

They were both silent for a few minutes. Nate ate more of the snack Gemma had made for him, though dredging up the unhappy memories had cost him his appetite. Finally, he pushed the plate away.

"And what about the midwife?" Gemma asked. "That Brendyce person? Did she go by only one name because she was skirting the law?"

"Probably. As far as we knew, she wasn't licensed or qualified to deliver a baby. I think she saw a young woman in trouble, thought she could take advantage of it and just took hold. Like a leech. Like Vaugrun had done. With Mandy's mental state, it was probably easy."

"Was there any sign of her after that?"

"No. That night, before my parents realized everything that had happened, Brendyce was gone—never to be seen again. They couldn't find a trace of her. Not even her real name."

"I can tell you for certain that she wasn't a trained midwife or she never would have put Mandy at risk. She would have known the signs of diabetes, checked her urine, taken every precaution and made sure she got to a qualified obstetrician right away. A midwife knows that some issues have to go straight to a doctor or medical facility."

"Like what happened with Misty today," Nate said in a flat tone.

CHAPTER TEN

COLOR WASHED INTO her face. "I wasn't going to bring that up, especially not now...after you told me what happened to your sister. But yes, today was different. I knew exactly what to do for Misty. I've done it before. I knew within minutes what was preventing the baby from being born and how to solve it. I knew what I was doing. It wasn't simple luck."

"It was a risky situation."

"Was it, Nate? Or are you biased because of the actions of the incompetent woman you hold responsible for Mandy's death?"

"I'd like to think I'm more professional than that, Gemma, but—"

"And I'd like to think that, too, Nate."

"If you'd let me finish," he said, holding up his hand, but she shook her head and went on.

"Do you honestly think the Sandersons,

Mr. Clegg and the other donors would have made funds available for the birthing center if they'd thought I was incompetent? It's more than their gratitude to me for delivering Max. They're business people who look at the bottom line and they expect to get value for their money." She made a waving gesture with her hand. "If they can trust me, you can, too."

"Trust has to be earned."

"And in your mind, I'll never earn it, right, Nate?" Hurt and anger filled Gemma's eyes as she said, "It doesn't matter to you that I'm one of the few people who's been on your side—"

"That's not true. I appreciate that, but I was going to do what needed to be done in Reston with or without your help—or your need to rescue me from the people of my hometown."

"Which you're leaving," she said. "As for my attempts at rescue, I obviously was wrong to do that. You don't need my help." She gestured toward his head, then down to his feet. "You're complete unto yourself."

When he started to respond, she said, "It's time for you to leave, Nate. We don't have anything else to say to each other."

He was going to argue. A dozen responses sprang to mind, but his common sense finally made itself heard, urging him to walk away. Turning, he did as she said and headed back to his car so he could get off her property. A glance in his rearview mirror showed him she had returned to work, even though it was beginning to rain.

COLE ARRIVED HOME to find that Yvette's car wasn't in the garage and there were no visible signs of dinner preparations. Tired, thirsty and annoyed, he grabbed a bottle of beer from the refrigerator, popped off the cap and took a long drink as he looked around, wondering what he could have for a snack while he waited for his wife to come home and fix him something to eat. That was when he spied the note on the kitchen table.

I've gone into town to help with the Extreme Paint Over at the hospital. I'll be back by dark. Love you, Yvette.

"A note?" he grumbled, frowning at the neat lettering. "Why'd she write me a note? Why not call or text?"

He thought about it for a minute. "Because I would have answered right away and she didn't want me to tell her not to go. Even though she knew I wouldn't want her to help Nathan, she went anyway."

He took another drink of beer. This was getting out of hand. Yvette knew he had certain expectations, but she insisted on defying him. He finished his first beer and opened another one. Still brooding, he flopped down in his recliner, shoved aside the six remote controls for his various gaming systems and grabbed the one for the television. He scrolled through the channels until he settled on a baseball game, but even after several minutes of watching, he couldn't have said who was playing or what the score was.

He didn't understand why Yvette wanted to get involved in painting the Reston hospital. Their baby wasn't going to be born there. Her doctor was in Claybourne. Cole would drive her there, be with her throughout labor—although the thought of that made him feel kind of sick to his stomach. He would be the one to cut the cord and show off his son to his mom and dad.

In fact, he didn't see the point of reopening the hospital in Reston. The town was doing fine without it. Maybe he should have brought that up at the town meeting, along with trying to get Nathan to admit what had happened to the funds his old man had stolen. Cole was still convinced Nate knew more about it than he was telling, but there might not be a way to prove it beyond getting Nate to confess.

Cole finished his second beer, tossed the bottle and pulled a fresh one from the refrigerator. He sat with his elbows on his knees as the game played in the background and he contemplated the carpet at his feet. Momentarily, he considered getting up and finding that snack he'd been looking for earlier, but his thoughts returned to the problem he was having with his wife.

He knew he could get her to see things his way. He just had to figure out how. He'd been shocked when he'd found her at Gemma's birthing center, taking a class on how her body was changing with the baby. He could have told her how. The baby grew, her stomach expanded and eventually the baby was born, leaving her with stretch marks. He'd have to encourage her to do crunches and sit-ups to return her belly to its former flatness. She would probably appreciate the reminder.

Cole admitted that he was having a hard time trying to figure out why she had defied him after he'd told her to stay away from Gemma. He'd always gotten his own way. His parents had made it clear that he was special and they expected great things from him. Well, at least until he'd injured his leg and had to quit football. And he'd gotten his own way until he'd wanted Gemma to be his girlfriend and he'd ended up in the lake, thanks to Nate. Their laughter still rang in his ears. They had humiliated him and taken away what he wanted, but he wasn't going to let that happen again.

How would he stop it, though? His eyes narrowed in thought as the alcohol began to work its way through his system. He wasn't going to let them take Yvette away from him, or influence her. He had to put a stop to it. Having her go off without his permission to help with painting...

"Painting," he said aloud, sitting up straight. Maybe he needed to do something she would like. She'd wanted to paint the nursery. He hadn't wanted to go to all that work, so he'd said the white walls that were there had been good enough for him. That was true, but maybe they weren't good enough for his son.

Cole drained the last of his beer and stood, staggering slightly. Maybe three beers on an empty stomach hadn't been such a great idea. It took him a second to get his balance, but then he was striding out to the garage, where he grabbed the cans of paint Yvette had purchased, along with the paint tray, brushes, rollers and drop cloths, and hauled it all back inside.

In only a few minutes, he had placed everything he could, including Cowboy Bear, into the crib and scooted the lot away from the walls. As he worked, he wondered what had happened to the big changing table and the rocking chair his parents had bought. He'd have to ask Yvette. She probably appreciated the fact that she didn't have to shop for anything for little Cole Jr.

Cole popped the lid off the first can, gave the paint a good stir, poured some into the tray and gleefully slopped the roller into it. Only a little spilled onto the drop cloth he'd been thoughtful enough to spread down first.

No point in getting paint on the carpet. There were a few stains on it, but it was still good.

He was tall enough to reach the top of the wall with the roller, but since he'd never painted anything before in his life, he miscalculated his aim and bumped the ceiling several times, leaving blue streaks in his wake. Also, he saw pretty quickly that he'd loaded too much paint onto the roller so that drips trailed down the wall. That was okay. He'd catch those later.

He was still trying to perfect his technique when Yvette walked in.

"Cole, what are you doing?" she asked, looking around at the piled-up baby things and the inexpert paint application.

He'd been so involved in the task, he hadn't heard her arrive. When he turned around, his head felt a little light and it took a moment to focus on her.

"I'd think you'd be able to figure that out, Yvette. I'm painting the nursery like you wanted."

Her mouth dropped open and he felt a moment of smugness when he realized he'd surprised her, but then she pointed to the wall and said, "I didn't want it painted like *this*."

"Whaddya mean? This is the paint you picked out."

She indicated the drips snaking down the walls. "I mean the way you're doing it. Haven't you ever painted anything before?"

"Never needed to. White paint was good enough until now, but you wanted this blue."

"I wanted everything fresh and clean and new for our baby, and—and I wanted it done well."

Cole dropped the roller back into the tray. "And I guess you know all about it since you spent the day at the Big Paint Out."

"Extreme Paint Over," she said, correcting him. "And, no, I know all about it because I used to work with my uncle, who was a housepainter."

"Well, you can't do this now because you're pregnant." He shoved his hands on his hips, spoiling for a fight. She'd ruined his plan to surprise her, hadn't shown any gratitude, made him feel foolish. He hated feeling stupid. "And what were you doing there, anyway? You can't be around all that paint and dust."

"I was sitting outside the front door in the fresh air, handing out the assignments. Most of the time, I even had my feet up on another chair. I met a lot of nice people. They asked where you were."

"I could introduce you to nice people if you'd asked."

"But you didn't, Cole. I'm home almost all the time. The only people I ever talk to are you and your parents, at least until the Sandersons' party, where I got to know Gemma, Carly and Lisa a little better."

The mention of their names infuriated him. "After I'd told you not to have anything to do with them!"

She stuck out her chin. "You can't choose my friends, Cole. You can't control me."

"I can take away your car."

Yvette crossed her arms over her chest. "Yes, you could, but it wouldn't matter. I have friends now. They would call or come to find out why they hadn't seen me, and, really, do you want it known around town that you took my car away from me because I wouldn't do what you said?"

His brows drew together, his eyes narrowed and his mouth turned down. This wasn't what he'd had in mind when he'd married her. She wouldn't have dared do something like this before Gemma and Nate had come back to Reston.

"Besides, Cole, the car's in my name. Remember? You made a point to do that so I'd have a safe car to drive. Legally, it's mine."

"Just like the baby is yours, right?" He stepped closer and pointed a finger at her. "It's time for *you* to remember that you wouldn't have anything if it wasn't for me."

"I know that, Cole, and I'm grateful, but…"

"But, what? You don't like what you've got? Don't like what I've done? You don't know what it means to be grateful. You had nothing before I came along."

"I know that, and—"

"You've let Gemma and Nathan poison your mind against me."

"That's not true, Cole. Gemma has never said anything against you, and I've hardly spoken to Nathan."

"And you're not going to, either!"

"You're—you're not going to control me, Cole." Even though her voice broke on the words, she was defiant.

Fury surged through Cole. Even more than he hated feeling stupid, he hated being contradicted. She wouldn't listen, wouldn't do what he said, and lately, she opposed every statement he made even though he knew he was right. Cocking his arm back, he formed his hand into a fist.

Terror bloomed in Yvette's eyes as she threw her hands up in front of her face and cried, "No, Cole. No!"

She jumped back, stumbling over a pile of the things he'd thrown onto the floor. Her shoulder slammed into the door frame, knocking her off balance. She slid to the floor, where she huddled, one arm protecting her head, the other cradling her belly.

Shocked that he'd raised a hand to her, that he'd threatened her with his fist, and sick with remorse at her reaction, Cole crouched beside her. "Yvette, honey... I'm..."

"Get away from me." Her arm flailed out, pushing him away. "I don't want you to touch me! Don't ever touch me again. You're not going to hit me. You're not going to hit my baby."

"No, no, Yvette, of course not. I..."

"Go away."

He tried once again to help her up, to show her he wouldn't hurt her, but she pushed his hands away and huddled, sobbing, on the floor.

Cole got to his feet and stepped back. He'd never seen her like this—never seen any woman like this.

"Yvette, I didn't mean it. I… I wouldn't…"

"No, and you never will." Tears were running down her face as she looked up at him, determination and anger in those blue eyes that had only ever looked at him with affection and amusement. "Gemma said I have to protect my baby and…that means—that means even from you."

"Gemma! What's she told you?"

Yvette shook her head. "Go away."

Furious, feeling helpless and confused, he rushed from the room, through the house and out to his truck. Rain was falling at a steady rate, running off the house and onto ground that was already soaked.

He started the engine and backed out of the driveway. His tires squealed as the truck fishtailed and he straightened it out. He needed to get away, fix this, get Yvette to calm down and listen to him. He wasn't sure what he was going to do yet, but he knew who was responsible, who to blame.

He planned to find them and make them understand they couldn't interfere in his marriage.

Pressing down on the gas pedal, he headed toward town.

"THIS IS THE last place I want to be right now," Carly said, looking around the high school gym. "Can't I go home and slip into something more comfortable instead? A shower and a deep coma, for example."

"No," Gemma and Lisa said in unison.

Gemma tried to keep from wincing at the headache-inducing wall of noise that had hit them as soon as they'd walked in—people talking, laughing, kids chasing each other and shouting.

"If we have to be here, you do, too," Lisa added. "Besides, almost everyone in here is as grubby as you and I are."

"Not Gemma," Carly pointed out with an exaggerated pout. She eyed her friend's clean slacks and top, then her own paint-stained shorts and shirt. "*She* managed to get cleaned up."

"And you can, too," Gemma responded. "As soon as we show our support for Frances and our gratitude to Marlene and her crew. Count your blessings. At least you got some dinner when the ladies from First Baptist delivered sandwiches to all the workers. Also, unlike the hospital, the air-conditioning works here."

"Believe me, I'm grateful." Carly pulled at the neck of her shirt and fanned herself as she took a slow look around. "Why did Frances want to do this today? When everyone's so tired?"

"I suspect because exhausted people are less resistant to her financial pleas." Gemma nodded to the Wilsons as they walked by. "Besides, she knows that if she offers our citizens ice cream and toppings, they'll follow her anywhere."

"She *is* very persuasive," Carly admitted. "Do you think she was the one who got the rain to stop? It was pouring a few minutes ago and now the sky is clear."

"It's entirely possible," Gemma said.

"And I'd still like to know how Frances arranged all of this in one day. Magic?"

Lisa grinned. "No, Carly. People won't say no to Frances any more than they would to Marlene. Anybody who didn't already have a job or two was sent out scouring for everything she needed. I'm betting there's not a spare quart of ice cream left in Reston County."

"In that case, before the ice cream runs out, I plan to overdose on a hot-fudge sundae. I'll probably pass out from sheer joy. You two will have to take me home and put me to bed. Come on."

"That's cool with me, but I'm not going to give you a shower," Lisa stated firmly.

Gemma smiled as they maneuvered through the crowd, but she didn't follow them to the other side of the big room, where a group of volunteers were filling plastic bowls with ice cream from huge tubs and adding toppings. Several people she knew had a bowl in each hand, although she didn't remember seeing them on any of the painting crews at the hospital. She decided it didn't matter. This was another way to build community.

A few people asked about Misty Summers's baby, commenting on how nice it was to have a midwife and a birthing center in town, and even praising Nate for being there to help her out. Gemma didn't bother telling people she hadn't needed help.

She looked around for Nate. Perhaps he hadn't arrived yet, but wherever he was in this crowd, she planned to be somewhere else. She'd had enough encounters with him for one day—for one lifetime, she added. When she didn't see him, she let her shoulders relax.

Gemma got her own bowl of ice cream from Tom Sanderson at the refreshment table. It made her smile to see him with shirt sleeves rolled up, plastic gloves stretched over his big rancher's hands, cowboy hat still on his head as he scooped out the frozen treat. She moved around the room, talking to people she'd known her whole life and making new acquaintances. The entire time, her mind was on Nate.

It would be so much easier if they weren't in the same profession, didn't have to work together. Even in a town the size of Reston she could avoid him if not for the hospital, the birthing center, and all the community relations and fund-raising that were involved.

As if the thought of fund-raising had conjured her up, Frances Sanderson appeared on a dais at the end of the gym. As always, she looked elegant in a sleeveless blue dress and high-heeled sandals. Microphone in hand, she called for quiet, then thanked everyone for coming and praised Marlene Fedder and her committee. She called them all onto the stage to thank them personally and invite applause.

Gemma grinned when she saw that Carly looked significantly happier with a big bowl of ice cream in her hand.

"Now remember," Frances called out. "There's still much work to be done to get the hospital reopened, so unchain your wallets, whip out those checkbooks and get ready to give." She graced the room with a sweet smile. "I'll be around to collect."

People groaned good-naturedly and then clapped when she said, "As a special last-minute addition to the festivities, we have Ron Jett and his Rocket Boys arriving right now to provide live music. Feel free to grab your partner and dance."

Gemma marveled at the delight in Frances's face and voice. Ron and his band were arguably the worst country-music band in southeastern Oklahoma—maybe in the whole country. The noise was only going to get worse.

As Marlene's committee members left the dais, Luke Sanderson approached Carly and pulled her aside. He leaned in to speak to her and Carly listened thoughtfully as she continued eating her treat. Gemma wondered why he was still in town since he lived and worked in Dallas. Whatever he was saying didn't make Carly look happy.

Gemma contemplated rushing to Carly's side, but when she gave Luke a firm look and began talking, low and fast, Gemma decided her friend didn't need any backup.

Calculating how long she needed to stay, and looking for an escape, Gemma turned away, only to spot Cole Burleigh coming in the door. When she saw the angry, purposeful light in his eyes, she stopped dead. He started toward her but a mass of people came between them, some heading to the area near the band, others trying to get as far away as possible. She scooted in with the fleeing group because she'd had enough drama for one day. She couldn't imagine why Cole wanted to confront her, but she had seen purpose in his eyes, so she wasn't going to stick around and find out. She didn't even glance behind her to see where he had gone. Instead, she spotted her receptionist, Rhonda Morton, talking to a group of women and invited herself into the conversation. A discussion of Marlene's mural designs and the day's painting achievements, or almost any other topic under the sun, was exactly what she needed.

When the music started, the group moved outside, where someone—probably Frances and Tom—had set up tables and chairs under the wide porch roof and provided citronella candles to help ward off mosquitoes. At one point, she heard an engine start up and twisted around to see Cole Burleigh's truck leave the parking lot. Relieved, she settled back in her chair and gratefully accepted a glass of lemonade from someone passing by with a tray of drinks.

Lisa was sitting nearby, deep in conversation with Ben McAdams—a conversation neither of them seemed to be enjoying. If they were having another argument, she knew she'd hear about it later, but as with Carly a few minutes ago, her first instinct was to rush to her friend's aid.

The door to the gym opened and a group of people surged out, including Reta Bunker.

She was a short, plump woman who usually had a sweet smile for everyone. Right now, she looked worried. When she spotted Gemma, she darted over, swiped the glass of lemonade from her hand, set it on the table-top and spoke urgently as she tried to haul Gemma to her feet. Everyone at the table fell silent as the drama began playing out.

"You need to hide, honey. Bunky is looking for you."

Gemma's toes had their usual reaction of curling into her sandals. When was she going to learn to wear steel-toed boots when there was even the possibility of dance music being played? Even when he was all the way on the other side of town, Bunky always seemed to hear dance music.

"Oh, no. Where is he?"

"Right behind me. It was pure luck that I spotted you before he did." Reta patted her arm. "I'm sorry, but you know he's like a bloodhound when it comes to finding his favorite dance partner."

Gemma looked around frantically. "I probably shouldn't try to hide, then. He'll find me."

"Um, you're right." Reta looked around, as well. Spying someone over Gemma's shoulder, she said, "You need to dance with another man." Reaching out, she snagged someone's arm and hauled him closer. "Come on, you need to dance with Gemma so my husband won't permanently cripple her feet."

Laughing, Gemma glanced up. Of course, it was Nate. Her smile collapsed.

She started to pull away. "That's okay, Reta. I'll go on home, and—"

"Too late. Save yourself." She gave Gemma a shove that sent her stumbling into Nate, who shot out an arm to keep her from falling.

Turning and squaring her shoulders, Reta's voice broke as she said, "Sometimes a wife has to do what a wife has to do. I'll dance with him." Marching forward, she grabbed her husband's arm and pulled him back inside.

The people Gemma had been sitting with waited in breathless anticipation as she looked at Nate. Unobtrusively, she tried to scoot away from him. The corner of his mouth kicked up as he said, "Shall we?" and held out a hand to her.

She was still mad at him, furious, in fact. But it was only one dance, and a tableful of their fellow townspeople were watching her.

Gemma put her hand in his. "As long as you don't murder my toes."

"I wouldn't think of it. I'm a pretty good dancer." His voice caught, but he smiled. "Mandy taught me."

They went inside the gym, where the crowd was beginning to thin out as parents scooped up cranky, ice-cream-smeared toddlers and urged their older children toward the door.

Before Nate took her into his arms, he said, "I owe you an apology, though."

Shaking her head, Gemma held him off. "One more thing. This has been a hard day. I can't handle another thing. No apologies, no arguments, no conflicts, nothing but the questionable beauty of the Rocket Boys and their music."

Nate gazed at her for a second as if he wanted to argue the point. She was beginning to understand that he didn't necessarily want the last word, he wanted to finish one issue before moving on to the next. The problem was that their issues never seemed to get resolved.

Finally, he said, "Agreed," and pulled her closer. Relieved, she rested her hand on his shoulder. He had showered, too, since their last encounter and was now dressed in jeans and a crisp white shirt, unbuttoned at the cuffs and rolled back a couple of turns. His subtle cologne teased her senses. She was becoming a big fan of that scent.

After a couple of minutes, she said, "This is going to get really awkward if we don't think of something to talk about—other than medical, or personal or…"

"Almost everything else."

This close, she could see the way his eyes crinkled at the corners when he was amused. "There's always town gossip," he said.

That startled a laugh out of her. "You've been gone from Reston as long as I have. Longer. Where would you hear gossip?"

"Brantley Clegg. He's a real busybody and bankers know almost everything that goes on in town."

"But should they *tell* everything?"

"Only if it's really juicy."

She lifted an eyebrow at him. "For example?"

Nate nodded toward the band. "The time Ron Jett locked his wife in a closet so he and his band could go play a gig in McAlester."

"No. Really?" She looked over at the band, where Ron was happily picking out a tune on his guitar and singing an old country classic. "What happened?"

"She got loose, headed straight for the bank, cleaned out their joint account and filed for divorce."

"Wow, she was really mad."

"It was their anniversary."

"Then good for her. I guess the moral of the story is don't ever come between a man and his music."

"I'm not sure locking up his wife was the best solution."

"It's hard to say. He and his band do sound a little better than they used to," she admitted.

"More time to practice since he doesn't have a wife to worry about anymore."

They laughed together and Gemma tilted her head as she asked, "What other gossip do you know?"

"Old Jesse Nevis, Marlene Fedder's dad, finally quit driving."

"Thank God," she said fervently. "He must be ninety years old."

"Ninety-two."

"How did they get him to stop?"

"His grandson had to arrest him for car theft."

Gemma laughed. "Jesse stole a car and Junior arrested him?"

"Yup. Seems the old man climbed into a truck that he thought was his when he came out of the Mustang Supermarket."

"Only it wasn't?"

"No. He couldn't find the key, thought he'd lost it, probably dropped it in that big puddle, so instead of getting out and looking for it, he hot-wired the truck and took off. The real owner took exception to that and called the sheriff's office. Junior had to chase Jesse down with lights and sirens—which, apparently, Jesse couldn't hear. Junior followed him all the way home before he could get him to stop."

"At least the old guy didn't try to make a run for it."

"Even if he had, Junior would have known where to find him."

Gemma smiled, glad this hard day was ending on a happier note. They clapped when the song finished and she said, "Thanks for the dance, Nate, and for the gossip."

"Anytime." Nate gave her a critical look as he held her away from him. "To use a strictly nonmedical term, you look dead on your feet. I know a lot of it's my fault, and I also know you don't want to talk about it right now. Can I drive you home?"

Gemma shook her head. "I've got my car."

"With four new tires and a decent spare, right?"

They both smiled at the memory. "That's right."

Nate stepped back, rubbed his earlobe, glanced away and then back at her. "Okay if I come by in the morning?"

"Sure. I'll be up early." She lifted her chin. "I have lots to do and a class on breast-feeding to teach at ten."

He blinked. "On Sunday morning?"

"It was the only time two of the moms could come."

He nodded thoughtfully. "See you early, then."

Gemma turned away, congratulated Frances on another successful fund-raising evening, told Carly and Lisa good-night, and then headed home. All the while, she thought about the day's exhausting events, from her satisfaction with the mural she'd helped create, to the exhilaration of the safe birth of Misty's daughter, to her conflicts with Nathan and what he'd told her about Mandy's death, to the sweetness of the dance they'd shared. It was going to take her a long time to process all of this, but if she and Nathan could have one adult, professional, nonemotional conversation, she felt they could finally begin moving forward.

Satisfied with that conclusion, she pulled into her driveway, splashed through puddles and shuddered over the ruts that marred the surface. Reminding herself to have it graded and graveled after the rains let up, she realized with a start that the big yard light high on a pole by the back door was out.

Shoulders slumping with exhaustion, she told herself to let it go. She couldn't fix it tonight even if she wanted to. The ground was too soft from the rain to hold a ladder safely. Besides, she was sure she didn't have a bulb to replace the one that had burned out. Clouds were moving in, obscuring the faint moonlight, and rain was beginning to fall again.

She parked her Rover and felt in the glove

compartment for the flashlight she usually kept there, but she couldn't find it. Annoyed, she carefully picked her way to the back door and fumbled with the key. Safely inside, she dumped her belongings on the kitchen table and headed toward her bed.

CHAPTER ELEVEN

THAT WOULD TEACH HER, Cole thought. Miss High-and-Mighty Gemma wouldn't like coming home to what he'd prepared for her. Good. Maybe she'd learn to mind her own business. She needed to know what it felt like to have someone interfering in her life like she'd interfered with his and Yvette's.

He sped down the highway, water from puddles arcing away beneath his tires. The rain was starting again, but he didn't slow down, too excited by the surprise he'd prepared for Gemma to pay attention to the weather.

Things had been fine between him and his wife before Gemma had started sticking her nose into their marriage and wrecking the life they had together. He was determined to get that life back. Yvette was upset right now, but time was all she needed. Time to think and appreciate everything he'd done for her.

Maybe he wasn't great at painting, but he could hire someone to do it for him. He could let his wife have what she wanted as long as she understood it came from him, that she would have nothing and no one if not for him.

Yvette wanted him to leave her alone, to not touch her. Fine. That's exactly what she would get. He'd leave her alone tonight, wouldn't call or answer her if she tried to call him. A flush of shame darkened his face when he thought of how he'd raised his fist to her, but he shoved the feeling down. He wouldn't have really hit her. He'd only wanted to scare her, remind her who was the boss, the provider in the family.

He eased to a halt at the four-way stop where Highway 6 crossed County Road 1282. The open sign of the Crossroads Tavern caught his eye. They had good burgers there, and cold beer.

Thanks to the interference from Gemma and Nate, Cole hadn't had any dinner. He was hungry and decided he deserved a treat. After crossing the intersection, he pulled into the tavern's parking lot. He'd stay gone for a while, he decided, as he stepped out of the truck. In fact, he'd stay gone all night if he wanted to. Maybe two nights. He hadn't liked it when he'd come home half-starved and tired only to find that Yvette was gone. It was long past time for her to learn a lesson, learn what if felt like to wonder where someone was.

He'd eat his hamburger, drink a couple more beers and then keep driving before he called to check on her and the baby. She needed to know what worry felt like.

GEMMA WOKE SLOWLY in the bedroom that had belonged to her parents. She was grateful for the extra thick curtains she'd put up to block the sun coming in the east-facing windows. She wasn't ready to confront the sunlight yet. But she had to. Sitting up, she swung her legs over the side of the mattress.

Once she was dressed in slacks, a shirt and sneakers, she wound her hair into a loose bun and secured it with a couple of small chopsticks her mother had sent her from Thailand.

She was heading into the kitchen to make coffee when a knock on the front door rerouted her. Pulling it open, she found Nate standing back to admire her house and front yard. He was dressed in what she had come to think of as his work clothes—khaki slacks and a shirt with the sleeves rolled up. This one was pearl gray.

He was freshly shaven and the faint scent of his cologne drifted toward her. Her stomach fluttered. This would all be so much easier if she didn't find him so appealing.

"I haven't really looked at this yet," he said, indicating the aloe vera plants in the abandoned car tires, and the bright paint on the door and trim. "It's...welcoming."

"Thanks. Blue is my favorite color."

He looked down and smiled. "I'll remember that. Okay if I come in?"

She stepped back. "Of course."

He came inside and when Gemma nodded toward the sofa, he sat, but scooted forward with his hands clasped loosely between his knees. "I won't stay long. I came to apologize—again."

"For?" she asked cautiously as she took the chair opposite him. There had been enough misunderstandings between them. She wanted to be sure she knew where they were going with this conversation.

"For what I said yesterday—and every other time. I need to explain." He grimaced. "Like most men, I'm no good at the whole idea of getting in touch with my feelings."

"What *are* your feelings?"

"Confused," he said on a sigh, then paused as if pulling his thoughts together. "And the confusion goes back years, to my childhood, to Mandy's death, my mother's depression and her death, but those were occurrences— tragedies, really—that I couldn't change."

Gemma sat still, unable to believe he was opening up about something so painful. He stared at the braided rug beneath his feet, probably not even seeing the pattern.

"I realized pretty early on that I wanted a different life than what my family had, what most people in Reston had."

"Which is why you won't be staying here." That knowledge hurt her deeply, but it also made her admit how attracted she was to him. His leaving wouldn't bother her if she wasn't so attracted to him and if he wasn't so in need of someone to love him.

"That's right."

The certainty in his tone made her heart sink. He looked up. "Believe it or not, I wanted what your family had, even though I thought your parents were a little crazy."

Gemma smiled. "They're proud of the fact that they're unique and don't fit into any mold, and most people in town accepted that. When I went off to college, I had to learn to be like everyone else in order to fit in." She shook her head. "Looking back, I'm not sure that was the best idea."

"I envied the way you, and your mom and dad, were so comfortable in your own skins, so at home in the world. There were times when I'd stay away from my house because the tension between my parents was so bad I couldn't stand to stay there. I used to sneak over to your lake, watch people fish, see kids playing in the water."

The starkness of his words was like a knife to Gemma's heart. She imagined the lonely boy he'd been, watching and listening, wishing he was part of a happy family, a carefree group.

"Oh," she said, sitting up suddenly and staring at him. "That's what you were doing the day Cole tried to grab me."

"Yeah." His lips twisted. "Pitiful, huh? I promise I wasn't stalking you. I saw him sneak up on you and I didn't like the look on his face. I knew I had to get between the two of you. I don't think I'd ever run that fast in my life. Still haven't."

Gemma thought about the boy he'd been then—shorter, skinnier, not nearly as big as Cole, who was almost a year older. If he'd thought about what he was going to do, he probably wouldn't have done it. But he hadn't thought. He'd simply acted to save her. She'd been right to be so crazy about him in high school, even though he'd barely given her the time of day.

"I'm glad you did. He scared me to death coming at me like that, announcing he wanted me to be his girlfriend."

"He *said* that? I didn't hear what he said. I only saw that you looked scared."

"Believe me, I was—and then he denied he'd been anywhere near me, the jerk." She paused. "Something's always bothered me, though. When I saw you at school, and tried to say thanks, you brushed me off as if it didn't matter."

Nate grimaced. "It mattered, but I was afraid of getting too close to you because then I might never get away from here, and that was the most important thing back then."

That hurt, but Gemma reminded herself that she'd been the one with the massive crush and he'd been trying to do what was best for his future.

Still, things must have improved for him once he was on his own. He'd gained an education and probably friends, including the one whose practice he was joining in Houston.

Gemma looked up and asked the question she'd had for weeks. "Nate, have you ever been in love?"

His head jerked back in surprise. "Why do you ask?"

"Because I want to know if you've ever been truly happy, been completely at ease with anyone. Have you ever been able to say what's on your mind, been loved unconditionally?"

He frowned. "Is this another attempt to save me from—"

"No. I'm curious. If you'd loved someone in Oklahoma City, you would have stayed there…" Her words trailed off because she didn't like where the next thought was leading.

"And if I had someone here, I'd be willing to stay in Reston."

Gemma glanced at him, then away. "Yes."

"I've dated lots of women, but mostly, I've been alone." His voice went soft, heavy with regret. "History, family history, the past, the sins of a father, the misery of a mother, death. They're all too heavy to live with after a while. In my case, after eight years. I'm leaving them buried here."

"And moving on."

"Yes." He sat back and asked, "How about you, Gemma? Ever been in love?"

"Sure. A couple of times, but it never worked out."

A corner of Nate's mouth lifted. "Is it possible things didn't work out because those guys didn't need to be rescued?"

"Certainly not," she answered, instantly annoyed, but then she shrugged. "At least I don't think so."

"Why do you have that need, Gemma?" Nate leaned back, stretched out his legs and laced his fingers over his stomach.

She stared at him. "Are you trying to analyze me?"

"If I can tell you why I want to leave here,

you can tell me why you need to rescue people."

"I'm a nurse, I—"

"But it started when we were kids with animals and birds. Begin there."

Gemma thought about it while he waited and watched. "My parents' example, I suppose. There were always people at the campground, some of them were down on their luck. My dad was a pretty good mechanic so he could fix their vehicles. Mom was a seamstress, cook, carpenter, knew a lot about herbal medicine. Mom and Dad could usually come up with a plan to help them, a place where they could find a job, or an agency or charitable organization to help them."

She sighed. "Although I can also remember my parents getting exasperated if those same people came back with the very same problems."

"Did they help them again?" Nate asked.

"Of course, but Dad always said if they had listened and done what he said the first time, they would have been better off."

"Or if they had been taught to do their own car repairs, carpentry and job hunting, they might not have needed help again."

Gemma let his words sink in as she wondered if that's what she'd been doing—jumping in and doing things for people instead of teaching them to do it for themselves? No, not in medicine. She taught mothers to take care of themselves and their babies, but outside of that? Well, maybe.

Sitting in her living room as Nathan told her about his life, things she'd wondered about for years, helped her understand him so much better—and made her love him more. Heat washed over her as the realization worked its way through her mind, past all the objections, the disagreements, they'd had.

She was in love with him. It wasn't something she'd ever asked for and she had no idea how he felt about her, but she knew the truth had been quietly waiting for days now, lurking until she was ready to acknowledge it.

His dark hair fell over his forehead as he continued to study the rug at his feet.

Look at me, she wanted to say. *I've got the answer. I love you.* But she didn't voice her thoughts. She hugged them to herself, knowing she would examine them later.

Right now, she had to focus on what they were talking about. It took her a few seconds to remember. Oh, yes, her need to rescue people instead of teaching people to do for themselves. But they had also talked about his need after high school to get away, how he couldn't spare time for her.

Exactly like now. He'd spent years trying to leave Reston and all its bad memories behind. He was determined to do it this time. Her feelings for him made no difference in light of his resolve to do what needed to be done and get away.

"In that case, I'm glad you got away."

"I was pulled back by what my dad did." Nate frowned. "It was so huge, so crooked and messed up, I couldn't understand it. Still can't. Brantley Clegg was the one who called me up to tell me so I wouldn't have to hear it on the news, or read about it in the paper." He looked up. "Is that where you heard it?"

"Carly called me and read the entire article in the *Reston Weekly*," she said.

"Most people did, including everyone I worked with or had classes with. Brantley apologized for not seeing what was happening, but my dad was a master at cooking the books so it's no surprise he wasn't caught."

"I understand that his crime is the reason you came back to Reston."

"When Brantley came to see me last winter, said the Sandersons and some others were interested in reopening the hospital, it was like I'd been handed a way to make up for what he'd done—to give something in return for what he'd taken. I made a vow that I would do everything in my power to provide excellent-quality health care, make sure nothing was slipshod or less than the best—at least while I'm here."

Gemma shifted in her chair, sure something was coming that she didn't want to hear.

Nate's serious gray eyes were trained on her. "That brings me to your birthing center. It's true that when I first came back, I would have shut down the birthing center before it opened—"

"Wait." She held up her hand. Struggling to keep hurt and anger at bay, she said, "I think we've got different ideas on what an apology is and I think we're about to have a serious disagreement. Again. I need coffee before we go any further. Do you want some?" Turning away, she headed for the kitchen without waiting for his answer.

She set the coffee carafe in the sink, began filling it with water and gazed out the window, grateful to see that the rain had stopped, although that meant it would be a muggy day.

Her gaze drifted from the sky to the saturated ground, where she saw, with a jolt, that her garden looked different. It took her a few seconds to realize what had happened and then, horrified, she shut off the water. Gemma jerked open the back door and ran outside.

Her plants had been destroyed. Herbs and vegetables had all been stomped on, overturned, rooted out. She spun in a circle, surveying the devastation. Nate hurried out after her.

Gemma's voice shook as she threw a hand out to indicate the mess and blurted the first thing that came to her mind. "Did you do this?"

"Gemma! Of course not." Looking as if he'd been slapped, he moved closer, examining the ground.

"You're set against me and—"

"I certainly wouldn't do something like this. Did this happen during the night? Most likely it was wild animals. I heard there's been a pack of wild hogs around."

"Wild hogs? Wouldn't they have eaten the carrots?" she asked, pointing to the vegetables scattered across what had once been neat rows. "And the beets? And wouldn't there be little cloven hoof prints if it was pigs?"

"Maybe. Maybe not. There's a lot of standing water here even though the dirt is soft, so the prints might have washed away. When do you think this happened?"

She rolled her eyes at him. "I don't *know* when this happened. I couldn't see anything when I got home last night because the yard light was burned out." She looked up.

"Not burned out, broken," Nate said, following her gaze up the twelve-foot pole to where the remains of the smashed bulb dangled from its socket.

They walked over to the base of the pole.

"Definitely not hogs unless they've learned to throw rocks." Nate pointed to the dozen or so rocks and bits of broken glass scattered around—along with boot prints. He crouched to examine them more closely.

"Cowboy boots, in fact," he said, pointing. "See the heel and the pointed toe?"

"Who would do a thing like this?" she demanded.

Nate shrugged. "Vandals. Kids looking to be destructive little thugs, trying to impress each other with how daring they are. Whoever it was, they had to work at it for a while if they needed to throw this many rocks." He stood up and lifted one of his mud-caked sneakers. "Whoever it was probably carried away some of this sticky mess. I'm already three inches taller than I was when I walked into your yard."

"I hope the rocks bounced off their worthless heads."

Tears spurted into her eyes as she looked at the unnecessary destruction. "Thi-this was no accident," she sobbed. "It was…per-personal. Someone targeted me."

Nate pulled her into his arms and she quickly soaked the front of his shirt. "We'll find out who did this, Gemma. Don't be so upset." He rubbed his hands over her arms and kissed the top of her head. "We can replant. Do we have to wait until the next full moon?"

That made her cry even harder. She was constantly off balance with him. One minute he was saying he would have shut down her birthing center and the next he was offering to replant her herbs. As if that wasn't enough, she'd realized she was in love with him. It was too big, and too hard, and too complicated.

When her tears finally stopped, Nate put his hand under her chin and tilted her head back. He placed a gentle kiss on her lips. "We can fix this, Gemma. All it will take is time."

The sweet taste of his lips, and his tenderness, almost undid her. Waterworks were threatening again, but she drew back and took a deep breath, forcing her emotions to settle down.

"Yes, we can." Turning, she went in search of her phone. "But first, I'm calling the sheriff."

An hour later, Junior Fedder had walked around Gemma's destroyed garden, surveyed the broken light, said "huh," about a hundred times and told her they would probably never catch the vandals. He took a picture of the boot print, wrote a few notes and clumped away on mud-caked feet.

Nathan had left because he had to get to the hospital, so their talk would have to wait. That was fine with her. She didn't need another argument with him. And she had so much to think about. It would take time to process it all.

Besides, she had to go teach a class. She also needed to contact Misty and make an appointment for a follow-up visit when the new mother was home from the hospital in Claybourne.

Hurriedly, she changed out of her muddy clothes, ate breakfast and started for the Sunshine as the heavy rain began once again. She had to pick her way around tarp-covered piles of building supplies, but two of the mothers-to-be showed up for the class so she didn't feel as if the morning had been wasted.

Disappointed that Yvette didn't attend, Gemma phoned to see how she was.

"I didn't want to bother you," Yvette said. "But I was going to call because I don't feel very good."

Gemma suppressed a frustrated sigh. Sometimes no amount of reassurance could convince a woman that the mother's care was top priority. In a cheerful voice, she said, "I'll be right there to check on you. Get into bed and tell Cole to help you prop up your feet and legs."

"Um, well, he's not here right now, so..."

"I'm on my way." Grabbing her medical bag, she hurried out through the pounding rain, grateful for her faithful Rover and its new tires.

On the way to the Burleighs' house, she was surprised to see that the elevated road that ran between the two halves of Reston Lake had water lapping at the shoulders. She wondered how close the lake was to flood stage when she slowed her vehicle on the bridge and saw water less than a foot below the structure. Glancing up, she spotted Cole and Yvette's house on its rise of land. She doubted it would flood, but if the water got any higher, it would be impossible to get in or out. She wondered why a road crew hadn't been there to set up a blockade, but maybe they were more optimistic than she was about the possibility of flooding.

At the Burleighs' house, Cole's truck wasn't in the driveway. Even though it would make things easier for her, she didn't like the idea of Yvette being there alone.

When Yvette opened the door, Gemma gave her a quick once-over and was relieved to see that her ankles weren't unduly swollen, and even though she looked tired, her color was good.

"Hello, soon-to-be mama. Let's get you back into bed so I can check you over." She gave her a warm smile as she glanced around. "Is Cole at work?"

"No. The sale barn is closed on Sunday." Yvette gave her a distressed look as she lay down on her bed and arched her knees so Gemma could scoot pillows beneath them. "I—I don't know where he is. We…disagreed. He thought he was doing something I'd like, and…" With tears in her eyes, she told Gemma about the fight. "I've called and texted and left messages to apologize, but he won't call me back."

"So you're here alone?" Gemma asked, trying to keep her voice calm. Even though she'd known Cole was a bully, she'd never thought he was stupid. As she removed the blood pressure cuff from her bag, she glanced across the hallway at the mess in the nursery. On the other hand, maybe Cole *was* stupid.

"All night, I thought he'd be home any minute. He's never stayed out all night before. I suppose I can call his parents. I know they'll come. They'll be concerned about the baby, and…"

"And about you," Gemma added.

A sweet smile touched Yvette's lips. "Yes, they will."

"Whatever the circumstances, Yvette, you can't be alone."

"Okay. I'll call them." The tone of Yvette's voice said she would rather be on her own, but she picked up her cell phone from the bedside table and called her mother-in-law. From the volume and length of the squawking that Gemma could hear, she guessed Mrs. Burleigh wasn't happy that Yvette hadn't called sooner.

When she hung up, Yvette smiled and said, "She's right. I should have called them last night."

Gemma finished her examination and said, "In spite of the stress you've been under, all the signs are good. There's no reason to think you won't have a safe, successful delivery of little Cole Junior."

"David," Yvette said, a determined light in her eyes. "I've always loved that name."

Gemma nodded and squeezed Yvette's hand. She had a policy of never getting involved in her patients' private lives and family dramas unless they were having an adverse effect on the health of mom and baby. Yvette was so young, and with only Cole and his parents to depend on, she had seemed afraid to stand up for herself. The fond tone in her voice when she'd mentioned her in-laws, and her statement about the baby's name, though, gave Gemma hope.

She pulled up a chair and sat beside the bed. "I'll stay and chat until the Burleighs arrive. Can I get you anything?"

"I missed your class," Yvette said, turning onto her side. "So tell me about breast-feeding."

NATE HAD DONE all he could do for the day. He'd talked to everyone he needed to at the hospital, taken care of details and it still wasn't even noon. The one thing he'd wanted to do, talk to Gemma and clear things up, wasn't going to be possible today. As usual, he'd started out by saying the wrong thing and there hadn't been time to make amends before she'd discovered the mess in her garden. He'd meant it when he said he'd help her replant and he hoped she believed him.

The best part of the morning had been holding her while she cried, not even caring that she was soaking his shirt. He had reveled in the feeling of his arms around her, the warmth of her skin and the tickle of her curly hair against his cheek. She was so independent, so sure of herself, so willing to rescue those she thought needed defending, including him, that he'd never thought he'd see her that vulnerable. He yearned for her in a way he never thought he would for anyone, and certainly not someone established in the town he was set on escaping.

That need clawed at him and warred with the certainty that he had to leave her once he'd fulfilled his reason for coming back.

Nate didn't like the way things had been left. He was tired of keeping everything in. He would try again later today, or even tomorrow. She had a class to teach, and he didn't want to stand around in the rain waiting for her, so he went home to finish up a few chores. When he opened the guest room closet to put away an extra blanket, he saw the sealed boxes he'd found in his mother's room. Staring at the triple thicknesses of packaging tape, he realized they were never meant to be opened, but his mother couldn't bring herself to discard the contents.

"This is as good a time as any," he murmured. He carried the three cardboard cartons to the kitchen table, then pulled a knife from a drawer.

The layers of string-reinforced tape that had been affixed more than ten years ago had fused together. Nate had to use a sawing motion to cut through it, but he finally got the first box open, flipped back the lid flaps and stared down at a collection of baby clothes—one stack of tiny pink outfits, and one stack of blue.

"Huh," he grunted. "I didn't know Mom was sentimental enough to keep things like this." He lifted out several sets of footed sleepers and realized the price tags were still attached. Also, they were all the same size, for a newborn, and had never been worn.

They were from an upscale department store in Tulsa.

Nate frowned as a memory surfaced of being home alone one day after Mandy had returned. The ever-present and enigmatic Brendyce had been napping—although Nate could never figure out what she did, besides eat, to make her so tired. Mandy had gone for a walk, a "wander," as he'd come to think of it. His mother had left early and returned to the house carrying bags from that store. She'd had him take them upstairs to her room but he'd never known the contents. He lifted out a frilly pink dress. These were things his mother had bought for Mandy's baby, not ones she'd saved from her own children.

He sat back and stared at the items in his hands, recalling how she had gone along with Mandy's wish to have her baby at home, with a midwife. Mandy had insisted she would buy everything her baby needed, but their mother had seen that no preparations had been made and took it upon herself to do so. That was typical of her, but he didn't know why she'd kept them after Mandy's death. She had simply sealed them up and put them away. They were as pristine as the day she'd bought them, frozen in time.

"Twenty years." If his nephew had lived, he would be a man now, starting out in life, working at a job, maybe going to college. And what about Mandy? Would she have overcome her demons, been a loving, involved mother? He thought so because even though he'd wondered about his parents' affection for him, he had never once doubted that his sister loved him.

Nate eyed the other two boxes. There were probably answers to his questions in one or both of them.

He was reaching over to open the second box when his phone rang. The call was from the sheriff's office so he answered right away.

"Doc?" Junior Fedder shouted. "I'm at the scene of a crash out on Sky Mountain Drive about a mile west of Highway Six. No one seems to be seriously hurt, but the paramedics can't get here because they're tied up with other accidents. Can you come?"

"Be right there." Glad of the distraction, for the chance to slip into professional mode and forget the ghosts that were haunting him,

Nate hung up, grabbed his medical bag and hurried to his car through rain that was falling sideways, in drenching sheets. He was going to get the hospital reopened, no matter what. This situation couldn't go on. People's lives were at risk with competent medical care so far away.

As he drove away, he thought about the boxes waiting for him. They would be there whenever he was ready to deal with them. That was one thing about his past. It was always there.

CHAPTER TWELVE

THE FIVE POINTS CASINO was a well-lit and inviting place, Cole decided as he squeezed his eyes shut and then popped them open wide, trying to see his poker hand. He appreciated that the Native American tribes were so enterprising that they'd built these casinos for people like him. They were places to get away, to leave your troubles behind, relax and have fun. And it was decorated with plush carpet and beautiful colors on the walls. Even Yvette would like it—if the paint job lived up to her prissy standards, that is.

He'd rolled in at about two o'clock in the morning and immediately felt at home. An employee had shown him the conveniently placed ATM so he could withdraw some cash to buy chips. A pretty waitress in a barely there dress had kept him supplied with drinks, and he'd made a new friend.

"Cole, are you in or out?"

Bleary-eyed, Cole looked at the man who'd introduced himself as Fennerman but hadn't said if that was his first name or his last. Didn't matter. He was a good old guy, about his dad's age, but bald and craggy looking, like he'd been in fights, or had too many bouts with a bottle. It was obvious that Fennerman had pursued a hard life that didn't look to be getting any better. Cole thought he seemed familiar, like they'd met somewhere before, but trying to make his alcohol-soaked brain remember where was too much trouble.

"I'm thinking," Cole said, closing one eye and trying to focus on his cards, but he couldn't tell if he was holding clubs or spades unless he put the cards close to his face. Maybe he'd had too much to drink. He was good at poker, usually won when he played with his friends, but so far, he'd lost more than he'd won. A lot more. Some spark of common sense and self-preservation surfaced. He put down his cards and looked at the wobbly figures of the other men at the table, all strangers to him. "Nah. I'm out."

"So am I," Fennerman said. "In fact, I think I'd better take my new friend here and let him sleep it off." He hooked an arm under Cole's and hauled him to his feet. "Gather up your chips," he ordered. "You're cashing in for the night."

Cole was grateful to have someone to lean on as they weaved their way to the cashier, then outside to a waiting car. Fennerman stuffed him into the backseat and Cole lay down on the cushioned softness. He barely noticed that his friend had slipped behind the wheel and started the car before he closed his eyes and passed out completely.

The place where he woke up wasn't his house, Cole realized. He had to peel his face off the plastic seat of a too-short sofa when he tried to lift his head. The action caused nausea to fill his throat. Climbing awkwardly to his feet, he knocked against a coffee table, causing it to skitter across the linoleum floor. He didn't know where he was, but he knew he had to find a bathroom, and quick. He opened a couple of doors before he found it and lurched inside.

When he came out of the bathroom, he tried to make sense of where he was, but now that his gut felt better, his head was pounding so hard he couldn't think. He zigzagged back to the sofa and passed out again.

When he woke the second time, he could smell food cooking, which made his stomach flip and he groaned. He couldn't manage to crank his eyes open until he heard a voice calling his name.

"Cole. Cole, I'm glad to see you're waking up. Come on, buddy, sit up and drink this."

Someone propped him up and wrapped his hand around a glass, then guided it to his lips. When he realized it was water, he gulped it greedily until the glass was empty. It was taken away and he managed to open his eyes enough to see an older gentleman leaning over him.

"Thanks," he croaked, then cleared his throat as he looked around. "Where am I?"

"Five Points."

"And who are you?"

"Name's Fennerman. We met last night. Played poker."

Automatically, Cole slapped his hand to his hip, looking for his wallet. Fennerman shook his head. "Don't worry. Nobody took anything from you. Everything you won is there, but it wasn't much." He went into the kitchen and came back with Cole's wallet and keys. "Your vehicle is still parked at the casino. When you're feeling better, I'll take you to get it."

"Uh, thanks." Cole couldn't resist checking his wallet for his credit and debit cards, as well as the cash. He wished he could remember exactly how much he'd lost last night. He looked back at Fennerman. "Is this your place?"

"Yeah, such as it is." The other man glanced around at the cheap furnishings. "Been here a few weeks. I work part-time at the casino, dealing blackjack."

When Fennerman turned his head, a memory stirred in Cole's mind, but he was still too hungover to make sense of it.

"I cooked some food. You need to eat something to counteract all that alcohol."

"Yeah, okay." Cole rested his head back against the sofa until his new friend put a plate of scrambled eggs and toast in front of him. With a nod of thanks, he took a few tentative bites to see if it would stay down. When it settled in his stomach and stayed there, he wolfed down the rest of the food. "That was good. Thanks. My wife never cooked eggs until…" A jolt raced through him. "Yvette."

"Is that your wife?"

"Yeah. I gotta call her." He looked around for his phone and checked his pockets. "My phone…"

"Must still be in your vehicle." Fennerman handed over his own phone then gathered the empty dishes and returned to the kitchen. He made a noisy show of washing up as Cole punched in Yvette's number and waited for her to answer. Instead, his mom picked up.

"Yvette's phone. This is Margery speaking," she sang out.

"Mom?" he said tentatively. "Where's Yvette? Why didn't she answer her phone? Is she all right?"

"Cole Destry Burleigh!" his mom shrieked. "Oh, as if you care. She's fine and the baby's fine. No thanks to you! Where are you? Why aren't you home with your pregnant wife? Do you realize she was alone all night waiting for you? She finally called us this morning after Gemma Whitmire got here."

"Gemma? Why was she there?" Through the fog that still clouded his brain, he remembered being plenty mad at Nathan and Gemma—mostly Gemma.

"She was doing her job of checking on her patient since you weren't doing your job as Yvette's husband." His mom started to yell at him some more, but then the phone was snatched away and his dad yelled at him for a while. Furtively, he covered the earpiece to block his dad's booming voice as he glanced over his shoulder. Fennerman had gone into the bedroom and shut the door. Finally, Cole shouted down his dad and insisted on talking to Yvette.

"Hello, Cole." His wife's soft voice in his ear brought him immediate comfort. "Are you okay? I called and texted but you never answered."

"I'm okay. I'll be home in a few hours. What happened? Why was Gemma there? You didn't call her, did you? You know you've got a doctor you can call, and it's not Nathan Smith, either."

His wife didn't even bother to answer. She hung up on him and when he called back, her phone went straight to voice mail.

He slammed his fist against his knee, then dropped his face into his hands. This was hell, he thought. He was losing control of his wife, of his whole life, and it wasn't even his fault.

Cole stood up shakily when Fennerman came into the room. He handed over the phone and said, "Thanks for your help. Can you take me back to my truck? I've got to get home."

"Sure, but with this storm, road conditions are terrible, and you're still in no condition to drive."

"I gotta get home."

"You can try, but there are road closures all over the place. It'll take you a long time to get back to Reston. Be best if you waited at least until the rain stops."

Cole ran a hand over his face. "Yeah, I guess." A thought swam up through the swamp of alcohol in his mind. "Hey, how did you know I'm from Reston?"

Fennerman shrugged. "I had your wallet, remember? Looked at your driver's license."

"Oh, yeah." Cole fell silent. Something about this still bothered him, but he couldn't quite pinpoint it.

Fennerman brought him a cup of coffee

and asked, "Have you lived in Reston very long?"

Cole couldn't figure out why the old guy was so interested in him but decided maybe he was trying to be polite since they were stuck there for a while. Besides, he could spare the time. If his parents were at the house, Yvette was okay, and her hanging up on him had convinced him she wasn't worried about him. Probably didn't care anything about him, anyway.

Cole watched the other man from his spot on the sofa. The old guy wasn't going to try to keep him here, was he? Physically, he was no match for Cole. If he tried to hold him, Cole was sure he could knock the old guy down, but he didn't want to do that. Maybe Fennerman was right. More sobering up was needed and rain was pouring down like he'd never seen it.

This wasn't the kind of rain they'd been having—relentlessly falling for hours on end. This was a mean storm, with a cutting, sideways wind that slapped the falling water across the pavement. Cole was amazed to see actual whitecaps whipping up on top of the puddles.

Distracted by the storm, it took him a while to bring his mind back to what Fennerman had asked.

"In Reston? All my life," he answered and went on to talk about his family, especially his wife, and the baby they were expecting. Once he started talking, he didn't stop, telling Fennerman about Gemma and how she was trying to turn his wife against him. Cole decided not to mention how she and Nate had humiliated him all those years ago. This was about the way she and Nate were screwing up his life now.

Cole looked around, wishing he had another drink. He could ask—after all, it was after lunchtime. And Fennerman looked like the kind of guy who was no stranger to the bottle. Then he recalled that he was trying to sober up so he could get home. Suppressing his need for something stronger, he drank some more water and had coffee instead.

"Things were fine until Gemma came back to town, and Nathan Smith, too."

"Nathan Smith." Fennerman looked up, but his tone was even when he said, "Tell me about him."

"Went off to Okie City and got himself

made into a doctor, but when some people in town decided to reopen the hospital, he had to get involved. Got this big idea to start a doctor practice, too, and be the one in charge of the hospital—the same place his old man ruined by stealing all the money. Yeah, we've been without a hospital for a while, but it's not that bad. Paramedics come if you call 'em. Everybody goes to Toncaville or Claybourne if they need a doctor. What I'd like to know is if old Nate's actually the one who's got that money, and where's it hidden. I've been asking that question, but I don't get an answer."

"What makes you think Nathan has it?"

Cole gave him an are-you-kidding-me? look. "His dad stole it, right? Nate says he didn't know, but I don't believe him. A lot of other people don't, either. You know what's funny, though?"

"What's that?"

Cole's new friend had an edge to his voice, but Cole ignored it. He liked being able to talk like this, tell someone exactly what he thought. "I heard they've been fund-raising like crazy, but they're still way short of the money they need to finish the renovations and get the place open." He snorted. "They even had a bunch of people from town coming in to do the painting, fancy murals all over the walls."

Fennerman stood suddenly, startling Cole, but the other man only walked to the window, crossed his arms over his chest and stood staring out at the raging storm. He didn't say anything for a long time. Cole emptied his coffee cup, set it down, then rested his head against the back of the sofa and fell asleep again.

He didn't know how long he slept, but when Cole woke, Fennerman was back in his chair and the rain had let up.

"Um, sorry," Cole said, sitting up and craning his neck to look out the window. The movement made the hammer-and-anvil action in his head ratchet up, but he tried to ignore it. "Rain's not coming down so hard. I'd better go."

"There's something I need to talk to you about before you do." Fennerman gestured toward the sofa. "Keep your seat. This won't take long."

Fennerman picked up a letter-sized envelope from the coffee table. "What would you think if I gave you money to take back to Reston to give to the hospital board of directors?"

Cole's nose wrinkled up as he stared in disbelief. "Why would you do that?"

"Charity. Being a Good Samaritan. Take your pick."

"How much money are we talking about here?"

When Fennerman told him, Cole stared at him, then glanced around the cheap apartment. "Where'd you get that kind of money? Rob a bank?"

Fennerman shrugged. "Gambling. Sometimes I'm really bad at it, and sometimes I'm good." He waved the envelope in the air. "This is a cashier's check for that amount, made out to the board of directors. If you don't take it now, I won't have it for long."

The old guy's face twisted as if he was fighting both anger and disgust. Cole took the envelope from Fennerman's now-shaky fingers.

"For the Reston Hospital?" Cole was having a really hard time processing this. "That's a lot of charity."

"What do you say? Do you want to do it or not?"

Cole scratched his head. "I don't know. Could I get in trouble for this?"

"Nah." Fennerman licked his lips and stared at the envelope as if he wanted to snatch it back. "You're just the delivery man. And the check can only be cashed at a bank by the people it's made out to, so it's not like you can profit from this."

"But why do you—"

"If you don't want to do it, I'll find someone else," Fennerman snapped.

"Wait a minute, wait a minute," Cole said. "I gotta think."

"No, you've got to go." The older man pointed toward the window. "Rain's almost stopped. You want to get going before it starts up again and if roads are blocked it'll take you longer to get home. All you're doing is making a delivery, and didn't you say you had to get home to your wife?"

Yvette. Oh, yeah. This whole mess had started because he'd been trying to impress Yvette with his painting skills. She'd be really impressed if he showed up with enough money to help the hospital project that was suddenly so important to her.

"Okay," he said, standing up. He wobbled a little bit, but he was okay. Cole glanced at the clock. He didn't know when his last drink had been, but he was sure it was many hours ago. "I'll do it."

He folded the envelope and stuck it in his back pocket.

Fennerman nodded, but his expression was regretful, only adding to Cole's confusion. "Good. Do you know who's on the hospital board of directors?"

"Well, yeah." Cole had to think about the people who'd been on the stage at the meeting he'd attended. "Brantley Clegg, for one."

"Then take the check to him. He can take it straight to his bank."

Fennerman hustled him out to his car and drove the few blocks to the casino parking lot, where Cole's truck was waiting. Once Cole was out of his car, Fennerman called out his thanks, gave a wave and was gone.

Cole climbed into his truck thinking there was something fishy about this whole setup, but he was too eager to amaze his wife to give it the thought it needed. He opened the envelope and looked at the check. Sure enough, it was a huge amount, more money than Cole had seen. Even the most prosperous cattle buyers at his family's sale barn didn't write checks this big.

Yeah, he'd take this to Mr. Clegg, and he'd look like a hero. Nobody would expect Cole Burleigh to save the hospital. He paused as something teased his memory. He didn't remember telling Fennerman that Mr. Clegg was a banker. Or had he? Cole was still too hungover to remember clearly.

Grabbing his phone, he called Yvette. This time she answered. Once he'd told her he was on his way home and been assured she was all right, he said, "I've got a surprise for you, Yvette. It's one you'll like."

"That's nice of you, Cole," she responded in a cool tone. "I'm glad you're going to do *something* I like. I'd better tell you now that I'm going to do something you won't like. I've decided that when the time comes, Gemma is going to deliver our baby."

"What? No! You've got a doctor, and—"
She hung up on him again.

THE RAIN STOPPED by midafternoon, but with the soaked ground unable to absorb any more water, it stood on the roads in deep puddles that camouflaged potholes and ruts, making driving dangerous. Not that the danger slowed down these Oklahoma drivers, Gemma thought. If the speed limit was fifty-five, that, or more, was their intended target, which made anyone on the road a target, too. Local drivers were often the worst when it came to ignoring the laws. They thought they knew the roads so well they would be safe driving anywhere in the county, and under any conditions. Circumstances often proved them wrong.

When she had left Yvette's house earlier, the water in Reston Lake was rising and road-blocks were being set up. She was the last one allowed on the road back to Reston before it was closed behind her. After she passed, deputies dressed in light-reflective slickers were turning drivers back the way they'd come, warning that if they tried to drive around the barricades, they would be arrested. Unfortunately, there weren't enough deputies in the county to watch every flooded road.

The water would keep rising for a while.

It was expected to peak soon and then begin returning to normal levels as no more storms were expected. She hoped people listened and obeyed the law. She'd seen the effects of careless drivers caught in floods and didn't understand why anyone would risk it.

Although Gemma was nervous, knowing she wouldn't be able to reach Yvette if she was needed, she had to remind herself that Yvette had a doctor and a birth plan that might not include her services. Yvette had said she wanted Gemma to deliver her son, but Cole probably wouldn't go along with that plan and Gemma didn't want to get into a conflict with him. It wouldn't be good for Yvette.

For now, Cole's parents were with Yvette, and deputies were nearby if needed. Since she had left the Burleighs' house, Gemma had been back to the Sunshine to take care of a few things and was now headed home. A peaceful Sunday afternoon in her snug cabin was just what she needed.

When she pulled into her driveway, she was dismayed to see that water completely covered the yard. She had to be careful to avoid going off the drive into the soft mud.

Because she already knew the backyard was a swamp, she went to the front door and hurried inside.

When she heard a vehicle laboring through the boggy mess, she looked out the window…at a sight that made her heart sink. It was Cole Burleigh's truck, with Cole behind the wheel, pulling up behind her Rover. She couldn't imagine what he could possibly want, but when he knocked at her door, she answered it.

"Hello, Cole." She took in his unshaven face, bloodshot eyes, blond hair standing up at all angles and rumpled appearance. "You look terrible. And shouldn't you be home with Yvette? She's worried about you."

"Never mind about my wife, Gemma. And you're not delivering our baby, either." His lip curled and his eyes glowed with malicious intent. "I came by to tell you that your birthing center is shutting down."

She drew back. "What? What are you talking about?"

"I gave a huge check to the hospital board," he bragged. "It might even be enough to finish the renovations without any more fundraising."

"Where did you get that kind of money?"

"Never mind. I got it and now..." He paused and his eyes took on a calculating gleam. "Somebody on the hospital board told me your buddy Nathan said he'd use it but only if your Sunshine Birthing Center is put out of business. Nobody needs it now that we'll have the hospital—least of all Yvette."

"So that's what this is about? Yvette?"

"No." He pointed a finger at her as his voice rose in fury. "It's about you minding your own business. You're not wanted here. Why don't you sell this place and go back to Tulsa?"

He whirled away from her, slipping in the mud and slamming against the door of his truck, which he fumbled to open. Once he was inside, he reversed away from the front of her house and turned, spewing up muddy water behind him as he went.

Gemma stared after him. It couldn't be true. She *knew* it couldn't be true. He was a mean, vindictive man who was only trying to cause trouble. She shut the door and turned away, shaken.

It couldn't be happening, she assured herself again, and yet she couldn't help recalling

Nathan's statement that he would have shut down the birthing center if he could have. Had his wish come true? Had Cole's check made it possible?

Gemma's knees gave way and she sat down in the armchair, replaying every disagreement she'd had with Nate, each time he'd revealed some painful part of his past or his family's that affected the present. Mostly, she thought about his story of Mandy's death and the midwife he held responsible.

Her initial shock gave way to annoyance, and then anger. If this was true, it didn't matter what she did or said, he would never see her as the professional she was, and the mothers and babies of Reston would be the ones to pay the price.

There was one way to solve this. She grabbed her phone and called him, hoping that, for once, the call would go through. She only got his voice mail and left a message for him to call her back. It was impossible to keep the fury out of her voice as she said, "It's not up to you whether the Sunshine stays open. I know how you feel and you're wrong."

She hung up and took a few angry turns

around her living room and kitchen, then ended up standing by the kitchen window, staring out at her ruined garden.

COLE FELT A surge of triumph as he drove away from Gemma's house. That would teach her. Now things would get back to normal. Yvette would listen to him again, do what he said. He'd have the life he wanted.

He was so elated that he barely remembered to reduce his speed to the ridiculous twenty-five-miles-an-hour pace required in the city limits. Looking around, he decided it probably wouldn't matter. No one was out, and on this Sunday afternoon approaching dusk, most businesses were closed. He knew Junior Fedder liked to park his cruiser behind the big sign advertising the beauty of Reston Lake, but he wasn't there today. Cole kicked up his speed and hurried homeward.

At the bridge over Reston Lake, he found out where Junior was, along with another deputy. Barricades and flashing lights had him pulling to a stop and putting down his window.

"Hey, Junior, what's going on?"

The deputy gave him an exasperated look.

"See the bridge ahead of you, Cole? It's underwater. You can't cross it."

"Whaddya mean? My truck can make it across. I gotta get home." Cole pointed ahead. "I can see the lights on in my house from here. I need to be with my wife."

"Maybe you should have thought of that before you took off yesterday."

Cole answered with a nasty snarl. "It's none of your business, Junior. Now get out of my way and let me cross."

"Cole, you're about the tenth idiot today who's told me his truck can make it across. It's not worth your life, or anyone else's who tries to rescue you, or my job, for that matter, for me to let you cross. And if you try to go around the barricades, I'll arrest you."

"You wouldn't do that."

Junior grasped the door frame and stuck his head into the truck's interior. "You better believe I would." His glance fell to the muddied interior of the cab, then down to the floor and back to Cole's puzzled face.

"What are you looking at, Junior?"

"Evidence of vandalism, I think. Dried mud with what looks like carrots stuck in it. Where'd that come from, Cole?"

"Um, well. I might have stepped in something…"

"Yeah, and we both know where, but we'll talk about that later. I can only handle one crisis at a time." Junior unhooked the handcuffs attached to his utility belt and held them up meaningfully. "I'm tired, I'm wet and I'm hungry. Do I *look* like I want to mess with you today?"

"All right, all right," Cole said. "But if something happens to Yvette, I'll hold you responsible."

"Good luck with that. Fortunately, your wife is smarter than you are. She's got sense enough to stay home."

Determined to have the last word, Cole said. "Well, for your sake, it's good that my mom and dad are there, or you'd be in real trouble."

Junior shook his head. "They left a while ago. I saw them heading back to their house—on the other side of the bridge."

"You don't have to remind me where my parents' house is." Cole put up his window and turned his truck around even as Junior's words echoed in his head. Yvette was alone.

Driving out of sight of the deputies, he pulled over and called her.

Yvette's first words were "Where are you? I thought you'd be home by now."

He told her about the road closures but didn't mention the man he met, the check or what he'd told Gemma. There would be time for that later. "I'm down by the bridge, but Junior won't let me cross. Where are Mom and Dad? Are you okay?"

"A neighbor called your dad, said his cattle were out on the road and asked for help getting them back in. Margery and Bob both went to help, but they'll be back soon. Right after they left, I…"

Cole gripped the phone. "What? What?"

"I started feeling weird, and my back hurts so much."

"What's wrong? Is it the baby?"

"I don't know. It's not time for the baby yet, but Gemma says he can come anytime now, but maybe this is because I didn't sleep much last night. I was worried about you."

Cole felt like he'd been kicked in the gut. He had thought worrying a little would serve her right, but he'd been wrong. "I'm sorry,

Yvette. I…didn't think you'd care if I was gone for a while."

She sighed. "Oh, Cole. How could you think that? I love you. Last night, when you raised your fist to me, I was scared. I never thought you'd do that. I've been hit before, but I never thought you'd try it. I wanted to believe you were good, that you'd be good to me, treat me right."

The tremor in her voice had him dropping his forehead into his hand. He'd been so caught up in making sure she appreciated the life he'd given her, he hadn't really thought about what her life had been like before. She hadn't told him much, but maybe that was because she knew he wouldn't listen.

"I'm sorry, Yvette. I promise I'll never do that again. I love you, too, and you can do whatever you want to the house—paint, new furniture, anything, just…don't leave me."

"Oh, Cole, I'm not leaving. This is my home. Mine and my baby's."

Humbled, he said, "Thank you, Yvette. I'll be home as quick as I can. Try to rest. I'm on my way."

Cole tossed the phone into the console and sat with the engine idling and his wrists resting on the steering wheel as he considered his options.

Junior had made it clear that crossing the bridge wasn't one of those options. There was a road over the dam, but it would probably be blocked, too. He could go all the way around the lake, but with road closures and flooding, it would either take hours, or he'd have to turn back.

He couldn't turn back. His wife needed him. Slipping the truck into gear, he headed toward town and the road that would take him to the boat ramp that jutted into Reston Lake. He wasn't surprised to see that it was deserted and high-water warning signs had been posted.

Parking by the boathouse, he jumped out and pulled a pair of bolt cutters from behind the front seat. With silent apologies to the owners, he cut off the lock and swung the big doors open to reveal an array of watercraft. He chose a canoe and a paddle then grabbed a life vest, which he fastened securely. Ordinarily, he wouldn't have bothered—his need to appear macho would have overridden his common sense. He couldn't take chances like that anymore. He had a family—a kid on the way and a wife who loved him.

Cole closed the boathouse doors, replaced the busted padlock so anyone passing would think it was still secure, then pushed the canoe into the water and climbed in. He knew a place where the lake narrowed. He would cross there, even though the water would be rushing dangerously high.

He had to get home. Yvette needed him.

CHAPTER THIRTEEN

"YES, GEMMA." Brantley Clegg's voice rumbled over the phone. "Closing the birthing center is something that Nate talked about, though not recently, and the donor of this big check did make that a condition. Or so Cole said, but we only got the money today. The board hasn't met. It's short notice, and the storm has everything stopped, so—"

"You—you mean you'd actually do it? Really even *consider* it? That's... I'm..." Gemma was so angry she could barely string words together, much less form a complete sentence.

"Now, now, Gemma. Calm down. I can't speak for the board, but we have to look at the big picture, not simply what one small group wants."

"Small group? You mean mothers and babies? Maybe that's something you should have thought of before I came back here."

She took a deep breath. "You're right about one thing, Brantley. I need to calm down, and talking to you isn't helping."

She hung up over his squawking protests and didn't answer when he called back. She set her phone down on the table and paced back and forth through her house for a few minutes, breathing deeply and trying to get her rage under control. Nate hadn't called her back, and he probably wouldn't once he understood why she had phoned.

The hurt, anger and betrayal she felt had only grown in the hour since Cole had dropped his bombshell and left. In spite of the tangle of emotions twisting inside her, she knew she had to call and check on Yvette. She could only hope she didn't have to talk to Cole. Ever again.

"Oh, hi, Gemma." Yvette was her usual friendly self when she answered, but Gemma heard a worried edge in her voice. She told Gemma that Cole's parents had left but would be back momentarily, and Cole had promised he'd be there, too.

"Okay, but how are you feeling?"

"About the same as this morning, but my back really hurts. I've been lying down on my side, with a pillow under my knees, but it doesn't help much."

Grateful for something to focus on, Gemma responded in a firm tone. "I'm coming right out there. All you have to do is relax and try to rest."

"But the bridge is closed. They won't let you pass."

"Don't you worry about that. I'll get across that bridge if I have to climb the girders and crawl across the top on my hands and knees, holding my medical bag in my teeth."

Yvette laughed. "Thanks, Gemma. I'll see you when you climb down, then."

Gemma hung up and grabbed her medical bag, checking it for any supplies she might need, then adding extras, which took longer than she had planned. Locking her house, she hurried out to her Land Rover and started off.

NATE CHECKED HIS phone and listened again to the garbled message from Gemma. Only a few words had come through clearly, something about closing down her birthing center. One thing he understood as clear as crystal— she was plenty mad. He wished he knew why.

He had helped at two different accident scenes and was on his way home when he decided to detour to Gemma's and find out what this was all about. When his phone rang and he saw the sheriff's office identification come up, he knew it was Junior again.

"Hey, Doc. You finished with that last accident?"

"Yes." Nate suppressed a sigh. "Where's the next one?"

"No accident this time, but something's going on at the Burleighs'."

"You mean Cole's house?"

"Yeah, I'm on the other side of the bridge, trying to keep people from doing something stupid, but I think Cole outsmarted me." He told Nate about their earlier encounter. "I don't know how he got home, but he and his wife came down to the road in her car a few minutes ago, then turned around and went back to the house. I called up there and he said his wife's in labor, so I thought I'd better get some help. Paramedics are still all tied up."

"Good call," Nate said. "See if Gemma can get there, too."

"Already done. She's on her way. And,

Doc? If you've got some boots or waders, bring 'em."

After hanging up, Nate turned around and started for the bridge. He didn't own rain boots or waders. Life in the big city had never called for them. He didn't know what Junior had in mind, but he was glad to help and anxious to see Gemma. Now maybe he could find out what she was so mad about, and possibly finish the talk they'd started this morning before she'd found her yard torn up.

When he pulled up to the bridge, Gemma was there ahead of him, and already wearing what he assumed were police-issue waders that were too big. She looked like a little girl, dressing up in her daddy's fishing gear, but that image only lasted until she turned around and gave him a look that would have curdled fresh cream. Whatever she'd been mad about before, she was still mad.

GEMMA'S BACK STRAIGHTENED when she saw Nate drive up, pull onto the shoulder and stop behind her car. When he walked up, she waved dismissively and said, "I can handle this. I'm sure you have other things to do."

He stopped short and his eyes narrowed. "Like what?"

Her lips tightened in annoyance. "It can wait" was all she said. "*I* have a patient."

Nate shrugged. "Fine, but I'm coming with you."

She waited as he kicked off his sneakers, pulled on the waders that Junior had found in the trunk of his cruiser and then tied his sneakers around his neck, as she had done. She turned to Junior. "Thanks for the gear, but how are we going to get across the bridge?"

"We can't risk driving, even in the cruiser, because we can't have a vehicle getting stuck and blocking the bridge. Once the water goes down, we'll need to clear the structure of debris as fast as we can. So for now, we'll have to tie ourselves together and walk across, then I have to come back and continue on my idiocy prevention duty." He nodded toward a pile of rope curled up beside one of the steel supports. "Let's go."

It took only a few minutes to tie the three of them together, then they stepped onto the bridge. Junior glanced back and saw her nervous look. "Don't worry, Gemma. The doc's got me on a diet, but I'm still hefty enough to keep you from falling in."

Nate chuckled, but she ignored him and prepared to move out. Junior was first, leading the way, and she was right behind him, holding on to the railing with one hand, clutching her medical bag in the other and moving slowly.

At one point a huge tree limb, caught by the rushing water, crashed against the bridge, sending branches flying over their heads. Instinctively, Gemma ducked and felt her feet slipping, but Nate's arm came around her. His medical bag banged against her hip, but he gave her a moment to get her footing. When she was steady again, she made a point of moving away from him.

Grateful for the protective gear Junior had provided, Gemma looked down at the mounds of debris that had caught against the supports and the railing. She tried not to imagine the damage that could have done to frail human flesh if someone was unlucky enough to get caught up in that water.

She glanced back at Nate and wondered if he was thinking the same thing, then recalled how furious she was with him, and concentrated on moving in lockstep with Junior. When they reached the other side, they quickly stepped out of the waders and put their own shoes back on.

"Will you be okay going back by yourself?" Gemma asked.

"Yeah. Go see if Cole's wife is okay."

Impulsively, she stood on tiptoe and gave him a kiss on the cheek. "You're a great guy, Wayne Fedder Junior. If you ever run for sheriff, you've got my vote."

He laughed. "I can think of easier ways to secure a vote. Better not kiss me, though. The doc is getting jealous."

Gemma gave him a look that said, "Yeah, right," but when she glanced at Nate, he was frowning.

Pointing to a lane that was a few hundred feet away, she said, "That's their driveway. Come on."

They followed the paved lane and were soon at the Burleighs' front door.

Cole threw the door open as soon as they knocked and looked at them with terrified eyes as he said, "Thank God you're here, Gemma. I don't know what to do. We're pretty sure Yvette's in labor." Looking past her, he saw Nate and said, "And Nate's here, too. Thanks for coming.

"Yvette's in the bedroom. We think the baby's on its way because her pains are coming every couple of minutes. I started to take her to the hospital, but the pains were so bad by the time we got to the bottom of the driveway, we were afraid we wouldn't get there before the baby came. We called the paramedics, but they can't get here because of the flood and accidents, and everything. The dispatcher said I'd have to deliver the baby. Me? I can't do it. I just can't do it," he babbled. "I've never delivered a baby—or anything else for that matter. Do you think she's going to be okay, Gemma? I can't lose her." Frantically, he grabbed Nate's arm. "I'm not going to lose her, am I?"

"Of course not," Gemma answered.

Before she could say anything else, Nate asked, "What's the matter with your arm, Cole?"

For the first time, Gemma noticed that he was holding it up against his chest.

"Ah, I think I sprained my wrist." He told them about paddling a canoe across the lake to be with his wife. "Everything was okay until I got caught up on some rocks behind my house. The canoe was knocked sideways and I tried to keep it from turning over but jammed my wrist. That was another reason we couldn't make it to the hospital. I was in no shape to drive."

"Let me have a look," Nate said in a no-nonsense voice.

While he did that, Gemma turned toward the bedroom, glad to be away from both Cole and Nate. It took all the professionalism she could muster to keep from telling them what she thought of them both. "I'm going to check on Yvette."

"She going to be okay, right, Gemma?" the worried father asked.

"Calm down, Cole. There's absolutely no reason to think this won't be a perfectly normal birth."

At that moment, the lights flickered and went off.

"And now there's no *light*. The electricity has gone off every day this week! What are we going to do? She can't have a baby in the dark," Cole said.

"Then let's find some flashlights, or lanterns," Nate answered in a calm voice. "You've got some, right, since the power's been going off every day? And then I need to wrap your wrist."

Since darkness hadn't completely fallen, there was enough light for Gemma to find the bathroom, where she scrubbed her hands and donned gloves before going in to check on Yvette. By then, Cole and Nate had returned with battery-powered lights, which created a soft glow in the room. Gemma hoped it would soothe her patient, who was in a position similar to the one she'd been in when Gemma had left that morning.

After setting up the lanterns, Nate finished examining Cole's wrist, told him it didn't appear to be broken and wrapped it with bandages he'd taken from his medical bag. When Nate was finished, Cole surprised Gemma by sitting in a chair beside the bed and taking his wife's hand. Nate waited by the door and Gemma tried to ignore him, knowing he was judging her performance as he had before, waiting for her to make a mistake. She didn't plan to oblige him.

When she finished her examination, she smiled at her patient and said, "Yvette, honey, you're going to have a baby tonight.

You're dilated to eight already and you were only at two this morning. Good job."

"It's not something I've been working at," Yvette said around a grimace. "At this point, I'm just along for the ride."

"Fortunately, your body knows what to do."

"Glad one of us does." When she experienced the next pain and grasped her husband's hand, Cole looked as if he might faint from terror.

"Cole," Yvette said. "If you don't calm down, we're going to have two patients here, and I won't let you steal my moment."

Gemma snickered, proud of the way Yvette was standing up for herself, and using humor to do it. She knew she should feel some kind of glee at Cole's distress after what he'd said to her earlier, but she only felt sorry for him. Nate was relaxing in the doorway, ankles crossed and arms over his chest, until she gave him a steady look. He must have caught her meaning because he gestured to Cole.

"Come on, Cole, you look like you need a break. Let's go in the other room for a minute. Gemma's got this." He gave Gemma an approving look that completely threw her.

Cole stood up. "Yeah, I can do that if Yvette thinks it's okay."

"Go," she answered with a wave.

He gave his wife a kiss and said, "Okay, then. I'll go…boil some water."

As he rushed from the room, Gemma couldn't help exchanging an amused look with Nate, who said, "Maybe he wants some tea."

Over the next hour, Gemma was too busy to give Nate or Cole another thought. She had Yvette up and moving so gravity could help with the birth of her son. She could hear Nate giving Cole a pep talk about being strong for his wife, not letting her down by passing out at the signs of her pain. By the time they came back into the room, the baby was crowning, Cole was able to be supportive of his wife and Gemma was in her element.

Safely bringing a baby into the world held a special joy that never got old. Whenever she assisted at a birth, Gemma saw it as confirmation of why she was on the earth, what she'd been born to do. There was always a challenge, but that's what made it appealing to her.

"You're doing a wonderful job, Yvette," she said. "One more push, and you'll be able to meet your son. Are you ready?"

"As I'll ever be," Yvette answered. Looking up at her husband, she said, "I love you, Cole." Then, with one more mighty push, her baby was born and the placenta came out a few minutes later.

Smiling proudly, Gemma held the baby firmly. Cole had tears running unchecked down his face. "Would you like to cut the cord, Cole, and meet your son?"

With a nod, he stumbled forward and picked up the scissors, but his hands were shaking so badly, Nate stepped in to steady him. When that was done, Gemma wiped off the baby, wrapped him in a blanket and handed him to his mother, who immediately unwrapped him to check all his fingers and toes.

"He's perfect," Yvette said. "I knew he would be." Tears overflowed her eyes as she said, "Thank you, Gemma."

As if his knees had suddenly turned to

noodles, Cole collapsed into the chair, exactly as Kelvin Summers had the day before. Gemma had seen that so many times it made her smile. Even though they'd done none of the work, the fathers were often the first to need a rest.

When he had recovered a little, Cole leaned in close to his wife. Placing one arm above Yvette's head on the pillow, and the other over hers, he cradled his family. Looking at Gemma, and then at Nate, he said, "Yes, thank you."

"I didn't do anything," Nate said. "This was all because of Gemma's know-how."

Gemma turned and looked at him. The joy of the past few minutes had almost made her forget his treachery. Why was he praising her now? It was time to get some answers.

Without her asking, Nate stepped forward to help her clean up. They finished at about the same time the lights came on once again. Exhaustion suddenly swamped her and Gemma sat in a chair in the living room. With her head against the cushioned softness, she closed her eyes and tried to relax and recharge.

She heard Nate come into the room, heard the movement as he sat in the chair opposite her. "You did a good job in there, Gemma."

"Much to your surprise."

"What? What do you mean?"

She tilted her head and opened her eyes. "I'm not going to fight you anymore, Nate. But I'm also not going to let you shut down my birthing center. I'll talk to Brantley, and Tom, and whoever else I need to, but you're not going to shut me down."

He shook his head. "Gemma, I don't know what you're talking about."

She sat up and for the second time that day, tears filled her eyes. Furiously, she blinked them back. "You can't deny you've been opposed to it from the beginning."

"I don't deny it, but—"

"You were going to call my medical director. You said more than once that you would shut me down, and now you think you've succeeded, but it won't work."

He held up his hands. "Wait, Gemma. Stop and back up. Where is this coming from?"

"The check that Cole gave the board. The funding you insisted had to include shutting down the Sunshine."

He stared at her. "I don't know anything about a check."

"Don't lie to me, Nate, not when—"

"I've never lied to you."

"I was the one who lied," Cole said from the doorway. "It was me."

He indicated the phone in his hand. "I've got to call my mom and dad, tell them about the baby, about Cole David Burleigh—we're going to call him Davy—then I'll tell you about what I did."

Gemma stood up. "While you do that, I'll check on Yvette and Davy." In the bedroom, she took the sleeping baby from his mother and placed him in a hastily prepared bassinet, checked Yvette for any signs of hemorrhage, and monitored her temperature and blood pressure. Pleased to see that the new mother was doing well and ready to fall asleep herself, she returned to the living room.

Cole was there, shifting from one foot to the other. "My parents are on their way," he said. "This is going to be a full house tonight. Once they get here, they won't leave."

"Why don't you sit down, Cole, and tell us what this is all about?"

Cole perched on the edge of the sofa as if ready to flee at any moment. "I was the one who tore up your yard, Gemma, ripped up your plants."

She stared at him. "Why?"

"I was mad, I'd been drinking and yeah, I know I shouldn't have been driving. Shouldn't have done…any of the things I did last night." His face was lined with shame. "I'll pay for the repairs, or replant, or do whatever you need."

Gemma raised an eyebrow at him. She wasn't going to make this easy for him. "Yes, you will."

Cole swallowed hard and went on. "I lied about that check, Gemma. Nate didn't know anything about it. Kelvin Summers told me Misty heard you two fighting about the birthing center when she had their baby, so I used that. I'm sorry."

"Was that your money?" she asked.

"Nah. I was mad at you and Nate, been mad at you since that time when I ended up facedown in the lake."

Gemma and Nate exchanged a look. "We remember."

"Since you came back to town, and Yvette got to know you, Gemma, I've been afraid." He stopped, his eyes showing that fear.

"Of what?" Gemma asked.

"Of losing her. At first, I thought that if she didn't have any friends here, she'd only depend on me, but then I knew that wouldn't work, that having friends would make her want to stay. But I didn't want you two to tell her what I'd been like. I thought you'd poison her against me."

"Cole, we never would have done that," Nate said. "And wouldn't other people in town have told her what you were like? Let's face it, you were a bully."

"Nah, I've pretty much lived that down, and besides, one way or another, we do business with almost everyone around here."

Nate and Gemma looked at each other, still puzzled. Cole saw the question in their faces and said, "I don't deserve her, see? She's sweet and good, and I never thought I'd get a girl like her. I kept remembering what my mother said—easy to win, easy to lose."

"But she loves you, Cole," Gemma said. "That's obvious."

His face reddened. "Yeah, believe it or not, she does."

Knowing this was something the two of them needed to work out, Gemma changed the subject. "Tell us about the check."

Cole gave her a grateful look. "Well, I went to Five Points, you know, to the casino, met a guy there named Fennerman."

Nate sat up suddenly. "What did you say his name was?"

"Fennerman. Why, you know him?"

"Yeah, I think I do. Go ahead with what you were saying."

Cole told them the whole amazing story, concluding with "I got the feeling he wanted to get rid of the check before he changed his mind, and I was the first person he'd seen from Reston." Cole scratched his head. "Why didn't he simply mail it to Mr. Clegg?"

"Because even though it's a cashier's check with no sender's name on it, he decided he didn't want it to be anonymous," Nate said. "He wanted people to know his name and that he was the one who gave the money."

"Fennerman." Gemma shrugged. "I've never heard of anyone by that name around Reston."

Cole said, "I guess if I hadn't been so hungover, I wouldn't have gone along with it, but… I don't know, I thought it would make me look good to Yvette." He couldn't meet Gemma's eyes. "Except for the lie I told you. I'm sorry, Gemma. There's no excuse for what I did."

Headlights flashed across the living room windows, and Cole looked up expectantly. "My mom and dad are here. Will it be okay for them to hold Davy?"

"Of course, but you'll want them to wash up before they do," Gemma said.

"What about if they breathe on him?"

"I've got protective masks if you want them." Nate gestured toward his medical bag.

Cole nodded. "I think that'll be a good idea."

Margery and Bob rushed in, excited to meet their new grandson. Even though they seemed taken aback to discover that Cole wanted them to be almost germfree before holding the baby, they went along with it and were soon oohing and aahing over the tiny boy, thanking Cole and Yvette again and again for bringing him into the world.

When things had settled down, Bob came back into the living room. After praising the wonders of Davy for several minutes, he pointed in the direction of the lake. "The water level is falling fast and they're clearing the bridge to let traffic through. I can drive you back to your cars as soon as the deputies take down the barricades."

Gemma checked on her patient, issued warnings about a spiking fever and watching for signs of hemorrhage. She was pleased to see Margery taking careful notes. Cole's mother was a strong-willed, pushy woman, but tonight, she seemed to have only Yvette and Davy's best interests at heart.

"I'm twenty minutes away if you need me, but you can also call Nate or the paramedics if something happens. I'll be back first thing in the morning."

Carrying her medical bag, she joined Nate in the living room. Cole looked as if he was ready to drop so Nate ordered him to bed. Before he went, though, he turned to Gemma. "I'm sorry for the lie I told you today, for trying to keep Yvette from seeing you and for what I did all those years ago, scaring you like I did. I was used to getting what I wanted, and I was a jerk." He paused. "And a bully. I won't let Davy be like that. I'll teach him—Yvette and I will teach him—how to be a good person and how to treat people right."

Gemma held out her hand and shook his. "You're forgiven, Cole. Now get some rest."

He answered with a boyish grin. "Yeah, I guess I better before the sleepless nights begin."

He shook Nate's hand, then indicated his bandaged wrist. "Thanks for fixing me up, Nate."

"You're welcome. That's my job." He paused, frowning. "Cole, the guy you got the check from, this Fennerman. What did he look like?"

Cole nodded toward Bob. "About Dad's age, maybe younger, but like he'd had a hard life. He was bald and, well, tired looking. Not a big man, smaller than me. Smaller than you, but it was like he'd shrunk."

Grimly, Nate nodded and started for the door. Bob drove them across the bridge, then said good-night, eager to return to his family.

They checked in with Junior, told him

about the baby's safe delivery and walked toward their cars.

"Gemma, we need to talk. I have a lot to tell you, and—"

"Not tonight, Nate. I've had a rough day. Two rough days."

"Yeah, I know, and a lot of it's my fault." In the flashing caution lights from the barricade, he looked exhausted and distressed, but he gave her a smile. "I'm sorry for everything I've said and done that hurt you. I've been trying to tell you that for two days, but something always came up."

She shrugged. "And a couple of times I stopped you because I didn't want to have another disagreement."

"No more disagreements," Nate promised, holding up his hand in a pledge. "At least not in the foreseeable future. Can you come over to my place in the morning? I've only got a couple of patients scheduled. I can get Stacie to move them to Tuesday. There's something I want to show you, and tell you—unless you've got patients or classes to teach?"

"Sure, I can do that." Before she climbed into her Land Rover, she asked, "That man Cole met, the one who gave him the check..."

"Fennerman?"

"Yes. Do you know him?"

"All my life. I think it's my dad. In fact, it has to be. His middle name is Fennerman."

CHAPTER FOURTEEN

GEMMA PULLED UP to the curb in front of Nate's house. She stepped out of her Land Rover, trying to avoid one of the puddles that lined every street in town. The rainstorms were finally clearing away and the flooded areas around the lake were receding, but there was still plenty of water and mud everywhere. She had been out to check on Yvette and her baby and was delighted to see her doing well, with her husband and in-laws attending to her every need.

It was going to be a hot and humid day, but Gemma didn't care—even if it meant her curly hair would be wilder than usual. In fact, she'd left it down around her shoulders because there wasn't much she could do about it, anyway. Besides, she thought it looked good that way with her favorite yellow sleeveless dress.

She'd woken up several times last night,

thinking about Nate, his promise of no more disagreements and his certainty that the man who'd given Cole the check had been his father, George. Of all the twists and turns of the past few weeks, that had to be the craziest one.

Her knock at Nate's door brought an immediate response. He swung it open and invited her in with a wave of his hand as his gaze swept over her. "Come in, Gemma. You look beautiful."

"Thank you," she said, smiling as she stepped inside.

"Want some coffee?"

"Coffee?" She shook her head, trying to clear it. "No, I had some at home."

"Come sit down, then." He urged her toward the couch, then sat beside her and turned so he could take her hands in his.

"I've been an idiot, and I'm sorry. I was so stuck in the past, so caught up in my family history, my determination to do what I had to do and then leave Reston for good. I couldn't admit that I was wrong."

"What do you mean?"

"My feelings about midwives. It was easy to fall into the trap of being dismissive about your profession, and it's widespread among doctors. I thought I had a good reason after what happened to Mandy, but you're right. Brendyce wasn't a midwife, or any kind of medical professional. I guess I knew that at twelve years old when I called the ambulance for Mandy."

"I'm glad to hear you say that, Nate." Her lips trembled into a smile. "I've got something to tell you, too. It's true that I have a habit of rescuing people. I see now that you didn't need me to stand between you and the town, after all. But it was a way to inject myself into your life."

"Why did you need to do that, Gemma?"

She answered with a small shrug. "Habit of a lifetime. And seeing you again made me think of how things were years ago." She raised her eyebrows and twisted her lips to the side. "When I had a huge crush on you."

"Oh, yeah?" Nate said, grinning.

"Yeah. And I still had some of those feelings when I saw you again, but your objections to the Sunshine were too painful."

"I'm sorry, Gemma. I respect you and everything you do. I was too far down the road of denial to admit I was being stupid and stubborn. You were right about the treatments for Yvette and Misty. They were lucky to have you."

This was so different from what he'd said before, Gemma couldn't help the lump that formed in her throat. "Thank you." She blinked back tears. "Is that all you have to tell me?"

"Nah, I'm just getting started."

Her hands tightened on his. She looked into his face, noting that he looked tired but at peace, and his eyes were clear, not the deep stormy gray she'd seen so often of late.

"That's good because I've felt, ever since the first night when you came into my yard, that something was eating at you, and that your objection to midwives was a cover—at least partly."

"You're right." He leaned forward and kissed her, then rested his forehead against hers as if pulling strength from her.

Nate stood and tugged three cardboard cartons from beside the sofa, sliding them over and flipping open the flaps on the first one. "It's true that I came back to Reston to try and make things right, reopen the hospital. I guess I wanted to be a hero, try and make my whole family look better." He reached into the box and pulled out a handful of baby clothes. "The truth is, I didn't even know my family. It blew apart before I ever learned what made them tick, what made us the way we were."

Gemma held the tiny clothes on her lap, running her fingers over the fabric, touching the softness as Nate told her how he'd found them in the box. "These are so sweet," she said, "but seeing them like this, price tags still attached after all these years, makes me want to cry."

"Yeah, I know. I think that buying these things for Mandy's baby was my mom's way of trying to show what she couldn't say— that she loved Mandy and she would love the baby, too."

"My family is way too open with our emotions, so it's hard for me to imagine what it was like for Mandy, having a mom who couldn't talk about how much she loved her." Gemma looked up. "I'm guessing she was that reserved with you, too."

"Yes, and I think I finally know why." He returned the baby clothes to the carton and set it aside. He opened the tops of the other two boxes and removed a stack of notebooks from each.

"What's this?"

"My mother kept journals, from the time she was a little girl. I had no idea, although I guess my father knew. He must have been the one to pack these up and seal them."

"Have you read them?"

"A few. I couldn't sleep last night, so I figured out which ones she'd written first and…"

He paused, his throat working as he fought his emotions. "Nate? What is it?"

"My mother was shy. It was a crippling shyness and I think she must have fought that, as well as depression, from childhood."

"Social anxiety," Gemma said.

"It explains why she stayed home so much, didn't belong to any of the local organizations, had few friends. It also explains why she cleaned house all the time. She had to have something to do."

"Being in her home probably made her feel secure."

"I think so, but it was like a prison. The fact that she had Carrara marble, mahogany floors and Oriental rugs at least made it a pretty prison." Nate shut his eyes for a moment and sighed. "My whole life, I thought she was just cold. Everyone must have thought that, everyone in town, but she was terrified of interacting with people, even her own kids."

"But she was married. Your dad…"

"She must have overcome it for a while. She mentions being on medication in one of the journals from forty-five years ago, probably some early version of antianxiety drugs, but those weren't the kinds of medications an ethical doctor would have let her take for the rest of her life, so at some point, she must have been taken off them."

"So her social phobia and depression returned."

"It must have been miserable, and I never knew. I learned a lot about her when I found the journals from when Mandy came home." He opened one of the notebooks and read aloud. "'So glad Mandy is home but she's sad because her worthless boyfriend left her. She's ready to have a baby any day! I can see in her the same darkness that I battle, but she refuses to stay inside, goes out walking every day—where people can see her. She's got some woman with her who claims to be a midwife and will deliver the baby. I don't like this, but I'll go along with it and I'll make sure George goes along with it, too, so our girl doesn't run away again. I know I was the one who drove her away before, but I won't let her go again. I'll do whatever I have to so I can keep her here.'"

Gemma wiped away the tears that had started when he'd read the first few words. "That's why she wouldn't go against Mandy, wouldn't call an ambulance. She was afraid Mandy would leave and never come back. Which is exactly what happened."

Nate closed the journal and returned it to the box. "There's a huge gap in these journals. For years after Mandy died, she never wrote another one."

"She was probably sunk so far into her depression, she couldn't."

"Until about ten years ago, when she seemed to get a little better, but then cancer took her. Since she rarely left the house, she didn't go to doctors, and…"

Gemma watched the sadness in his face, reached over and took his hands again. "There's nothing you could have done, Nate.

It's impossible to force someone to get medical care."

"I could have been a better son, been more understanding. I was in med school, learning how to take care of people. You'd think I could have learned to have compassion for my own mother. But I didn't know how bad she was until it was too late. Selfishly, I didn't want to come home if I didn't have to—not even for holidays. Dad didn't call and let me know what was happening until she was actually in the hospital."

"That must have been agonizing for her, having strangers taking care of her, asking her questions…"

"It was. I can see that now, but at that time… I was mad, mad at her for not being who I thought she should be, not being a fighter, giving up on life. I was mad at my dad…"

The emotions on his face changed from sorrow, to anger, to determination.

"My dad needs to answer for some of this. Sure, he must have felt helpless against her anxiety and depression, but that doesn't excuse what he did."

Nate stood and held out his hand. "Gemma,

will you go with me to Five Points? I've got to see a man about a theft."

THE FIVE POINTS CASINO was bustling for a Monday morning, Natc thought. The parking lot was full of cars and buses.

"Don't these people have jobs?" Gemma asked as they stopped near the welcoming front entrance. The facade was angled in so it could funnel people into the double front doors. It made him think of the mouth of a shark, one that had an electronic sign over its snout that advertised fun, entertainment and riches untold.

"Not when there's money to be won," he answered. He was so glad Gemma was with him since he had no idea how this was going to play out. The day had started on a promising note when she'd told him she still had some old, good feelings for him. He was deeply grateful for that admission. She was easy to love. Him, not so much. His family, *really* not so much. He only hoped that after they talked to his father, she would be willing to marry him.

Once they were inside, Gemma asked, "Any idea where to look?"

"Poker used to be his game, probably still is—at least it was last Saturday night from what Cole told me." He nodded toward the arched doorway of a room full of poker tables. "I'm guessing that's where we need to go."

"I've never been a gambler, never played poker," Gemma said.

Nate pulled her close to his side. "Don't ever start. With your expressive face, you'd lose every time."

She bumped her hip against him, making him laugh as they walked into the poker room. There were games going at several tables, but at one, a man was sitting alone, playing solitaire.

Nate couldn't help the way his body stiffened in response and he knew Gemma had felt it because she gave him a questioning look.

"There he is," he said, walking toward his father with his heart pounding and a sick twist in his gut.

George Smith barely glanced up, but waved to indicate the other places at the table. "Hello, son. I wondered when you'd show up. Have a seat."

Nate pulled out a chair for Gemma, then sat beside her, across from the man he once thought he knew. Gemma scooted her chair closer and slipped her hand into his.

"Hello, Dad," he responded.

George looked up from his game, even while his hands hovered over the cards, as though he expected this wouldn't take long.

"So Cole Burleigh delivered the check, did he? I wasn't sure he would, being so hungover and all. I recognized him as soon as he walked in here. It was fate. I'd had that check for only a day when Cole walked in. I was going to mail it, but having him deliver it was better, even if he was acting like an arrogant badass."

"Cole's all right," Nate said. "He's not a thief."

George shrugged and went back to his game while Nate took in the grayish cast of his father's skin, his sunken cheeks and balding head. "You don't look well."

George tossed down his cards and sat back in his chair. "Well, apparently this is what happens when you pursue a life of crime. It ages you pretty fast."

"Are you saying you've committed other crimes, besides embezzlement?"

"Nah, that's my only one. So far."

His father's cavalier attitude had the sickness in Nate's gut transforming into fury. He scooted to the edge of his chair and leaned in, speaking in a low, enraged tone. "One was enough, Dad. Why did you do it?"

Gemma tightened her hand in his as she said, "You hurt a lot of people, Mr. Smith."

He looked her up and down. "You're that Whitmire girl, aren't you?"

"Yes. My name is Gemma now, and we're here for answers."

Nate felt a surge of pride in her forthright manner, acknowledging that he had been annoyed when she'd turned it on him. It was exactly the right note to take with his father.

"Answers," the older man snorted. "I don't have answers, don't even have good reasons. All I ever had was gambling, looking for excitement, for a big score so I could get out of Reston, and…"

"Away from the memories," Nate added. "Away from Mom…and me."

George pointed a finger at him. "Hey, I provided some money for your education.

You wouldn't be a doctor now if it wasn't for me."

"If I'd known the money was stolen, I never would have taken it."

"Well, good for you. You don't have to worry about it, though, because that check will pay back what I stole."

Nathan gaped at him. "No, it doesn't, Dad. It's pennies on the dollar."

"Yeah, I know." George gathered up his cards and stacked them neatly, tapping the edges against the table to make them perfectly even. "But that's probably all there's gonna be. If I held on to what I'd made gambling, I could win more, maybe even the full amount I took, but—"

"You could also lose it all."

Nate saw a flicker of regret in his father's eyes before his cockiness returned. "Maybe, but I figured, what the heck, give some back, so I got the cashier's check and gave it to Cole."

"Because if you'd kept it any longer, you would have canceled the check and gone right back to a high-stakes poker game," Gemma added, her hand tightening on Nate's.

"Easy come, easy go."

"But why now?" Nate asked. "After all these years?"

"It was time."

Nate glanced at Gemma, who met his gaze with sympathy and nodded toward his father. Taking a breath to settle his confusion and anger, he slipped into physician's mode and gave his father a clinical assessment.

"You're sick, aren't you, Dad? What is it?"

"Liver, kidneys, take your pick." George tilted his head to the side. "That's what people do, isn't it? They try to make amends when they think they're dying."

Sick regret roiled in Nate's stomach. "Is that what you're doing, Dad? Dying?"

"Not quite yet."

"There are treatments…"

"I'm going to have to go to jail first. Don't worry. You won't have to call the sheriff and turn in your old man. I already did that. A couple of deputies just walked in the door. I wasn't sure you'd come find me, but I knew you were smart enough to figure out where I was, and I wanted a chance to talk to you before I go to jail." He looked past Nate and nodded at someone.

Nate and Gemma turned to see Junior

Fedder and another deputy walking toward them. Nate stumbled to his feet, pulling Gemma with him. He felt the color wash out of his face, and then rush back in when Junior gave him a regretful look. Solemnly, the deputy unhooked his handcuffs and snapped them onto George Smith's skinny wrists.

The entire room had gone silent so when George spoke, his voice rang out loudly. "I'm sorry about this, Nathan. I'm sorry for what I did to you and to the whole town of Reston. When—*if*—you want to talk, you'll know where to find me. I'm broke now, and I don't expect anyone, not even you, to post my bail."

As the authorities marched George out, the silence lasted a moment longer, and then all the gamblers in the place seemed to be talking at once. Gemma stepped close and slipped her arm around his waist.

"Come on, Nate. Let's get out of here."

When he lowered his head, she tightened her arm to make him stand straighter and urged him toward the door. Once outside, they saw the Reston County Sheriff's Department cruiser they hadn't noticed on their way inside. Junior was holding the door while George slid into the backseat.

Nate wanted to pull her away from the scene, but Gemma said, "No, Nate, from here on, you need to know everything that's going on with your dad. People will ask, and you've got to have an answer."

He watched the deputies drive away with his father. Even though they were taking in the biggest criminal Reston County had ever known, they didn't feel it was necessary to pull out with lights flashing and sirens blaring. He appreciated that.

"You're right." He rubbed his hand across his forehead, trying to clear his mind. With his arm still around Gemma's shoulders, he started walking toward his car. "I have to admit that I hope he pleads guilty and... wait..."

"What, Nate?"

"It's been eight years. Hasn't the statute of limitations run out by now?"

"I don't know. The law isn't my area of expertise. Maybe it's different if he turns himself in."

"Or maybe he knows he got away with it, and..."

"Nate, did you get a good look at him? He hasn't gotten away with anything. He's been miserable. He's paid the price for what he did and paid back a little of what he stole."

"And now he's broke, or so he says." Nate rubbed his forehead again. "I'm too tired to think. I don't know if being broke is some kind of justice or not."

Gemma held out her hand. "Why don't you let me drive home? I've got to pick up my car at your house, anyway."

Nate handed over his keys, grateful to be in charge of nothing for a while and to sit, thinking things over, while Gemma drove back to Reston. He'd experienced a number of shocks and surprises in the past two days. He needed to make some decisions about his future, but one of them had suddenly become remarkably clear.

He looked over at Gemma. Her hair fell to her shoulders but was brushed back by the blast from the air-conditioning. *With that red hair,* he thought once again, *and in her yellow dress, she looks like a burst of sunshine.* He dozed off with that thought in mind, and woke when she pulled into his driveway.

"Nate, we're home."

He sat up and yawned. "Yes. Yes we are." He hurried around the car to hold the door for her. "Gemma, thanks for coming with me."

She dropped his keys into his hand and smiled. "You're welcome. I would say 'anytime,' but I'm hoping this is the only time we'll have to do this."

"Me, too." When she started to walk away, he said, "Gemma, okay if I come over later?"

"Of course, but…"

"I'll bring a picnic for dinner."

"Seriously?"

"It's a campground, isn't it? Picnic tables, and so forth."

Gemma gave him a puzzled smile, but she nodded. "Well, yes. If you're bringing the food, I'll provide the mosquito repellent."

"Sounds fair."

With a wave, she climbed into her Rover and drove away. Nate hurried into the house. He had plans to make. Things to do.

GEMMA DRESSED IN linen slacks and top, and pulled her hair up off her neck, hoping she could remain cool in the evening's lingering heat and humidity. Her preference would be to stay in the house with the air-conditioning blasting, but Nate seemed set on having a picnic.

Nate arrived at six and when she opened her front door, presented a big basket with a flourish and said, "Let's go."

"Um, okay," she said. "But wouldn't you rather eat inside?"

He shook his head. "No. We're having a picnic. I've never been on a picnic."

"Never?"

"My family wasn't the picnicking type."

"Right." Gemma looked at him for a second, saw hope and happiness in his eyes that she'd never seen before. "Picnic it is. I'll get the mosquito repellent."

Their walk through the humid evening was worth it when they reached the picnic table near the pavilion and a breeze kicked up.

Nate told Gemma to sit and relax while he spread out their feast of sandwiches, salads and wine. They ate and talked about all that had happened in the past couple of days as the shadows grew long.

"You seem happy, Nate. I've never seen you like this."

"I've never felt like this. I'm ready to leave the past behind."

Gemma sighed and looked down. "I know, and you'll be leaving Reston as soon as…"

"No." Nate took her glass from her fingers and set it down, then clasped both of her hands in his. "No. I'm not leaving Reston. In spite of everything, it's my hometown, and… I'm needed here." He said it slowly as if he was becoming used to the idea.

Joy filled Gemma's heart. "Yes, you are. The town needs you." I *need you*, she added silently.

"I don't know what I was thinking. It would be crazy to do all the work to reopen the hospital and establish a medical practice, then leave it behind."

"You were thinking you would be able to make a clean break with the past." Gemma smiled. "But it's always with you. The trick is to not let it control you, ruin your future."

"You're right." Nate leaned over and kissed her, his lips meeting hers in lingering sweetness. "Speaking of the future— would you like to share mine?"

She blinked at him. "What?"

"I love you, Gemma. I think I started falling in love with you when I came across you planting herbs by moonlight."

"You did a good job of hiding it all this time."

"I had things to work out. How about it? Will you marry me?" He gave her a wicked grin. "I mean, after all, you've had a crush on me for a long time."

"I never should have told you that. It's gone straight to your head. In spite of that, yes, I'll marry you. I love you, too."

Nate kissed her again and Gemma responded by putting her arms around his shoulders and running her hands through his hair. Love for him filled her, along with gratitude that he had conquered the demons from his past.

EPILOGUE

GEMMA STOOD WITH her hand resting in the crook of Nate's elbow as she waited for the music to begin for their first dance as husband and wife. He looked incredibly handsome in his black suit with a silver-gray shirt and tie.

Nate looked down at her. "Have I mentioned how beautiful you are today?"

"A few times, but I can always hear it again. I have to admit, I love this dress." She smoothed a hand over the lace-covered, strapless bodice, and straightened the satin ribbon that encircled her waist above the full skirt. Her bridesmaids had similar dresses, Carly's in a soft yellow, and Lisa's in blue.

He leaned down to kiss her. "You look beautiful, and I can't believe you pulled this wedding together in less than a month."

When he tried for a second kiss, she held him off. "You were the one who insisted on speed."

"No reason to wait, and we're not getting any younger."

She laughed, but she knew the real reason. Everyone in town had been upset when it was announced that George Smith wouldn't be prosecuted for his crime. The restitution he'd made had helped calm some of the anger, but most people thought he'd been let off too easy. They were right, and the fact that he lived only fifty miles away didn't help. Nate had been to visit his dad a couple of times, arranged medical care for him, but she knew they hadn't yet talked about Virginia and her battles with anxiety. She thought it would probably be a long time before that happened, but Nate had begun to forgive himself for not being more understanding and compassionate toward his mother.

The people of Reston no longer blamed Nathan for his father's wrongdoing, and the number of citizens who had stepped up to help with wedding preparations was proof of their forgiveness.

This was one of the reasons she'd moved home, Gemma thought, proud of her hometown. And she was glad that Nathan had a reason to be proud, too. She hoped he would be able to form some kind of relationship with his dad, but she knew it would take a while.

Even Cole Burleigh had changed completely and had fulfilled his promise to replant her garden. She and Yvette had spent a wonderful evening chatting, sipping iced tea and holding Davy while Cole sweated and strained, planting herbs by the light of a full moon. He had also paid to have her yard light repaired, and, still feeling guilty, had graded her driveway and covered it with new gravel.

Smiling at the memory, Gemma looked across the expanse of the pavilion to where Yvette and Misty Summers were talking and laughing together while they ladled out punch and their husbands held their babies.

The musicians finally started, hit a few sour notes, laughed at themselves and started again.

Gemma shook her head. "I can't believe you hired Ron Jett and the Rocket Boys to play at our reception."

"It seemed like the most appropriate choice, and—"

"They were the only ones available, weren't they?"

"You guessed it," Nate answered, turning her into his arms as the music finally started on the correct note. "I even paid them to put in some extra practices."

"That was money well spent. They sound better than usual."

As they moved around the dance floor of the campground's repaired pavilion, Gemma saw the joyful faces of her parents. She wiggled her fingers at them as she sailed past, glad they had come from Africa to help with the wedding preparations. They planned to stay around for a while, living in the cabin while she and Nate occupied the house he was renting in town. Someday, she and Nate would build a house of their own, free of any ghosts from the past.

"I'm amazed that Wolfchild is wearing a suit and tie," Nate said.

"I think he is, too. Mom insisted, said I'm their only child and this will be my only wedding, and that he needs to look civilized."

Nate grinned. "He got a haircut, too. Makes him look like a banker. How does your mom know this will be your only wedding?"

"Because she's a smart woman. She knows I've been crazy about you since high school. There's no way I'll ever let you go."

Nate pulled her closer and kissed her again. "That's good to know because I'm never letting you go, either."

* * * * *

*Don't miss the next book in
Patricia Forsythe's*
OKLAHOMA GIRLS *miniseries,
available February 2017!*

LARGER-PRINT BOOKS!

GET 2 FREE LARGER-PRINT NOVELS PLUS 2 FREE MYSTERY GIFTS

Love Inspired®

Larger-print novels are now available...

LILP15

LARGER-PRINT BOOKS!

GET 2 FREE
LARGER-PRINT NOVELS
PLUS 2 FREE
MYSTERY GIFTS

Love Inspired®

SUSPENSE
RIVETING INSPIRATIONAL ROMANCE

Larger-print novels are now available...

WESTERN WP PROMISES

B.D.

LARGER-PRINT BOOKS!
GET 2 FREE LARGER-PRINT NOVELS PLUS
2 FREE GIFTS!

 HARLEQUIN®

super romance®

More Story...More Romance

YES! Please send me 2 FREE LARGER-PRINT Harlequin® Superromance® novels and my 2 FREE gifts (gifts are worth about $10). After receiving them, if I don't wish to receive any more books, I can return the shipping statement marked "cancel." If I don't cancel, I will receive 4 brand-new novels every month and be billed just $5.94 per book in the U.S. or $6.24 per book in Canada. That's a savings of at least 12% off the cover price! It's quite a bargain! Shipping and handling is just 50¢ per book in the U.S. or 75¢ per book in Canada.* I understand that accepting the 2 free books and gifts places me under no obligation to buy anything. I can always return a shipment and cancel at any time. Even if I never buy another book, the two free books and gifts are mine to keep forever.

132/332 HDN GHVC

Name	(PLEASE PRINT)	
Address		Apt. #
City	State/Prov.	Zip/Postal Code

Signature (if under 18, a parent or guardian must sign)

Mail to the **Reader Service:**
IN U.S.A.: P.O. Box 1867, Buffalo, NY 14240-1867
IN CANADA: P.O. Box 609, Fort Erie, Ontario L2A 5X3

Want to try two free books from another line?
Call 1-800-873-8635 today or visit www.ReaderService.com.

* Terms and prices subject to change without notice. Prices do not include applicable taxes. Sales tax applicable in N.Y. Canadian residents will be charged applicable taxes. Offer not valid in Quebec. This offer is limited to one order per household. Not valid for current subscribers to Harlequin Superromance Larger-Print books. All orders subject to credit approval. Credit or debit balances in a customer's account(s) may be offset by any other outstanding balance owed by or to the customer. Please allow 4 to 6 weeks for delivery. Offer available while quantities last.

Your Privacy—The Reader Service is committed to protecting your privacy. Our Privacy Policy is available online at www.ReaderService.com or upon request from the Reader Service.

We make a portion of our mailing list available to reputable third parties that offer products we believe may interest you. If you prefer that we not exchange your name with third parties, or if you wish to clarify or modify your communication preferences, please visit us at www.ReaderService.com/consumerchoice or write to us at Reader Service Preference Service, P.O. Box 9062, Buffalo, NY 14240-9062. Include your complete name and address.